No place is safe anymore.

Matt and his crew know it all too well—and it's especially true now as the war with the Alraki has reached the heart of Federation space and struck close to home. Suddenly, Matt is faced with a difficult choice. He has the opportunity to sway the tide of the war and rectify a past wrong by helping the Fleet obtain a groundbreaking Alraki technology. But to do so, he must risk his ship and the lives of his crewmates.

With Matt's archenemy, the infamous Captain Rodgers, still on the loose and bent on revenge, the Alraki aren't the only ones who pose a deadly threat to Matt and the people most dear to his heart. With danger and betrayal haunting their steps, Matt and Ryce must find a way to save their friends even as sinister secrets from the past threaten to tear them apart.

This time, the price of staying afloat might be higher than what Matt is willing to pay.

Afloat is the third book in Isabelle Adler's exciting debut series, *Staying Afloat*, and concludes the series. For best enjoyment, advise reading the books in order.

AFLOAT

Staying Afloat, Book Three

Isabelle Adler

A NineStar Press Publication

www.ninestarpress.com

Afloat

© 2021 Isabelle Adler

Cover Art © 2021 Natasha Snow

Edited by Elizabetta McKay

This is a work of fiction. Names, characters, places, and incidents are either the product of the author's imagination or are used fictitiously. Any resemblance to actual persons living or dead, business establishments, events, or locales is entirely coincidental.

All rights reserved. No part of this publication may be reproduced in any material form, whether by printing, photocopying, scanning or otherwise without the written permission of the publisher. To request permission and all other inquiries, contact NineStar Press at the physical or web addresses above or at Contact@ninestarpress.com.

Printed in the USA

ISBN: 978-1-64890-210-9

First Edition, February, 2021

Also available in eBook, ISBN: 978-1-64890-208-6

WARNING:

This book contains sexually explicit content, which is only suitable for mature readers. Depictions of violence, abduction, physical injuries. Mentions of torture, mutilation, alcohol abuse. Allusions to past rape. Deaths of minor characters.

To all the amazing readers and friends who encouraged me along the way.

Chapter One

"Can't wait to get the hell out of here," Matt muttered to himself.

A Federation space map slowly revolved on the large canopy screen, illuminating the darkened bridge with the light of distant stars. A red dot flashed sedately at the very edge of the map, marking their current location. The Elysium system was as remote as an inhabited corner of the galaxy could possibly be.

Unfortunately, as it turned out, "remote" didn't always mean "out of harm's way."

Matt set the empty coffee mug on the edge of the console and leaned back, linking his hands behind his head as he considered the vastness of the galaxy, sprawled before him in all its unassuming majesty. At first glance, it appeared to hold endless possibilities, but as it turned out, they were unfortunately limited by constraints that had nothing to do with Matt's dreams and preferences. Even the parts of the galaxy ostensibly under Federation control weren't always safe for humans, and out of those, quite a large number of places weren't safe for him personally.

"Permission to come on the bridge," a voice chimed over the speaker. Matt smiled and spun around in his chair to greet Ryce as he walked in.

"So formal. Are you going to salute me next and call me 'Captain'?"

Ryce grinned back at him and leaned down for a quick kiss before sitting beside him in the copilot seat.

"Now who's being kinky? I thought adherence to a chain of command wasn't your thing."

"It's not. But it'd still be nice to get some respect around here."

"Knowing your crew, there's not much chance of that," Ryce remarked and cocked his head as he studied the map. "Have you been here all morning?"

"Pretty much. And where were you? I didn't see you at breakfast."

"I was playing chess with Val in the rec room."

"Really? Two geniuses playing chess? Could you be any more cliché?"

"Neither of us is technically a genius," Ryce observed, his eyes still glued to the screen.

"Close enough from where I stand."

"Val and I have also tested the new power converter for the engine, and, as far as he's concerned, it's all systems go." The digitalized starlight reflected in Ryce's eyes as he pulled up the specs at the bottom of the screen, making Matt's attention momentarily slip. "We can be out of this system the second you decide where we're going. Have you?"

Matt sighed and ran a hand through his hair. His auburn locks had grown a bit too long for his taste, but with everything that'd been going on lately—namely, his engineer having been kidnapped and his pilot having been roped into participating in deadly drag races—he hadn't had a chance to cut them.

"Not really. Since we've changed registration twice in one year already, there are only so many sectors where we could apply for a working permit, and a lot of the others are now a warzone. This whole war business is a real nuisance when you're on the run."

"Do you think Griggs is still after us?" Ryce asked. "It has been rather quiet lately."

"I don't know, but I'm not planning on hanging around much longer to find out."

Griggs, the black-market king of the Freeport 73 station, was the man behind their crew's recent misadventures, and though they'd managed to strike an uneasy truce, Matt wasn't naive enough to believe the crime lord would swallow the bitter pill of blackmail without some kind of payback. Having to—literally—piece his engineer back together was more than enough incentive for Matt to look for opportunities elsewhere.

"Tony says we're due a vacation, and for once, I tend to agree with her. We've all been through some tough shit in the past few months, and we all deserve a break while we have the cash to afford it. But before we go booking that luxury resort stay on Nova, I'd like to have all my bases covered."

Matt shook his head and looked at Ryce.

"What about you? Is there anywhere you'd like to go, even if it's just for a little while?" he asked gently, reaching out to stroke the other man's hand. "Have you considered getting in touch with your mother?"

"I don't think it's time for that yet," Ryce said, looking away. "I'm grateful for the money she sent me, of course, but it still doesn't mean she wants to see me."

There was something evasive about the way he said it, as if he wasn't completely sure or completely truthful in his answer.

"Okay," Matt said slowly.

It really wasn't his place to pry or push Ryce into being more open about this particular subject; God knew, Matt was prickly about discussing his own family with other people. But he couldn't help but feel a pang of disappointment. It was silly, really, but there he was, unable to hold back a frown because it implied Ryce didn't trust him enough to share something a little more personal.

But his disappointment was his hang-up, not Ryce's. So instead of quietly sulking, Matt squeezed Ryce's hand in reassurance. The feel of Ryce's skin against his was still wondrous to him, despite them spending barely any time apart, his own private miracle. Not only because he still couldn't quite believe a man like Ryce could love someone as flawed as him, but because after everything they'd been through, they were incredibly fortunate to be alive to enjoy their happy ever after. This was what he should be focusing on, not some imaginary slights he was learning to recognize as self-sabotage.

Ryce smiled and covered Matt's hand with his own, his cool touch sending sparks of excitement down Matt's spine. "What are you thinking? You have that funny look on your face."

"Must be the aftermath of last night's dinner."

Ryce scoffed. "You didn't have to be quite so unequivocal about how bad you thought it was," he chided, but there was a spark of laughter in his eyes.

"I'm actually glad you suck at cooking. Just goes to show nobody can be perfect at everything. And if you're not perfect, there's hope for the rest of us mortals."

"Remind me to gloat with the same level of delight when I discover something *you* suck at."

"So pretty much anything?"

"I can think of a few things you're good at," Ryce murmured, sliding from his seat and onto Matt's lap in a fluid motion.

Matt's heart sped up. He pulled Ryce closer, greedily drinking the kiss as he closed his eyes and lost himself to the whirlwind of stars around him.

He slid his hand over the front zipper of Ryce's fatigues, but then Ryce withdrew abruptly, frowning, and touched the adapter on his temple, the one linked to *Lady Lisa*'s computer.

"There's an incoming call," he said.

"They'll call later," Matt said impatiently. Whoever it was, they could damn well wait another ten minutes. "We're kind of in the middle of something here."

"It's a military channel." Ryce's frown deepened, and he stood up to sit back in the copilot seat.

"Damn it." Matt sat up in his chair, pushing down on his arousal and frustration. His disdain for authority didn't extend as far as ignoring contacts from the military. This could be Nora, of course, but his sister rarely used encrypted communications simply to check up on him. "Bring it on-screen."

The face that appeared in front of them wasn't Nora's, but it was familiar. The bright white background didn't look like the bridge of a ship. Something beeped steadily just out of sight, jolting unpleasant memories of Matt's several stays in medical facilities.

"Commander Walker," Matt said, trying to keep the worry out of his voice. "Not to sound rude or anything, but why are you calling?"

Matt had been questioned ad nauseam by the man almost eight months ago, after their unfortunate stint on the Colanta-3 moon and the discovery (and subsequent destruction) of a Mnirian superweapon. He hadn't liked Walker then, and he wasn't thrilled to see him now, but he couldn't deny he owed the commander his life after being saved from a slow, oxygen-deprived death in the depths of the alien bunker.

"I'm contacting you on behalf of Major Cummings." Walker sounded unusually subdued. The stress lines around his eyes and mouth seemed deeper, marring his otherwise classically handsome features. "I thought you should know your sister was gravely injured in the line of duty."

Ryce's sharp intake of breath indicated that Walker had said something terrible, but for some reason, the moments stretched and stretched until the meaning of the words finally registered in Matt's brain, hitting him with the force of a freight barge.

"How gravely?" he asked, digging his fingers into the arms of his chair.

Walker pursed his lips. "Enough for me to contact you on my own initiative," he said, his voice clipped.

"What happened?" Ryce asked while Matt was busy remembering how to breathe.

"We were deployed back in the Sonora sector, and our ship, the *Lennox*, was on her way from Freeport 16 to the Sonora-11 outpost when we were attacked."

Even though they weren't touching, Matt felt Ryce tense beside him.

"Attacked? By whom?"

"An Alraki frigate," Walker said after a pause. "A torpedo took out a portion of the bridge. Major Cummings was lucky to be able to get out before the shields gave and the section was sealed off."

Matt and Ryce exchanged a look. Judging by Ryce's startled expression, the same thought must have occurred to him, one that made Matt's stomach, already tied in knots by the news, lurch with awful premonition.

"I haven't heard anything about the fighting reaching as far as Sonora," Ryce said, frowning. "The military bases in this sector are designated mainly for training and redeployment."

"It hasn't," Walker said. "This was...an isolated incident."

"An Alraki frigate attacking a destroyer battleship in the heart of Federation space?" Matt said, barely recognizing his own voice for the strain. "That's—"

"Disturbing. I know," Walker said. For the first time since Matt had met the man, he looked troubled, but a second later, he visibly pulled himself together, as stern as ever in his officer uniform. "By rights, I shouldn't even be telling you this. But I know how much your sister cares for you, and I thought you should be here by her side. Before it's too late."

*

"My god, Matt. I'm so sorry," Tony said. "Of course you should go see Nora right away."

They were all huddled in the tiny galley where Matt had called for an emergency crew meeting. Despite the basic utilitarian decor, it had always felt more welcoming and homelike to him than the kitchen of the house he grew up in.

"We'll all go," Val said. All traces of the torture he'd suffered were gone from the engineer's face, but Matt still had that twinge of guilt (misplaced though it might be) every time he caught a glimpse of the new scar tissue that surrounded Val's index finger. "Moral support aside, it's a bad idea to split up when there are still folks out there with scores to settle. Neither one of us should be alone right now."

That was certainly true—perhaps even more than Val realized since Griggs might not be the only one hot on the trail of *Lady Lisa* and her captain. Matt hadn't told anyone about the call he'd gotten from Dylan Rodgers, his old-time enemy (and, coincidentally, one of the most dangerous people in the known galaxy), not even Ryce. He hated to admit it, but the little reminder that he wasn't off the pirate's radar had left him rattled, though he did his best to forget about it and focus on things that had to be done. But whether real or not, that particular threat was a worry for another day while there were much more pressing concerns to busy himself with.

Like his sister dying.

"Her ship is stationed in Sonora," Matt said, firmly stomping down on that particular avenue of thought. "I wasn't planning on showing our faces there for a long time. As you might remember, there's still the little issue of Pat Gentry believing we owe him money for his lost cargo."

"And he settled that score by selling us out to Rodgers, remember?" Tony said, making a face of disgust and tugging on her long braid. "As far as I'm concerned, you guys are even."

"Besides, with all due respect to the scope of Gentry's system-wide black-market operations, he's hardly omnipotent," Ryce added. "Sonora is a huge sector, and after coming in through the Freeport 16 jumpgate, we'll effectively be out of his reach—especially considering we'll be meeting a Federal Fleet battleship."

"Well, that's true. Thanks, guys." The tightly wound band of anxiety around his heart eased a fraction as he looked around the small round table at his crew members. No, he amended. Not just his crew—his family. And family stuck together through thick and thin and vengeful criminals with homicidal tendencies.

"So when are we leaving?" Val asked.

"As soon as we can. I've already booked us a jump with Station Control."

"I'll make sure we have enough fuel, and then we'll be ready for liftoff," the engineer said and headed for the doorway.

"I guess I should say goodbye to some people before we go," Tony said. "Not that I'm sorry to leave this place, mind."

"Your friends at the IMA?" Matt asked.

Tony nodded. "I'm glad I've had this chance to reconnect and put some old issues to rest." Her voice took on a note of sadness. "It was nice to finally get some closure. But there's a good reason the past should stay in the past."

She nodded again to Matt and Ryce and followed Val on her way out.

"Unfortunately, the past has a nasty habit of surfacing and biting you on the ass when you don't expect it," Matt grumbled. He sat down heavily on one of the white plastic chairs, staring moodily at the shiny tabletop. A familiar yearning itched at the back of his throat, but he couldn't afford wasting time on getting sloshed, no matter how comforting the promise of alcohol-induced stupefaction was.

"Like that Alraki frigate," Ryce said quietly, sitting down opposite him. "Do you really think it could be the same one?"

"I don't know. Walker wouldn't give any more details, so we'll have to find out what's it all about when we get there." Matt drummed his fingers on the table. "But if it was the one to attack the *Lennox*, and Nora doesn't make it, I'll never forgive myself."

Ryce reached out across the table, stilling Matt's fingers with his palm.

"You couldn't have known. And it was a long time ago."

Matt only shook his head. Granted, those eight months since his decision to take on the ill-advised job offer that threw Ryce and him in each other's paths seemed like an eon ago. But with everything that had happened in the interim, it hadn't been enough time to forget the Alraki almost taking over his ship. Ryce's skill as a pilot and his quick thinking had allowed them to escape that lonely frigate coming at them from the middle of nowhere during their run in the Sonora system, with them losing Gentry's volatile cargo in the process while using it as a makeshift IED. But it was entirely Matt's fault for keeping his mouth shut about it all to avoid being accused of illegal smuggling.

"You're the one who wanted to report the Alraki attack to the authorities, and I stopped you. This one's on me."

Ryce made a noncommittal sound. "I admit I haven't given it much thought, seeing as we were otherwise engaged at the time, but now that I think of it, I can't come up with a reasonable explanation for this ship being in Sonora at all. I haven't heard anything about the Freeport 16 jumpgate being hijacked around that time. There's something terribly wrong about all this."

The comforting warmth of Ryce's hand soothed, and Matt wished he wouldn't let go for a little while longer. He didn't want to think about all these things right now, even as his mind kept running frantic circles around his guilt. All he wanted was to get his ship in the air and through that jumpgate to see his sister. Perhaps it was a small comfort, but she deserved to know that Matt loved her, that he always had, even when they'd spent years pointedly not speaking to each other.

"I know Nora is a career soldier, and with the war going on, there's always a risk, but...I just can't get my head wrapped around it. I can't imagine her...not being there anymore."

"Were you two close in the past?" Ryce asked quietly, still holding his hand.

"Not really. We were very different, ever since we were children. Nora was always the serious one." He smiled faintly, sorting through the half-faded memories. "If she wanted something, she'd stop at nothing to get it, and she was willing to work extra hard to achieve her goals. That was what our father admired most about her, that dedication and focus. I was never that disciplined. But she was a great big sister, and she never failed to be there when I needed her help. Nora talked me into sticking with college when I got overwhelmed with it at first, before Father could find out I was slacking. She just...did so much for me even when I was too proud to ask for it. Breaking away from her was the hardest part of cutting ties with my family."

Matt shook his head and took another breath. He hadn't talked about it for so long, it felt like pulling a scab off a wound only partially healed, but there was something comforting in knowing Ryce wouldn't judge him in the same way all the people in his life had when he'd made those fateful decisions.

"I guess I thought she'd back me up and defend me to our father when I quit the Fleet, but she didn't, and that was it. We hadn't spoken in years, but I always kept tabs on her. When she got her command, I was happy for her, even if I couldn't tell her that. I knew it was what she'd always wanted."

"You two may be more alike than you think," Ryce said, a small smile playing on his lips. "You're both stubborn to a fault, and just as caring."

Matt blinked, willing away the sudden tears.

"She did come through for me, didn't she? Even when she didn't have to, even when she had so much to lose by trying to keep me out of trouble. But she still helped me, like she'd always done. And I've done absolutely nothing to repay her. If anything, I've made it all worse."

He bit his lip, looking down.

"We have no choice but to stay positive. She will be fine, and then you'll make it up to her," Ryce said firmly. "The major is tough as nails. She'll pull through."

Matt nodded, but for the first time in his life, he couldn't bring himself to believe a lie he was desperate to hold on to.

Chapter Two

The robust shape of the destroyer loomed on the screen, dull silver against the gentle blues and yellows of the Sonora-11 planet and the ringed structure of the maintenance station that served the ground military base. Tiny repair pods scurried across the damaged parts of the ship's hull, like insects crawling over the carcass of a dead giant.

For once, Matt had no patience to appreciate the oddly serene beauty the view offered. All he wanted was to make sure *Lady Lisa* was safely docked in the *Lennox*'s pod bay, and then find the infirmary.

He had to hand it to Commander Walker—whatever the man's private opinion of Matt was, he'd made all the arrangements for him and his crew to receive the security clearance that would get them on board with no additional fuss. Even their arrival at the Freeport 16 jumpgate and subsequent sojourn to the outer planet region had gone smoothly. They hadn't had to dock at the station proper, thus avoiding running afoul of the locals, though Matt had no doubts his name on the arrival registry would set off quite a few alarms across his old stomping ground. But it wasn't something he had to deal with now, so he put it out of his mind.

When he'd worked in the Sonora system, he'd brag about having the fastest ship in the sector. Matt had no idea if this was still true, but making the run all the way to Sonora-11 in just under three days had to be some sort of record.

The layout of the *Lennox* was the same as other destroyers of its class, and thus uncomfortably familiar, harking to Matt's days as a

Federal Fleet officer. He could have reached the hospital wing without the escort, but the young (and armed) private Walker had assigned to chaperon him wasn't there to make sure Matt didn't get lost or to show him the local attractions.

The commander hadn't said Matt could bring anyone else with him, but he'd asked Ryce to tag along anyway. Matt wasn't above admitting he could use all the emotional support he could get, and besides, Nora liked Ryce, which meant she probably wouldn't mind having him visit her as well. At least, that was what he kept telling himself when they strode down the brightly lit, utilitarian corridors in complete silence.

His heart hammering, Matt followed the private into the corridor that led into the infirmary, but they didn't have a chance to go inside. The sight of Commander Walker waiting for them just outside the wide transparent doors was like a punch in the gut, and Matt stopped dead in his tracks, forcing both Ryce and their escort to halt there beside him.

Matt opened his mouth, but no words came out through the dryness in his throat.

"Commander," Ryce said, coming to his rescue and stepping forward. "Is there any news?"

Walker threw him a glance. In person, the haggardness in his face was even more pronounced, his lips pressed into a hard, unhappy line, and dark circles shadowed his brown eyes. A nasty bruise lurked at the edge of his hairline.

"Major Cummings's condition has deteriorated in the last twenty-four hours," he said curtly, addressing both of them. "Her lungs had been punctured when she was crushed by the armature, and the doctors are afraid they might give out entirely. She's currently in ICU, in deep sedation, and can't have visitors. They're doing everything they can."

Matt swallowed hard as his heart seemed to drop into his stomach like a lump of ice, but he only nodded, forcibly pulling himself together. As much as he wanted to succumb to despair, he refused to do it in the middle of a battleship corridor, surrounded by people who couldn't care less about his private pain.

Perhaps he wasn't being entirely fair to Walker though. The man was holding a tight rein over his emotions, but even Matt, in his current state of distraction, could see he was overwrought. Clearly, Matt wasn't the only one who had been hit hard by the news of Nora's turn for the worse.

"When can I—" Matt began.

"I'll see to it that you're notified immediately of any developments," Walker said, cutting him off. "Now, if you'll please excuse me. We have a situation."

"What's going on?" Ryce pressed, steely notes ringing through what Matt had dubbed his "command voice." Granted, he could hardly pull rank on Walker even if he hadn't been discharged from the Fleet, but it was difficult to ignore Ryce when he was determined to make something his business.

"Please wait for Mr. Spears and Mr. Easom by the elevators," Walker told the private, who saluted and sprinted back down the corridor. He then lowered his voice. "The Alraki frigate that attacked the *Lennox* was spotted near Atasia, one of the far moons of Sonora-11. I'm directing the ship there now. Hopefully, we can get there before the Alraki decimate the place."

Matt and Ryce exchanged a startled glance.

"From what I've seen, your bridge is severely damaged," Ryce said cautiously.

"It's a destroyer; even damaged, it can take out a frigate," Walker said, scorn tinging his voice. "The last time they came at us out of nowhere, but now we'll be ready for them. I'll be damned if I let those fuckers get away from me again after what they've done."

"Commander, I really should ask you to reconsider—"

"No," Walker said with unexpected vehemence. "I shouldn't even be talking to you two. I've extended you a courtesy for your sister's sake, Mr. Spears. Don't make me regret it."

With that, he turned on his heel and strode down the corridor.

"He's taking this very personally," Ryce said into the ensuing silence, frowning. "Him not thinking clearly might get us all into trouble."

Matt sighed and rubbed his forehead. He didn't know the commander nearly well enough, but this insistence on engaging the enemy from a position of disadvantage seemed uncharacteristic of him. Walker didn't seem like a man who let anger guide him, but right now he was positively incandescent with it. Still, whatever the man's reason, Matt could understand Walker's eagerness for a confrontation—it gave him a something else to focus on other than desperate helplessness. Had Matt had the command of an entire destroyer entrusted to him under such circumstances, he might have done the same thing.

But he didn't have the might of a Fleet battleship at his beck and call, and while there was nothing he could currently do for Nora, aside from wishing and hoping, he still had his own crew to think about.

"I wasn't counting on landing smack in the middle of another war." He sighed. "We have no idea what's going on here, and neither does Walker. If the Alraki amass forces in the sector..."

He trailed off, the implication heavy in the air.

"It is still Sonora," Ryce said. "The heart of Federation space. Walker can call on all the backup he needs if he runs into trouble."

"Oddly, I don't find that at all reassuring," Matt said.

*

In the end, Matt's concerns proved unfounded—but not in a way he'd hoped for.

The human settlement on Atasia was small, an agricultural community that grew water-based crops on the moon's subterranean lakes. The sight that greeted Matt and the others upon arrival was one of complete desolation, water vapors mixing with black smoke rising from the charred remains of the eco domes.

None of the *Lady Lisa* crew had been invited to the command room from which Commander Walker coordinated the operation, so they huddled on their bridge, silently watching the *Lennox*'s external camera feed on the canopy screen, right there in the destroyer's spacious docking bay.

It was clear they'd arrived too late. The raid had been swift and brutal, the settlers having nothing to protect themselves with against an Alraki ship swooping in on them. By the time the *Lennox* arrived at Atasia, joined by a Federation emergency response vessel, the enemy craft was long gone, with nothing indicating its next destination. It was as if it'd disappeared off the radars—either by magic or by some previously unseen stealth technology.

It was a worrisome notion piled on top of more trouble.

"Are you all right?" Matt asked in a low voice, turning to Ryce, who was leaning against the pilot chair currently occupied by Tony's petite frame.

Ryce's fingers were white where he clutched the tall back of the chair, but he nodded, his jaw clenched. His adoptive parents and almost the entire community he'd grown up in had lost their lives in a similar attack only a few years ago—not that the destruction wasn't a horrible thing for anyone to witness.

"I never thought something like this could happen in Sonora," Tony said, watching the tiny rescue pods scurrying between the ruined domes. "The Alraki so rarely opt for direct confrontation. It's always the small, distant colonies being hit out there in the boonies." She glanced at Ryce as she said it, but she wasn't wrong, exactly.

Val grunted in agreement. "There's weird stuff going on."

Matt tended to agree with him. It was exceedingly strange to the point of it all feeling like a bad dream. Attacking a massive destroyer with a single frigate coming out of nowhere, annihilating a civilian outpost of no tactical or strategical importance, and vanishing again without a trace, all in the space of a few days, in a sector notorious for heavy military presence? There was definitely something sinister brewing, and Matt *definitely* didn't want to stick around to see what it was. Once he was sure Nora was out of danger (and he refused to consider any other option), he was getting his ship the hell out of this system.

The question was, where could they possibly go to escape the war? If the fighting had reached Sonora, no place was going to stay uninvolved for very long.

"Humans are running out of safe spaces," Ryce said tightly, echoing Matt's thoughts. "It seems no sector remains unaffected these days."

"How many survivors?" Val asked, nodding toward the screen.

"They're not sure yet," Matt said. "The search and rescue parties are still down there. But the current count is about two dozen."

There was another silence as they all digested that. It was such a small number compared to the thousand or so population of the settlement.

"This is awful." Tony faced Matt. "We have to help somehow, Captain."

"Like how? None of us has the skills to man a rescue salvage mission."

"I don't know, but we should do *something*." The stubborn set to her mouth and a warning gleam in her eyes indicated she wasn't about to let it go.

Matt turned to Val and Ryce for support, but they were both looking at him with the same expectant expression.

"All right." Matt sighed. "I'll contact the emergency coordinator and ask it they need an extra hauler to transport people and equipment."

He understood their sentiments; it seemed wrong to stand by watching others do the heavy lifting in a massive disaster relief operation while *Lady Lisa* sat idly in the pod bay. He couldn't keep his crew out of it if they were all raring to go. Besides, it would give him something else to focus on other than fretting over whether or not Nora was going to make it.

*

It seemed the Alraki had been intent on a show of strength rather than looting, so while most of the outer domes and the infrastructure were severely damaged, making them unfit for habitation, much of the underground agricultural systems had survived the attack. It was a matter of sealing them off while waiting to rebuild, even if the current crops were lost.

What couldn't be replaced, of course, were the human casualties. Matt tried hard not to dwell on the death toll as *Lady Lisa* made a quick run to Sonora-7 to fetch more supplies for the temporary field camp being set up for the survivors on the military base on Sonora-11. But the images of the carnage being broadcast from Atasia were hard to ignore. The practicalities of hauling a large cargo weren't enough of a distraction, and the crew had been subdued and tight-lipped for the entire run—especially Ryce, though he insisted he was fine.

The truth of the matter was none of them were fine. The elation they'd been feeling after their narrow escape from Griggs's clutches and then receiving the unexpected cash gift from Ryce's birth mother—which had gotten them out of a seriously tight spot—had all but dissipated over the course of the last week or so. First, with Nora being injured, and then this new atrocity—it had taken them unawares, and it hit where it hurt.

Immersed in thought on his way back from the bridge to his quarters, Matt was startled to find himself standing at the entrance to the rec room. Deep down, he knew what he was doing there, of course. The familiar siren song of the whiskey bottles hidden in the liqueur cabinet drew him with irresistible force, promising sweet, if temporary, numbness.

Ryce looked up at him from where he was curled up on an old sofa, reading something off his commlink, and Matt imagined he could detect a flicker of disapproval in his gaze. Seeing him made Matt hesitate, since it was clear what his partner thought of his little drinking habit, but he went inside, affecting nonchalance.

"Where's Val and Tony?" he asked, heading straight for the panel that hid his precious bottles.

"Tony needed to make some personal calls. And Val is reconfiguring the air-conditioning wiring."

"Again?" Matt felt Ryce's gaze at the back of his neck but refused to acknowledge it as he poured himself a shot.

"He said the cargo hold was freezing."

"It's cargo; it doesn't care if it's cold," Matt said, a bit grumpily, though he couldn't fault Val for tackling a project to keep himself busy. He swirled the amber liquid inside the tumbler, savoring the woodsy, slightly bitter aroma, but didn't drink it right away, instead just watched a tiny maelstrom form inside the glass.

There was no reason for him to stay sober anyway. *Lisa* was flying on autopilot, and Ryce could take care of anything should the need arise. There weren't any pressing needs that required Matt's urgent attention. With all the stress being piled up on him, he deserved some time to unwind and have a glass or two if he wanted. Didn't he?

"What are you thinking?" Ryce asked softly, startling Matt out of his unhappy reverie.

"Do you notice how trouble just follows me around wherever I go?" he said. "Everyone around me keeps getting hurt. Hell, not even around; people I have never heard of got hurt because I was too damn selfish to warn everybody about the danger."

"I hardly think you can take credit for every development in the human-Alraki war," Ryce said in that annoyingly reasonable tone.

"Only those I could've prevented."

Matt's body thrummed with yearning to down the drink in one long gulp, and if Ryce hadn't been there, *looking* at him, he would have. It wasn't even about appearing weak—Ryce knew Matt's weaknesses better than anyone, maybe better than Matt. It was about forcing himself to be as strong as Ryce believed him to be.

He set the tumbler down on a side table and turned around just as Ryce sat up and put away his comm.

"Come here."

Matt joined him, settling on the sofa, and Ryce threw an arm around his shoulders. He didn't say anything else, but some of the tension gradually drained out of Matt's body. None of his anxiety went away, but now it seemed a bit less all-consuming.

"There was hardly any talk of Atasia in the news," Ryce said, stroking Matt's hair. "And none of the reports mention anything about the Alraki. They say the eco domes collapsed, without going into much detail."

"I guess the Feds don't want to rouse panic just yet," Matt said. "Sonora's been quiet so far."

"That won't hold for long."

"Maybe I should visit the Alraki home world and see if I can't push some of my bad luck their way," Matt said, but the attempt at humor fell flat. He eyed the whiskey glass longingly and closed his eyes before he could change his mind again.

"Do you think—" he began, but then his commlink buzzed.

Sighing, he sat up and pulled it out of his pocket. His heart did a little flip when he saw Commander Walker's contact.

"Commander," he said, bringing him on-screen and hoping he sounded level and not at all freaked out.

"Mr. Spears," Walker said. "What's your ETA?"

Matt exchanged a glance with Ryce before answering, "We should arrive at the Sonora-11 base tomorrow morning. We'll head over to the *Lennox* right after that. Why?"

"They took Major Cummings out of the ICU," Walker said.

A sprig of hope, fragile and tenacious like a flower striking out from beneath the snow, unfurled in Matt's heart.

"That's good, right? That means she's better," he said, wishing he wouldn't have to crush that tiny bloom.

"She's stable, for now. It's the best I could get out of them. You can see her upon your arrival, if you want."

"Of course."

"Let me know when you dock, and I'll meet you at the infirmary." Walker disconnected without wasting time on further niceties.

As far as Matt was concerned, the commander could be as curt as he wanted as long as he made sure Nora was being properly taken care of.

"I knew she was going to pull through." Ryce clapped Matt on the shoulder and smiled encouragingly.

Matt smiled back at him, but despite the rise in spirits, he couldn't wholeheartedly share in his optimism. Not while the talk about his shitty luck was still too fresh in his mind.

Chapter Three

Twenty minutes after docking back at the *Lennox*'s pod bay, a nurse admitted Matt and Ryce into the infirmary. The private who'd escorted them stood guard in the corridor. What she had to guard against, Matt had no idea, but he guessed, with the ship's senior commanding officer still fighting for her life, no one wanted to take chances, even with said officer's own brother.

It was somewhat sobering to see how many infirmary beds were currently occupied. With his focus on Nora and her injury, and then on the Atasia raid, Matt had forgotten there were other people on the *Lennox* who'd been hurt during the fight with the Alraki. And a lot of them hadn't been lucky enough to have been hospitalized.

Ryce discreetly touched his hand before guilt could surge again at the realization that Matt was—however indirectly—responsible for this, and Matt turned to offer him a quick, strained smile. It was amazing how well Ryce had learned to recognize Matt's moods and inner struggles, sometimes before he could identify them himself—a gift Matt would try his damndest not to squander.

"This way, please," the nurse said, ushering them into a separate room after sanitizing their hands and clothes. The matte glass doors swooshed closed behind them, and Matt stopped cold.

It wasn't the sight of Nora's pale face or the tubes coming out of her nose and mouth, or the quiet beeping of the machines that were keeping her alive. He'd been in enough hospital rooms throughout his life to not be shaken by their stark reality.

A tall man in a pristine Fleet uniform stood next to the bed, watching the monitor. As Matt and Ryce entered, he turned sharply in their direction, fixing them with a dark look.

"Father," Matt said, wondering why his voice sounded as if coming from far away—and why he'd automatically fallen into the formal address that had been instilled in him as a child. "When did you get here?"

Both Matt and Nora took after their late mother, so it was small wonder there wasn't much familial resemblance to Foreign Intelligence Admiral Cummings's features, aside from the shape of the mouth and some intangible but eerie similarity of expressions. The man was just as imposing as Matt remembered, carrying himself with the authority of a monarch, but he looked significantly older now, his dark hair generously peppered with white, his forehead creased with deep furrows. The war must have taken a harsh toll even on the top brass.

"Matthew," Admiral Cummings said, somehow managing to cram a lifetime of disappointment into two syllables. "I arrived this morning."

For some reason, the possibility of their father visiting Nora's sickbed had never crossed Matt's mind—perhaps because never, in all the years he'd spent away from the family nest, had Thomas Cummings bothered to check up on Matt when he was in a hospital.

Maybe he wasn't being fair. After all, Matt was the one who'd insisted on keeping the ties severed. And maybe it was for the best anyway, because there was only so much condescension Matt could stomach while convalescing. But he couldn't help the childish hurt that stirred in his chest at the thought.

"This is Ryce Easom," he said before his father could correctly interpret his expression and inquire why he was sulking. "My pilot. And my boyfriend."

"Pleasure to finally meet you, Admiral," Ryce said in his best just-this-edge-of-polite voice as he drew up to Matt's side.

The admiral's gaze flickered, taking in Ryce's stance and the military-grade flight adapters on his temples. He nodded curtly but offered no greeting in return.

"Nice of you to join us, son," Cummings said, turning his attention back to Matt. "Though I must say I'm surprised."

"She's my sister."

"I didn't realize it meant anything to you."

Apparently putting old grudges to rest was a foreign concept in their family.

Sometimes Matt envied Ryce's knack for donning a full armor of icy indifference to prevent people from getting under his skin. He could have used that kind of protection when dealing with his father.

"Okay, yeah, I deserve that," he said, grasping for patience. "I get it. I didn't come for Mom's funeral. But Mom didn't care anymore. She was dead. Nora"—he nodded toward the bed—"is still alive. I'm not here to pay my respects and graciously accept condolences from people I despise. I'm here for her, if she needs me."

The admiral pursed his lips. "Nora told me about your little... escapade last year and everything she did to get you and your crew off treason charges. Are you sure you're here for her, rather than for yourself?"

"With all due respect, sir, this is hardly helpful," Ryce interjected. "I'm sure this bickering can't be conducive to Major Cummings's recovery."

The admiral's eyes narrowed. For a moment, the room was so utterly silent the only sounds came from the machines surrounding Nora's bed. Matt braced himself for the imminent lashing, but thankfully, right then the door opened again, admitting Commander Walker, who saluted the admiral.

"At ease," Cummings said, and Matt let out a discreet breath. "I gather this is your doing, Commander?" He nodded toward Matt and Ryce as if they were a sticky mess Walker had spilled over the shiny laminate floor.

"I assumed the major would want all her family close by, sir." Walker's attitude was guarded and showed no obsequiousness, a fact that raised the commander's stock in Matt's eyes.

"Looks like you've made a string of unfortunate decisions so far, Commander," the admiral said, rounding on Walker. "Culminating in directing a half-defunct ship into a possible engagement with a hostile vessel with unknown potential instead of calling in readily available reinforcements. This is not the time to let emotions cloud your judgment."

Matt felt a reluctant stirring of sympathy for Walker—assuming command of a battleship while taking heat, deserved or not, from higher up the ladder must've been hard.

Matt stepped closer to the bed, leaving Walker and the admiral to sort things out between themselves. With all the tubing and the tape, Nora's face was hardly recognizable. Her hand rested on the stark white cover, and Matt tentatively stroked it, running his fingertips over her scraped knuckles. He hadn't held Nora's hand since they were both children, and perhaps he wouldn't be able to do it ever again.

"Nora? Can you hear me?" he whispered, leaning closer. "It's Matt. You're gonna be all right. Okay? Everything is gonna be all right. Please don't die."

Nora's eyelashes fluttered, but otherwise, she remained unresponsive. He didn't really expect her to answer, as heavily sedated as she was, but seeing her like this, fighting silently for her life, hit Matt harder than he expected. He bit his lip, holding himself from breaking down right there in front of his father.

Ryce moved closer and put a hand on Matt's shoulder. He didn't say anything, for which Matt was grateful. Empty words were just that, and no tragedy had ever been mended with platitudes.

But actions did mean something, and there was still something Matt could do, even if it fell into the "too little, too late" category.

"About that Alraki ship," Matt said, stepping away from Nora and interrupting whatever it was Cummings and Walker were arguing about.

Walker expression instantly shuttered. "What about it?"

"I don't think the altercation with the *Lennox* was their first run of the Sonora sector."

"Exactly how much classified information have you divulged to a civilian, Commander?"

Admiral Cummings's steel-grating tone was usually enough to instill dread in the hearts of the hardiest opponents, so Matt had to give Commander Walker credit for not cowering under his glare.

"I've judged it permissible, under the circumstances, to waive discretion," Walker said, folding his arms over his chest. "The major was in critical condition, and she'd made it clear on several previous occasions that she trusted her brother. As for Mr. Easom here, he's a retired flight lieutenant with a previously high level of clearance. They've been of great help with the Atasia situation, as well."

"I hate to break it to you, but the Alraki basically having free range with our outposts isn't something you can keep a secret for much longer," Matt said. His father was already angry at him for being there; he might as well deflect the admiral's wrath off Walker and direct it back where it belonged. "The *Lennox*'s crew, the station's personnel, the response teams on Atasia, the survivors' families—there are already too many people talking. And I guarantee this won't be the last ship or the last settlement to be attacked around here."

"How can you be so sure?" Walker asked.

"Because it wasn't the first," Ryce said. "The *Lady Lisa* encountered an Alraki frigate in this sector eight months ago. We managed to escape, causing some minor damage to their ship."

"Why didn't you say anything about it then?" the admiral demanded.

"I was instructed by my then commanding officer, Commodore Archer, to avoid any contact with the authorities that would jeopardize the secrecy of the mission he'd charged me with," Ryce explained.

Oh, no. Like hell Matt was going to let Ryce take the heat for him on this one.

"We didn't say anything about it because I didn't want to be busted for trying to smuggle illegal cargo on Freeport 16," Matt said, probably a little more harshly than strictly necessary. "I'm a criminal, remember? Now can we please get back on topic and—"

"Let's not discuss it here," the admiral cut him off. He glanced at Nora but headed straight for the exit. "Commander, I'll meet you in the major's office in an hour."

"Yes, sir," Walker said, but Cummings was already out the door.

"I'm sorry about that," Matt said into the pregnant quiet.

Walker looked at him askance and then shrugged.

"I've submitted my report of the recent developments to Central Command, and Admiral Cummings insisted on taking control of the situation."

"I'm guessing my presence isn't exactly helping things," Matt said. "But whatever my father says, I want to stay here until Nora recovers."

Walker nodded. "I know the major would want you by her side. If I'm wrong in my assumption, she can get out of that sickbed and tell me so herself."

*

"Ugh." Matt plopped into a chair in the infirmary waiting area and ran his hands through his hair. He really should cut it, he thought absently.

"Walker is right, you know." Ryce was watching the screen that showed the local news on mute but looked at Matt when he raised his head. "The only thing that matters is Nora's wishes, not your father's."

"Well, she can't voice them now, can she?" Matt said sourly. Perhaps not ever, a panicked voice whispered in his mind, but he shoved it aside. "And until that happens, my father is the one calling the shots. It was a mistake coming here."

"But we're here, and we may as well do what we can to help them sort out this thing with the Alraki."

"I doubt my father would want my help. He'll probably just make me sign a nondisclosure statement and push me into the jumpgate himself. Unless he finds something to charge me with and get me thrown in jail, so I won't get the chance to embarrass him any more than I already have."

"Then we'll deal with it when it happens," Ryce said firmly. He came up to Matt and gently took his hand before he could pull some more hair out. "Nora will be proud of you when she wakes up and hears you came all this way to do the right thing."

Matt shook his head. "I'm shit at doing the right thing. Always had been. It seems no matter how hard I try, I end up making a mess of things. Haven't we been through this already?"

"Do you really regret every single one of your life choices?" Ryce asked, his gray eyes impossibly bright in the sickly fluorescent lighting.

"Well, I can't deny there've been some exceptions to the rule," Matt relented, squeezing his hand. "Buying *Lady Lisa*. Hiring Tony and Val. Charming my way into your good graces."

"Oh? The hardened cynic admits falling in love was a good decision?"

"It wasn't really a decision. It was more like fate." A blush crept up his cheeks, but Matt didn't care how trite he sounded, as long as it was true. "Best thing that ever happened to me."

"Why is that?"

"Because you're an amazing person, and you make me want to be better to deserve you," Matt said, looking up. "Anything that can do that must be fucking miraculous."

Less than a year ago, he wouldn't have dreamed of saying something like that out loud, let alone mean it. Ryce had been generous when he called him a "hardened cynic." Jackass would've been a much more accurate description. It was ironic, really, and yes, miraculous, that he could go from being so jaded and broken to having faith, both in himself and in others. But for once, he was grateful for the universe having a joke at his expense. It could laugh at him all it wanted, as long as Ryce was by his side—and as long as Ryce was happy with being there.

A smile touched Ryce's lips, transforming his beautiful face into a living, breathing work of art, and then he leaned in to plant a light kiss on Matt's forehead.

"We're lucky to have someone we both feel about in the same way," he said, almost shyly. ""Fucking miraculous,' indeed."

"It's a good thing we're in a hospital already. I might faint if you keep using that kind of language."

"Unfortunately, you don't have time for fainting. Visiting hours are almost over." Ryce took out his commlink and checked the time. "Look, you can submit a statement to Walker regarding our run-in with the Alraki and go somewhere else to wait. No one said you had to stay and be humiliated by your father."

Matt rubbed the bridge of his nose. "No. I can't really leave while Nora's like that, even for a little while, not after everything she's done for me. Whatever crap the admiral piles on me, I can handle it. After all, I've had plenty of practice."

*

"Do you want me to stay with you tonight?" Ryce asked when they stepped into *Lady Lisa*'s airlock. They walked down the main corridor toward the cabins. Both the galley and the rec room were dark and quiet, meaning Tony and Val must have gone to sleep already.

"Yes. Thank you."

Matt had never thought he'd be one for cuddling. There'd been a time when he couldn't stand the sight of anyone lounging in his bed after they were done with sex. But with Ryce it was different, just like everything else with him was different. His closeness was like a soothing balm slathered all over the scabs of Matt's past wounds. Ryce lying next to him, their quiet breathing mixing in the cool artificial darkness, had become almost an addiction. It was a feeling of home, of loving the person beside him and knowing he was loved in return, a drug so powerful he could never get enough of it.

Hand in hand, they reached Matt's cabin, greeted by the familiar sight of upturned sheets and dirty coffee cups stacked on the little side table. Thankfully, by now Ryce was familiar enough with his housekeeping habits not to be taken aback by the mess. Had to be one of the perks of being in a long-term relationship.

"I think I'll take a shower first," Ryce said, running his hand through his short-cropped blond hair and heading for the en suite bathroom. "Do you have any fresh towels?" His muffled voice came from inside.

"Um—" Matt began, but was saved from having to come up with an excuse by his commlink beeping.

The number was unfamiliar, but Matt answered anyway, sitting down on the edge of the bed and propping up the commlink on the table.

Despite his fear, the call didn't come from the hospital, but he nearly gasped when the image showed the face of a serious-looking man in a Fleet uniform. He was a year or two younger than Matt, with pretty brown eyes and a sensual curve to his bottom lip. He hadn't changed much since Matt had last seen him, aside from losing some youthful lankiness.

"Grayson," Matt said, unable to hide his surprise. "It's been, like, what? Six years?"

"Give or take," Grayson said in a brisk, businesslike tone. "I'm Admiral Cummings's aide now."

Oh, dear God. Matt just knew his father wouldn't let him off the hook so easily. Now he was siccing his ex-boyfriend on him?

"Does he know about us?" Matt asked because he just couldn't help himself.

"Not that I'm aware of." Grayson's voice grew dryer by the second. "Should he?"

Not if you want to keep your job, Matt thought, and shook his head.

"Probably not. I'm sorry; it's just a bit of a surprise. I didn't know you served in the admiral's office."

It shouldn't have come as a shock, really. When they were dating six years ago, just before Matt quit the military, Grayson Lee was an ambitious intelligence officer, eager to embark on a journey of climbing the Fleet career ladder. Matt's preoccupation with fighting his own battle for independence and his growing contempt for the military ethos were the main reasons they'd broken up.

"I was assigned to this post about a year ago. I'm a lieutenant," Grayson said.

Of course he was.

"Look, I'd love to catch up and all, but it's kind of late. Was there something you wanted?"

"My apologies," Grayson said with an unruffled smoothness that reminded Matt of Ryce's demeanor when addressing someone acting particularly unreasonably—which of course irked him even further. "The admiral would like to schedule a meeting."

"You can tell the admiral to go and—" Matt took a deep breath, cutting himself off just in time. "—tell him I'm not interested."

"I'm afraid the admiral insists," Grayson said. "This is a matter of grave importance. He's also requesting Mr. Easom be present, as well as Commander Walker."

Matt's eyebrows shot up. He doubted his father would require all this audience just to scold him. He could find many faults in Admiral Cummings, but an affinity for public whippings wasn't one of them. No, this must have something to do with their impromptu report on the Alraki ship. Could it be that the mighty admiral needed his help after all?

"All right," Matt said slowly, wondering if he was going to regret it. The mere use of the phrase *grave importance* suggested he would. "When?"

"Tomorrow at 2100 hours, in Major Cummings's office. I'll arrange for your escort," Grayson said and disconnected before Matt could issue an objection or change his mind.

"Fuck," Matt muttered. Unsurprisingly, he had a very bad feeling about this—even if it did look like he'd have his chance at doing the right thing after all.

Chapter Four

Ryce kept an ominous silence as he and Matt headed to the major's office, once again escorted by the same sour-faced private. Matt really couldn't blame her for being unsociable; he'd probably be put out, too, at having to pull a late shift tagging along with a bunch of strangers and making sure they didn't snoop around.

At least she wasn't quietly judging him for getting soused right before an important meeting. Matt hadn't been planning to drink, but the longer he thought about being in a room full of Fleet officers, chief of whom being his father, the more he felt like he needed to fortify his nerves. Which, of course, resulted in him chugging one too many glasses of whiskey in the comfort of the dimmed rec room, fretting as he ran possible scenarios of confrontation in his head, each more daunting than the next. By the time he met up with Ryce on their way out, he had a serious buzz going, and his boyfriend didn't fail to notice his condition—or let him know exactly how he felt about it.

It was too late to cancel the meeting, and anyway, it wasn't as though he was ready to pass out. The drink only served to dull his anxiety, as well as lower his inhibitions—which, considering the setup and Matt's current mood, could well be a recipe for disaster.

"I doubt Lieutenant Lee will be pleased when he sees you like this," Ryce said at last as they passed into the administrative area.

Matt glanced at him askance and shrugged. "You're making too much of this. I'm not that drunk, honestly. Not slurring my words, am I?"

Ryce huffed without looking at him.

"Besides, it's not Grayson we're dealing with, it's Admiral Cummings," Matt continued as they rounded a corner. "Whatever he says, don't let him get to you. You're not military anymore. You don't have to come running when he snaps his fingers."

"I'm not here for him," Ryce said with a touch of exasperation. "I'm here for you. Let's just see what they want."

Grayson—Lieutenant Lee, Matt reminded himself—met them at the door. He appeared just as attractive as he had on the commlink, but the flat look he gave them spoiled the overall effect.

"Matthew, Mr. Easom. I must ask you gentlemen to leave your commlinks with me before entering." He made no effort at sounding apologetic and didn't comment on Matt's noticeable state of inebriation or the smell of alcohol on his breath.

Matt and Ryce exchanged a look. Finally, Ryce shrugged and handed over his device. Matt reluctantly followed suit. Not that he had anything incriminating stored on his commlink, or that he thought Grayson would go through his personal stuff on the admiral's orders, but surrendering it didn't sit well with him.

Both Commander Walker and Admiral Cummings were already waiting for them, seated at a long table. A holographic star map, displaying all the familiar routes of the Sonora system, slowly rotated above it. The admiral impatiently drummed his fingers on the table's smooth surface, and Matt had to resist the sudden urge to apologize for keeping him waiting, even though they weren't late for the meeting.

Instead, he sat down, crossed his arms over his chest, and pointedly sprawled as far as the chair would allow. Ryce sat between him and the admiral, straight and poised, his face blank but attentive, as if he were an officer attending a briefing. This was what he must have looked like during the countless briefings in the short years of his military service, sans the uniform. There was no doubt he fit right into the situation. It was as if all four men besides Matt—including Grayson, who followed them into the room after storing away their commlinks—had an aura about them, something that marked them as being used to commanding and making choices that could spell the difference between life and death. But, even if they were no strangers to fighting themselves, it was usually other people's lives and deaths that hung in the balance. And, as past events had proved, not even a decent and noble man like Ryce was immune to morally ambiguous decisions.

If Matt needed another reminder that he didn't belong here, this would definitely do the trick. He slumped back further in his chair, glaring at the huge Federal Fleet emblem painted on the opposite wall.

However, if one were to look closely and refuse to be intimidated by the concentration of medals and commendations shared by the other men in the room, it quickly became apparent the veneer of assumed confidence was wearing a bit thin. If anything, Walker looked more harried, which could be attributed to the admiral's presence (and the talking-to Walker must have received during their absence).

"What's the matter with you?" Admiral Cummings asked, frowning as he raked his gaze over Matt.

"Nothing, I'm fine. So what's this all about?" Eager to get the meeting done with as soon as possible, Matt was already itching to get out of this room and into his bed back on the *Lisa*. Despite the number of drinks he'd had, his brain wasn't so fuzzy as to not notice the atmosphere of tension in the room, and he didn't really want to find out the cause.

"In a minute. First, I want to hear what happened with you and the Alraki ship." The admiral's attention was focused on Ryce now. He hardly spared a glance in Matt's direction, so his efforts at being insolent were sadly wasted. "I gather this occurred while you were piloting the Phaeton hauler?"

"She's called *Lady Lisa*," Matt said sullenly.

Cummings shot him a look. Matt naming his ship after his late mother surely hadn't escaped the admiral's attention and had undoubtedly been added to the long list of Matt's transgressions.

"Yes," Ryce said quickly. "I was piloting."

At the admiral's impatient gesture, he proceeded to relate the encounter in minute detail, some of which made Matt wince internally.

"Do you mean to tell me you fought off a frigate using smuggled explosives?" Walker said when Ryce was done.

Matt cringed and looked away. He caught Grayson regarding him with a calculating expression on his face, but the man immediately averted his eyes when he saw Matt looking back at him.

"The source of the available ammunition aside, I must say that kind of ingenuity is impressive," Admiral Cummings said. "Your astuteness is commendable, Mr. Easom. I can see why you held such an excellent record in your squadron prior to this unfortunate business with Commodore Archer."

"Thank you, sir." Ryce's voice, politely bland, showed no surprise at the fact that the admiral must have pulled his personal file before setting up this meeting.

"What I can't find commendable is your choice to withhold this information from both your superiors and the Freeport 16 command," the admiral continued before Matt's jaw could drop at the praise. "Had the Fleet had knowledge about the Alraki ship roaming the sector this early in the game, this entire situation could have been avoided."

"This isn't Ryce's fault. I told him to keep his mouth shut. It was my decision as captain. We were in the middle of a job—"

"I heard your excuse the first time, Matthew," the admiral said. "And buying a ship doesn't make you a captain. However, what's done is done."

He nodded to Grayson, who tapped on his own commlink. The revolving star map was replaced with a detailed image of an Alraki ship, its twisted shape as foreign to the human eye as the aliens themselves.

"Is this the vessel that tried to capture you?" Cummings asked.

Ryce leaned closer, his eyebrows knitted in concentration as he studied the holograph.

"I think so," he said finally. "The general specs seem to match what I remember of the enemy ship. Is this the same one that attacked the *Lennox* and the settlement on Atasia?"

"Yes," Walker said. "The image was reconstructed from live footage."

"Great," Matt said. "Now, do you have any idea where the hell this thing came from?"

Walker reclined in his chair, looking uncomfortable. The admiral's expression became even stonier than before.

"I assumed the Alraki managed to temporarily hijack the Sonora jumpgate from their side to transport their vessels into the system, or there was some malfunction in the machinery. It's rare, but it's been known to happen," Ryce said. "I imagine the military would want to prevent something like that from leaking out, but we were at Freeport 16 shortly after our own scrape, and I didn't get the impression of anything being amiss from the personnel."

"There was no hijacking," Walker said.

"That makes no sense." Matt looked from one man to the other with growing confusion. Granted, he wasn't an astrophysicist or a xenoarcheologist, but he'd spent enough time as an independent pilot to know that space travel was impossible without the wormhole-generating technology of the laser-activated jumpgates left throughout the galaxy by the extinct Mnirian civilization. Something didn't add up, and his brain wasn't *that* addled. If anything, he was sobering up by the minute. "What are you saying? There's another Mnirian jumpgate hidden somewhere in Sonora that the Alraki are using?"

Walker looked at Admiral Cummings, who spread his hands on the table.

"This is part of the reason I'm here in Sonora," Cummings said. "The main part, if I'm being honest. What I'm about to tell you is highly confidential and will require complete secrecy on your part."

"Why tell us at all?" Matt countered. He could feel Ryce's gaze on him, but mistrust won over decorum—not that it was a fair fight to begin with. "We're just civilians now, remember? And not very law-abiding ones at that."

Grayson scoffed, but the admiral met Matt's defiant look impassively.

"Because, as surprising as it might sound, there may be something you could do to help us counter this threat and amend your past mistake. Now, if you cannot guarantee compliance with our rules, you are welcome to leave, Matthew. As I recall, it's a tactic you readily embrace."

Matt gritted his teeth. The most infuriating thing about this conversation was that his father wasn't wrong. It was so much easier to walk away. In fact, every ounce of common sense in his body was imploring him to do just that. His instincts, honed to needlepoint sharpness over years of self-preservation, told him in no uncertain terms that he was about to do something spectacularly stupid—and yet, when he remembered how ashen Nora's face had looked in that sterile hospital room, he knew backing down wasn't an option.

Whatever his father wanted him to do, it definitely wasn't going to bring his sister from the brink of death or recoup all the lives that'd been lost in the raids. But he couldn't deny the recent attack was, at least partially, a consequence of his inaction, and that made him culpable. It seemed no matter how much he tried to run from trouble, trouble always caught up with him, or worse, with the people he cared about the most. When he ran, people got hurt. So, he couldn't run anymore.

He looked at Ryce, seeking if not his permission, then his approval. There was no need to explain his meaning. Ryce gave an infinitesimal shrug and nodded.

"I'm listening," Matt said, turning back to his father.

"Good," the admiral said dryly. "You've guessed the Alraki might be using another jumpgate, and that may not be far from the truth. Except it's not really a jumpgate per se. Central Foreign Intelligence believe the Alraki may have obtained—or developed independently—a new technology that would allow them to bypass the existing jumpgates altogether, creating wormholes without the need for Mnirian infrastructure."

The silence following his statement was so absolute that Matt's own breathing sounded loud.

"Is that even possible?" Matt asked at last, sitting up straight and looking around the table. "All interstellar traffic goes through the jumpgates. An alternative network sounds like...science fiction."

"It's possible," Ryce said from beside him, drawing everyone's attention. "Theoretically, a wormhole can be created without the need for a stationary jumpgate activated by laser excitation. In practice, no one has ever been able to recreate this phenomenon outside of one. To my knowledge, no one even completely understands how the jumpgates work."

"Nevertheless, we believe the Alraki are now in possession of this capability," the admiral said. "Moreover, we have reason to believe this technology is mobile enough to be installed on a single ship."

Matt had rarely seen Ryce look confused, especially in front of strangers, but this was mind-blowing enough for him to let his iron self-control slip.

"You think this Alraki frigate—the one that had attacked Atasia, the *Lennox*, and attempted to raid the *Lady Lisa*—can generate its own wormhole to traverse space from any point it chooses?" Ryce asked slowly.

"We have the intel to support it," Grayson said. "It appears the technology is still experimental, and the Alraki are field-testing it on this particular vessel."

"Are you saying the Alraki have managed to do something the Mnirians couldn't?" Matt asked. "A ship that can jump to any place in the galaxy, possibly even beyond? This would revolutionize space travel as we know it. As every other race knows it."

"It would seem we may have underestimated them," Cummings said. For a brief moment he looked much older than his years, the weariness etched into every line of his face. "They have far surpassed our assessments of their scientific advancement."

Matt said nothing, still trying to wrap his mind around this revelation. The Alraki were a bad enough enemy, with their superhuman strength and casual brutality, without them popping up unexpectedly all over Federation space.

"Needless to say, gentlemen, if this technology proves applicable and the Alraki deploy it across their military contingent, it could be a tiebreaker in the war," the admiral continued, echoing Matt's thoughts. "Imagine what would happen if they launched surprise attacks against distant colonies or major Freeports. Maybe even entire planets."

Matt could never fault the vividness of his imagination, and right now it readily supplied him with images of Alraki forces laying siege to the most densely populated human home worlds. Cygnus-1. Sonora-7. Nova. Mars. Earth. How could humanity, scattered hundreds of light years across the galaxy, possibly stand against an enemy that could appear anywhere at any given time, with the sole intention to plunder and destroy?

He glanced at Ryce. He must have had the same idea, because his mouth was set in a hard, thin line. As someone whose entire adoptive family had perished in an Alraki raid, Ryce knew exactly what kind of potential damage they'd be facing.

"You said I had a chance to correct my mistake," Matt said, turning back to his father after taking a second to gather his thoughts. "What is it you want me to do?"

What use could one small-time smuggler be when you had all the might of the Federal Fleet at your disposal, he wanted to ask, but this time, he held himself in check.

"To be honest, I didn't want to involve you in any of this," the admiral said with a slight frown. "But the commander proposed a plan that I believe has a chance of working, however slim. Perhaps he should be the one to tell you about it."

"Thank you, sir." Walker took the dubious vote of confidence in stride. "As a matter of fact, the plan is simple—to infiltrate the Alraki vessel and take possession of the alien technology. Optimally, we'd be able to subsequently destroy the frigate to eliminate evidence of our presence."

"Wow," Matt said. "Seriously? *That's* your solid plan? Stealing aboard the alien ship and…what, impersonating the Alraki crew? Did you grow an extra set of limbs or bio-mech armor while I wasn't looking?"

"That's actually where you come in."

"Me? Do you want *me* to grow the extra limbs?"

"No. In fact, you're not supposed to be there at all," Walker said with a great deal more patience than their exchange warranted. "All we need is your ship. We'd like to hire it for the collection and extraction mission."

"The last time a Fleet official hired my ship, it didn't end well for anyone involved," Matt said with a sidelong look at Ryce.

"I'm aware," Walker said. "But this is different. There would be nothing illicit about it."

"Why would you want my ship? It can't exactly take on a frigate, alien or not. Weapons regulations and all that."

"Our first priority is obtaining the technology," Admiral Cummings said. "Blowing it up all to hell without accomplishing that is the absolutely last resort. This should be a stealth operation, not an altercation. That's why we're not sending in another destroyer or a cruiser to chase it. We know that right now, this particular ship is cruising Sonora. We can't risk spooking the Alraki and it disappearing God knows where."

"Going by your own report, Mr. Spears, the Alraki have shown themselves willing to go after what they must consider easy targets even while on an ostensibly covert mission," Walker said. "A lonely hauler randomly crossing their path would certainly appear so, just like it had in the past. Your ship would serve as bait, to be captured and boarded by the Alraki. It would allow our team to gain access to the frigate and canvass it from the inside."

Matt opened his mouth and closed it again. He'd been sure there weren't many things that could render him speechless, but it just went to show there were no safe bets in this world.

"Forgive me for saying so, but the chances of the Alraki randomly attacking *Lady Lisa* are...low, to put it mildly," Ryce said into the silence while Matt was busy doing an impersonation of a fish out of water. "If they indeed have the capability to jump independently, you have no means of predicting their route."

"No," Walker agreed. "We don't. In fact, there are a lot of things we don't know, including the physical limits of this technology, what source of energy they are using, and how many jumps they can make consecutively."

"We assume their resources aren't infinite," the admiral added. "Our best bet would be to monitor any reported sightings. If the frigate has to recharge between jumps, we stand a chance of coming upon it while it's still restricted to the same area."

"Great. Then, there's this small matter of being ripped apart when they board us," Matt said. "No matter how good your special ops team is, they can't take on a fully manned battleship. This ain't the fucking movies."

"And this is not a smugglers' canteen," the admiral snapped. "Watch your tongue, Matthew."

Matt scowled and opened his mouth.

"How can you ensure the safe return of Mr. Spears's ship?" Ryce asked, quickly changing the subject. "I'm sure it's only a freight vessel to you, but for us it's home."

"We can't guarantee it with a hundred-percent certainty, of course," Walker said. "Just like we cannot guarantee the overall success of the mission. However, all efforts will be made to compensate Mr. Spears in the event of any damages caused to his ship, in addition to the payment for his services."

It didn't sound particularly reassuring, but Matt suspected this was the best he was going to get.

"I'd have to run this past my crew before I make any decisions," Matt said. "But I wouldn't get your hopes up just yet."

He could tell none of the present officers liked that, but that was just tough luck. Not that he was in the habit of discussing every aspect of business with his crew members; but this time there was so much more than just their livelihoods to consider. And, if he had to be totally honest, he was stalling. He knew what he had to do, but he couldn't shake off the feeling of being cornered and put on the spot, and it was something he resented almost as much as having to surrender his ship to the organization he'd vowed never to have anything to do with again.

"Just remember what's at stake here, Matthew," Admiral Cummings said as Matt rose from his chair.

"Trust me, I remember," Matt threw over his shoulder as he headed for the door. "It's the only thing that's keeping me from telling all you gentlemen to go to hell."

Chapter Five

"I wish you hadn't been quite so flippant," Ryce said as they dragged themselves through mostly deserted hallways back to the pod bay where *Lisa* was docked. It didn't come off as an accusation, exactly, but Matt could definitely detect notes of reproach.

"You know—so do I," Matt said wearily, glancing sideways at their ever-present escort. The headache he'd be nursing in the morning was beginning to set in, and his mouth was parched. "For what it's worth, I'm sorry about all that. What can I say, being around my father always brings out the best in me."

They said nothing the rest of the way back to the dock and until they were finally alone, safely inside *Lisa*'s dim main corridor. But there was another thing Matt couldn't stop thinking about since they'd left the major's office.

"Did you mean what you said in there? About *Lady Lisa* being your home?"

Ryce stopped and turned to look at him, surprise fleeting over his near-perfect features.

"Of course it is. You didn't know that already? I thought me staying on rather gave it away."

"Yes, but..." Matt stopped, too, somewhat at a loss as to how to phrase his concern in a way that wouldn't make him sound either like an insecure dolt or an ungrateful bastard. "It's not just because you were out of options, is it?"

"I did have other options." Ryce's voice grew clipped, his earlier frustration resurfacing. "Come on, Matt, we've been through this. You may have forgotten all the nonsense you spewed about letting me go so I'd have the freedom to pursue my dreams, but I haven't. We aren't about to have that argument again, are we?"

"No, no. I'm sorry. It's just that I'm not used to—"

"People saying they want to be with you?" Ryce said, much more softly. "That happens more often than you think if you would just pay closer attention. You have to give those who love you more credit, Matt—and cut yourself some slack."

Matt shook his head, trying to dislodge the funny lump that had settled in his throat. "Anyway. Let's just sleep on it and call for a crew meeting first thing in the morning," he said, looking away. "It's been a long day."

"Something tells me tomorrow won't be much different," Ryce said.

*

Crew meetings aboard the *Lisa* were always an informal thing, held wherever it was easiest to convene—which was usually the rec room, the kitchen, or the bridge. This time, they met in the galley, with Matt figuring breakfast was as good a time as any to deliberate on their immediate future prospects—after he'd given himself enough time to have his first coffee of the morning to chase down the traces of a light hangover.

Commander Walker had gone as far as sending him a draft of the contract late last night, sans the sensitive particulars of the job. Matt forwarded the document to everybody's commlinks while making himself a second cup of coffee and waiting for the others to settle around the dining table with their plates.

"How's Nora?" Tony asked, opening the message but pausing to give Matt a concerned look as he sat down beside her.

"Still touch and go. But I was given to understand the doctors are optimistic. It was good to see she's getting the best possible treatment."

Tony reached out to give his hand an encouraging squeeze, accompanied by a tight smile. She had an uncanny ability to see right through his bullshit, but this apparently wasn't the time to call him out on it.

"I don't understand," Val said, frowning as he scrolled through the contract on his comm. His tall, powerful frame occupied almost half the table, leaving Ryce to huddle closer to Matt—not that he complained about the forced proximity. "You snagged a job with the Fleet? What would they need an independent hauler for?"

"Not exactly." Matt took a swig of his scalding-hot coffee, then a deep breath, and launched into explanations regarding the previous night's events.

"Wow," Tony said when he was finished. "Your dad's here? Talk about a small galaxy."

"Considering we're both here for the same reason, it's not that much of a coincidence," Matt said. "Though I'm not sure what was more important in his case—being by his daughter's side or being the hero who outguns the Alraki."

"You're not being fair, Matt," Tony chided.

"It's as if fairness isn't my strong suit."

Tony rolled her eyes.

"It's a nice chunk of change they're willing to shell out to hire us," Val said bluntly, looking at him across the table.

"Yep. Enough for this venture to be lucrative—in theory. Whether it's really worth the risk..." Matt shrugged and spread his hands.

"It might not be, but you're going to do this anyway," Tony said, her dark eyes intent on him even though Matt was doing his best to avoid her gaze. "I know that look, Captain. It's the 'I'm going to do something foolish no matter what everybody else says' look."

"I don't have a look for that," Matt protested. "Besides, I do care about you guys' opinion. Especially considering I'm pretty torn on this one. And by 'torn' I mean I'd rather do literally anything else."

"Sonora's a big sector. What makes them think the Alraki would stumble on our ship, out of all the transport vessels traversing the system, and then decide we're worth looting? Sounds a little farfetched, if you ask me," Val said, echoing Ryce's earlier concerns.

"They were being deliberately vague on this point," Matt said. "There's a lot more going on than they're telling us, and I'm pretty sure they have their contingencies covered. Willing to bet a hundred to one this isn't the only plan the admiral has up his sleeve. He's the kind of person who always has a backup plan, and this is definitely not an all-eggs-in-one-basket type of situation. But whatever they've come up with, they're not sharing it with us. It doesn't matter anyway. All we have to decide is whether we are willing to turn *Lisa* into a Trojan horse."

There was a pause as everyone seemed to consider his words.

"I know Walker's plan is dangerous," Ryce said finally. "Possibly even reckless. But this isn't a typical situation. In my experience, conventional methods of engagement aren't as effective with the Alraki, which is precisely why it could actually work."

"Of course *you* would think it might work," Matt said, rubbing the bridge of his nose. "Damn Fleet operatives. You're all fucking crackers."

"No one has ever won a war by being timid," Ryce pointed out.

"True. But, frankly, their plan working is what worries me. Whether the Fleet manages to get their hands on this new technology or not, the *Lisa* might not survive the encounter."

"If we're quick enough to bug out at the first sign of trouble—" Tony began.

"Oh, no," Matt said. "If I decide to go through with this—and it's a big 'if'—none of you folks are coming along. This is way too dangerous. Walker's team can handle it on their own, and I'm sure they won't want any civilians getting under their feet anyway."

"What about you?" Tony asked, once again cutting straight to the point Matt wished to avoid.

"I'm her captain. I don't let anyone else fly my ship."

Ryce raised an eyebrow and leaned back in his chair, crossing his arms over his chest.

"You know what I mean," Matt said irritably.

"Yes, I do. That's precisely why I'm not letting you tag along on a special military operation on your own."

"You can't 'let me' do anything," Matt said, trying to channel that signature Cummings haughtiness, but Ryce wasn't impressed.

"And you can't make me leave you," he said, doing a much better job of sounding authoritative than Matt could ever hope for.

"Boys," Tony said in a warning tone.

"This whole argument is moot anyway." Matt swirled the last of his coffee in the mug and gulped it down. It was unpleasantly lukewarm by this point, but he wasn't about to waste perfectly good coffee. "I seriously doubt I'm gonna accept their offer. This is way too risky, and the possibility of losing the ship... Yeah. As far as I'm concerned, if the Fleet wants this Alraki frigate so badly, they're welcome to shoot it out of the sky without getting the rest of us involved."

*

"You think it'd be wrong of me to decline," Matt said as Ryce and he walked to the bridge.

It wasn't so much a question as a statement, really. By now, Matt had a pretty good grasp of Ryce's various types of silence, and this one reeked of disagreement.

Ryce shrugged noncommittally. "This is ultimately your decision. And I can certainly understand all of your misgivings."

"But?" Matt prompted as he sat in the copilot chair and then tapped on the control panel to power it up.

Ryce didn't answer immediately; Matt got the impression he was carefully choosing his words.

"Perhaps I'm not the right person to be giving advice on this," he said at length. "Considering... Well. Considering my past choices. But if you want my opinion, I'd say we should do this."

"Miss the action, do you?"

Ryce gave him a long look.

"Sorry." Matt slumped in the chair, shaking his head. "I don't know why I'm being such a douchebag about it."

"I might have an inkling as to why. But you should remember that your ultimate decision has to factor considerations other than the desire to spite your father."

Matt scoffed, but mercifully, his commlink buzzed before he could answer.

"Oh God, what now?" Matt said, recognizing Grayson's number. He brought the call on-screen. "If Admiral Cummings is getting impatient, tell him to sit tight because I'm not goddamn ready to give my answer yet."

"It's not about that, Matthew," Grayson said. "I'm calling regarding Major Cummings."

Matt's breath caught as his heart plummeted into his stomach.

"What about her?" he asked, his voice shaking dangerously. "Is she..."

"No, no," Grayson said. "It's actually good news. Your sister is awake and feeling better."

There was a pause as Matt struggled to compose himself.

"I'd have thought Commander Walker would be the one to tell me that," he said. "Sorry for snapping at you."

"No harm done," Grayson said smoothly. "Her doctors have informed the admiral of her progress, and I've taken the liberty of passing it on to you as well. You may come to see her now if you like. I'd be happy to escort you to the infirmary myself."

"Yes. Yes, of course. I'll be right out. Thanks."

He ended the call and turned to Ryce, who patted his shoulder reassuringly.

"Go," Ryce said, his voice taking on a gentleness that almost made Matt cry. They could bicker all day long, but in the end, it was little moments like this that really mattered. "You should be with her now."

"What about you?"

"I'll use the time to do a bit of research. I might have an idea of how we could detect the Araki ship coming out of the wormhole, but the implementation could be a little tricky."

"You do your genius thing, then. I won't be long," Matt said.

Ryce shook his head. "Take your time. And send the major my regards."

*

The bright pristine hospital room looked exactly as it had last time, but a subtle, almost imperceptible change in the ambient energy greeted Matt as he walked in. It was as if he could sense the life returning to its occupant.

Nora lay in bed, still surrounded by a network of tubing like a fairy-tale princess asleep behind a lattice of brambles, but she looked a lot less sickly.

"Matthew," she said, catching a sight of him as he paused over the threshold. Her hand, resting on the crisp white sheet, twitched, but she was obviously too weak to lift it. "You came."

"Of course." Matt pulled up a chair to sit beside her. Grayson, who'd walked him right to the door, tactfully remained outside.

Matt thought about holding her hand but was too afraid to touch her, frail as she was, so he ended up clasping his hands awkwardly in his lap to stop them from shaking. He realized that up until now, deep down, he'd been afraid that despite everyone's assurances to the contrary, Nora might not make it. "Commander Walker called me. Please don't be cross with him."

"I'm not." Nora's voice was as feeble as she looked. "John—I mean Commander Walker—has done so much to make sure I was comfortable."

"So I've noticed."

Twin spots of color bloomed on Nora's cheeks, and Matt had to stop himself from grinning.

"Father is here too. He just left." She changed the subject.

"Yeah," Matt said, keeping his tone neutral. "I've met him."

There was a short, uncomfortable pause.

"Ryce, Tony, and Val all send their well wishes," Matt said. "They're all so happy to hear you're feeling better."

"I feel like I've been run over by a barge. I'm sure you can sympathize."

Matt didn't want to think of all the ways in which it was true.

"The important thing now is that you get plenty of rest and let them pump you full of whatever medications they deem fit."

"I don't have much choice." Nora closed her eyes, a grimace of pain briefly twisting her features. "Sorry. I'm still a little fuzzy. And talking hurts."

"You should sleep now. I'll be back soon, all right?"

But Nora was already asleep again, her chest steadily rising and falling underneath the sheet. For a moment, Matt just stood there, looking at her, letting himself breathe alongside her as something that had been constricted inside him eased.

He briefly considered staying there until she woke up again, but with Grayson waiting for him outside and the very real possibility of him running into his father again, he decided to ask the nurses to notify him when it'd be best to visit.

"How's Major Cummings?" Grayson was reading something on his commlink but got up when Matt stepped into the waiting area.

"Much better. Thank you again for arranging for me see her."

Matt was still slightly baffled because when Grayson first called him, Matt had gotten the distinct impression he'd done so reluctantly. They hadn't parted on the best of terms, to put it mildly, and neither of them had made any effort to keep in touch since the breakup. Matt doubted Grayson (or the admiral, for that matter) even knew what had happened to him during the last few years—or that he cared. And, if he was being honest, he hadn't been any different regarding them either.

"No problem." Grayson bit his lip, glancing to the sides. "Listen, Matthew... I was wondering whether I could have a word with you?"

Matt's eyebrows shot up despite himself. "Sure," he said warily.

Grayson sat back in the plastic chair, and Matt had no choice but to sit down beside him. He couldn't help but notice they were occupying the same spot as Ryce and he had the day before yesterday—and how different his current mood was.

"First of all, I wanted to say I'm very happy to see you doing so well," Grayson said, his tone taking a serious turn. "I know things went a bit downhill for us, but I never wished you ill."

Matt didn't know what he was expecting, but this wasn't it. Grayson was being nice, almost apologetic about their whole situation, and Matt felt he owed him some honesty in return.

"Thank you. I appreciate it, really."

Matt couldn't say he wished things had gone differently. Losing Grayson, on top of losing the connection with his family, had been painful, but without that, he wouldn't be where he was today. He wouldn't have bought the *Lisa* and hired Tony and Val. He wouldn't have met Ryce.

"You're welcome. But there's something else I want to show you." Grayson tapped on his comm and handed it to Matt.

The footage showed a black, starry expanse framed by part of a ship's hull. Matt recognized the outline of the main bridge of the *Lennox*, filmed by what he guessed was one of the portside cameras. The distant stars tilted as the ship spun, and flashes of explosions momentarily eclipsed their brightness. A dark shadow moved across the screen, all jagged edges and strangely curved lines, typical of Alraki vessels. The mere sight of it made Matt's pulse ratchet up and then nearly stop as the alien ship fired a volley of torpedoes in the direction of the bridge. The angle of the camera didn't offer a direct line of sight, but there was no mistaking the debris that catapulted into space, including tiny, cartoonlike figures.

Matt pushed down on the sudden nausea. Walker had been very vague when describing the skirmish with the Alraki, and Matt preferred it that way. He knew Nora had been lucky not to have been in the compartment that had sustained the most damage, but being nearly killed by falling armature wasn't much better. He really didn't need to see people being sucked into the void first thing after leaving a survivor's hospital room.

"Why are you showing me this now?" he asked, shoving the commlink back at Grayson.

"I know you're still debating whether or not to accept the job." Grayson slipped the device back into his pocket. "I thought this might tip the scale."

Matt pursed his lips. "That's a rather blunt manipulation," he said, striving for composure. "Betting on the softness of my heart? I was expecting more finesse from the admiral."

"The admiral has nothing to do with it," Grayson said. "I'm here on my own initiative, and this conversation is off the record."

"Why? And why are you all so keen on *Lady Lisa*? It's not the only small hauler ship out there ready for hire."

"That's certainly true. But you and your ship are here, now." Notes of urgency entered Grayson's voice. "And you and your crew have proved you can be counted on for discretion, as per Commander Walker. Soft heart or not, you must understand what the Federation stands to gain if this operation is successful. What a resounding victory this would be for humanity."

"Not to mention all the accolades for the admiral and a big fat promotion for you," Matt couldn't help but point out.

At least it solved the mystery of Grayson going out of his way to be nice to him all of a sudden. Every career Fleet officer he'd met his entire life had some ulterior motive that dictated their actions. Sometimes it was a savior complex disguised as heroism, but more often than not, there were much simpler motivations at play, such as greed and ambition. In a way, it was much easier to deal with those than with unexpected acts of kindness that Matt wasn't sure how to interpret.

"Whatever my reasons are, or what you believe they are, they don't change the fact that you know I'm right about this." Grayson nodded toward the infirmary door. "You saw the havoc a single Alraki frigate can wreak, here and on Atasia. Anyone, anywhere, could be the next victim. Any station, outpost, and colony in Federation space. I'm sure not even the most jaded person would just let it happen while knowing he could have done something to prevent it. And I know you're not as jaded as you want to appear, Matthew."

Matt frowned. These arguments reminded him, quite eerily, of the points Ryce had touched upon when he'd defended his old commander's quest for a Mnirian superweapon to defeat the Alraki. Only this time, as it turned out, the potential tiebreaker was out of the humans' hands.

It all came down to that, didn't it? Could he just stand aside while innocent people, both military and civilians, got hurt and killed, their homes and lives destroyed, as had happened to so many over the course of this exhausting war? Matt had done it before, opting to save himself rather than try helping his comrades. His father was right about running away being his tried and true modus operandi. But what had that ever gotten him but a wounded soul and a haunted conscience? If the last year had taught him anything, it was that some things were too important to give up on—friendship, love, acceptance. All the things crucial to the survival of mankind.

The man Matt desperately wanted to become—the kind of man his friends and partner believed him to be—would know what to do. And it was supremely and annoyingly the sort of "right thing" he shied away from.

"Fine, Grayson," he said with a heavy sigh. "Go tell the admiral I accept the job. May God have mercy on all of our souls."

Chapter Six

It was late by the time Matt got back to the *Lisa*. The communal areas were dark and quiet, the crew having retired for the night. He headed for his cabin, but changed his mind at the last minute, opting instead for Ryce's.

Ryce sat on the edge of his bunk bed, scrolling through something on the commlink that rested on the small side table. He started guiltily when the door opened and shut it off quickly.

"What are you doing?" Matt joined him and planted a kiss on his cheek. "Still researching wormholes?"

"No. It's nothing." Ryce pushed the commlink away and settled back on the bed.

"Too bad." Matt yawned and stretched before unzipping his fatigues. "I was hoping maybe you were looking up something kinky you wanted to try."

"No," Ryce said hastily. The way he'd blush over the most innocuous things was absolutely endearing. "I'm sorry, I..." He bit his lip, looking away.

"Hey." Matt reached out to take Ryce's hand. "What's wrong? Did something happen?"

"No. It's silly, but I don't like keeping things from you. Not being open with each other has gotten us in enough trouble before."

"Okay," Matt said slowly. He didn't mind talks or even serious discussions, but long and rambling prefaces made him nervous.

"I've been trying to trace the message that came along with the money transfer." Ryce sounded guilty, as if Matt had caught him in the middle of doing something naughty.

"The one that came from your mother?" Matt asked, baffled. "I thought you didn't want to seek her out until she was ready to contact you of her own volition."

"I didn't. I don't. But—" Ryce sighed and shook his head. "I just want to find out who she is, in case…in case either of us ever decide we should meet."

Matt squeezed Ryce's hand in reassurance. "Did you?" he asked softly. "Find out who she is?"

"Not through the message." Ryce scooted closer to Matt, and they snuggled comfortably, holding each other. "But when we met Prof. Brinan at that IMA function on Freeport 73, he mentioned he'd been her research supervisor on that off-world mission to Gemma-8 when they were attacked by pirates. I searched the web for whatever I could find on Brinan—his academic record, his publications, his scientific credentials—to see if I could find some connection. I found the names of the young scientists and students he mentored and narrowed it down to those who had accompanied him on that expedition. The incident hadn't gotten much coverage on the news at the time, but I was able to match the names."

He took a deep breath. "I think I know who she is. I was reading up on her just before you came."

Matt didn't say anything for a while. He understood Ryce's yearning for a family, but he couldn't say whether tracking down this woman was a good idea or not. Especially seeing as she hadn't contacted Ryce directly, even when she had every opportunity to do so.

"Is she as smart as you are?" he asked, keeping his tone light.

"She's a xenobiologist," Ryce said. Matt couldn't see his expression, but his voice had softened a fraction, losing its earlier tension. "I read up on her research on cryopreservation of microorganisms in extreme environments. It's quite fascinating."

"A study into immortality," Matt joked.

"Something like that. Though it remains a long stretch from permafrost microbes to human applications."

"Did you find her contact information?"

Ryce made a sound of assent. "I saved it to my commlink. But I'm not going to call her just yet. Not before I think it through."

"That's a good idea," Matt said gently, burying his face in Ryce's hair and breathing in the scent of him, familiar and intoxicating. He still had to tell him about his conversation with Grayson and his decision to go along with the admiral's plan, but that could wait till morning. "Sending you the money was a nice gesture, but coming to terms with having a child or a parent you've never met takes more than that. Perhaps you both need more time to process."

Ryce shook his head, but Matt couldn't tell whether it was in negation or rueful agreement.

"I'm sorry I haven't told you about this before," Ryce said. "I'm not sure whether I should be doing any of this at all."

"I understand." Matt hoped he was able to keep his expression neutral. "Don't mention it."

He was the one deliberately keeping a secret from his partner—a big one. And even if he did it to protect Ryce, he wasn't comfortable with the knowledge. This whole talk about mothers and parents and doing the right thing reminded him too acutely about the other part of the equation, the one in which Ryce's father—or the man Matt believed to be Ryce's father—was still a threat to them both.

Ryce didn't respond. Instead, he pulled away and raised his head, gazing solemnly into Matt's eyes.

"Do you ever think about...having a family of your own?" he asked, his voice subdued.

"You're my family," Matt said, just as quietly. "You, and Tony, and Val, and the *Lisa*. We all have one another's backs. That's what counts, right?"

Ryce's fingers tightened on Matt's hand.

"Yes. Of course we are family. But it's not what I meant."

Matt bit his lip. He knew exactly what Ryce meant, but the thought of having someone else dependent on him terrified him. Sure, he shouldered the responsibility for his crew's livelihood and wellbeing, but it wasn't the same as raising a child.

"I...don't think it's for me." Matt's heart dropped even as the words were out of his mouth. What if this wasn't what Ryce wanted to hear? What if he was ruining everything, again?

"Why not?" Ryce asked, his eyes serious. "Are you really that scared of the commitment?"

"It's not the commitment. It's the responsibility. You know me; I'll be sure to find some way to screw everything up. A kid doesn't deserve a parent like that."

"My mother abandoned me when I was a baby, and I'm still ready to forgive her," Ryce said gently.

"You're a better person than me."

"And you're not your father," Ryce said. "If you're capable of acknowledging your mistakes and be willing to do your best to rectify them, your child will forgive you for them."

Matt swallowed, trying to push down on a cold sticky lump that suddenly seemed to be lodged in his throat. Ryce was too astute not to realize where Matt's fears stemmed from, especially after meeting the formidable Admiral Cummings in person. That wound was still bleeding, no matter how much Matt wanted to pretend not to notice the scar.

"Where is this coming from?" he asked, desperate to change the subject to something less raw.

"This whole thing with my birth mother made me start thinking about having children myself someday," Ryce said, and then shrugged. "I'm sorry; I didn't mean to put you on the spot. It's not like I have any plans for our immediate future. We don't have to have this conversation now."

Matt shook his head. "If life has taught me anything, it's that I can't make any promises. I can't deny the idea of having children scares the shit out me, for so many reasons. But...if that's something you want, we can...I don't know, work it out somehow. In the future, when I've had time to adjust to the idea."

"Sure," Ryce said, a little smile playing on his lips. At least Matt's quiet freak-out hadn't seemed to upset him. But then, Ryce had always exhibited the patience of a saint when it came to dealing with Matt's various hang-ups.

Matt dropped his gaze to where their hands were entwined, still holding tight to each other.

"If I ever do start a family," he said, his voice barely a whisper, "it'd only be with you."

Ryce drew a deep breath. He reached out and touched Matt's face, tracing the stubbly line of his jaw with his long elegant fingers, making him look up again. His gaze now held a different kind of intensity, and his lips parted in anticipation.

Matt's pulse quickened, blood rushing in a tidal wave to the southern regions of his body. But he waited, unmoving, letting Ryce make up his own mind about what he wanted to do. It was only after Ryce leaned in, pressing their lips together, that Matt grasped his shoulders, deepening the kiss with the abandon of a dying man struggling for his last breath.

"Stay with me tonight," Ryce said when they released each other, gasping. His gray eyes were dark, shadowed by his long lashes. "If you want. Unless it's still—"

"No. I want to. So much." Matt stroked his hair and placed a hand on his nape to draw Ryce into another kiss. All the anxiety of the last few days, all the anger and the resentment and the worry drained away as he melted into that kiss, their lips and tongues locked in a dance as gentle as it was passionate.

Ryce stretched back, pulling Matt on top of him, sighing softly when Matt slid his hand under his T-shirt. His sigh changed into a muffled moan when Matt covered his mouth again with his own. Shedding their clothes became an awkward tumble as they seemed unable to tear away from each other long enough to undress.

"You're beautiful," Matt whispered, kissing the tender skin beneath Ryce's jaw. "You're perfect."

Ryce chuckled, throwing his head back to allow Matt more access. Pressed together as they were, the shiver that ran through his body echoed in Matt's, fueling his already flaring arousal. His fingers tangled in Matt's hair, nudging him gently downward as he spread his legs in unequivocal invitation.

Matt could take a hint, more than happy to oblige Ryce's silent request. He shuffled to the foot of the bed, pulled off Ryce's pants and underwear, and was greeted by the sight of his erection, long and graceful and eager.

As much as he wanted to pounce on that prize right away, he took a few seconds to shuck off his own fatigues and undergarments. There was no way he was going to deny himself the sweet luxury of skin sliding against naked skin while pleasuring his boyfriend.

And it was all about the uncomplicated pleasures and comfort they could share, whether by worshiping each other's bodies, or simply embracing through the night to hold the demons of the past at bay. They were here, ready to take on whatever the universe threw at them because they would face it together; and together, they were so much more than two people groping blindly to find their way in the world. Together, they could do anything.

The bed creaked as Matt repositioned himself between Ryce's legs. He wasted no more time taking Ryce's cock into his mouth, rewarding his earlier patience, and put his lips and tongue to work, reveling in the loud moans his efforts elicited. Ryce clutched at the sheets, rumpling them even further, arching off the bed.

"God, it feels so good when you do that," he panted.

Matt hummed in agreement, too intent on his task to offer a more eloquent answer. It felt good on his end, too, perhaps a bit too good, if his own aching erection was anything to go by. But it could wait for a few more minutes. Tending to Ryce's needs was a much more pressing concern, and Matt applied every ounce of skill he had to achieving that goal.

The minute reactions of Ryce's body were as familiar to Matt now as his own, and he couldn't miss all the tell-tale signs of impending orgasm—the way his restrained thrusts became shallower and his abdomen muscles tensed and rippled. Matt relaxed his jaw, taking him deeper, his throat working as hard as his lips and tongue.

Ryce made a high-pitched keening sound, bucking off the mattress. He was much more reticent during sex than most of Matt's previous partners, so he relished every little noise the man made, studying them like he would a fascinating new language.

"Matt," he said breathlessly, and this was Matt's only warning before the powerful jet of Ryce's release hit the back of his throat.

He swallowed sloppily, not worried about finesse at the moment. The second Ryce slipped from his mouth, Matt took ahold of his own cock, stroking it frantically as he leaned over Ryce's prostrate body, propping himself up on one arm. His first instinct was to close his eyes as he climbed toward his own climax, but the look on Ryce's face as he watched Matt touch himself, a dazed expression mixed with raw lust, urged him to keep them open. That look, combined with the urgency of his arousal and the taste of Ryce's come in his mouth, blended into an unstoppable force that shoved Matt over the edge of a precipice. He cried out as he came, hard and relentless, over the flawless expanse of Ryce's stomach beneath him.

Once again unheeding the mess he was making, Matt collapsed on top of him, shaking with ebbing pleasure. For a while, they simply lay there together, breathing in unison.

"That was so good," Matt murmured, angling his head to nuzzle Ryce's neck.

"Mmm. But don't think I'm done with you yet." Ryce ran his hand through Matt's dampened hair.

"Oh, my. Hope I'm up for the challenge, then." Matt rolled onto his back and stared contentedly at the ceiling.

"Can I ask you something?" Ryce propped himself on one elbow looking down at him.

"Anything."

"Lieutenant Lee and you. You were...a couple."

It wasn't framed as a question, exactly, and Ryce sounded uncharacteristically timorous. The abrupt change of subject (if it could be called that since they'd been communicating mostly in grunts and moans a minute ago) threw Matt a bit, but he didn't mind discussing this particular part of his biography. Even though bringing up his ex while they were in bed felt a little weird.

"For a short while, yeah. It was before I filed for a discharge. I was a flight controller; Grayson was with Field Intelligence then."

"Was it serious?"

Matt weighed the question. He'd been heartbroken over his breakup with Grayson, of course, but he realized it was more about the overall sense of betrayal that had sent him reeling back then than about their romantic relationship fizzling. They hadn't been together long enough for him to actually mourn their connection, and in the following years, that particular ache had faded in comparison with everything else he'd had to deal with.

"I wasn't about to propose, if that's what you're asking," Matt said, keeping his tone light.

Ryce hmphed. "Don't you find it strange that your ex-boyfriend is your father's aide?"

"It's a small world, I guess," Matt said.

It really wasn't, but he couldn't blame Grayson for setting his sights on the admiral's office. For someone so ambitious, serving as an aide to the Director of Foreign Intelligence was one hell of a stepping-stone.

"I guess," Ryce said, but he didn't sound too convinced, and his face clouded.

It was high time they talked about something else if Matt wanted to maintain their earlier frisky mood.

"Can I ask *you* something now?" He scooted closer to Ryce and ran a finger down his chest and abdomen, smearing the drying splashes of his come across the stretch of his boyfriend's pale skin.

"Sure."

"Have you ever wanted to try talking dirty in bed?" Matt raised an eyebrow suggestively.

Ryce was already flushed a healthy shade of red from his earlier exertions, but now the color in his cheeks deepened even further.

"I don't know," he said hesitantly. "I might be too self-conscious to do that. It's...embarrassing."

His answer gave Matt pause; he'd never considered his enjoyment of sex in all its variations something to be embarrassed about. Then again, sex was more personal and intimate to Ryce than it had ever been to him, until now. He stroked Ryce's side gently, mulling it over.

"What if you use a foreign language?" he asked, half jesting. "Something I won't understand. You could say all sorts of naughty things without it being awkward."

"Ugh..."

"Come on," Matt urged, too curious now to let it go. "Just try it."

"*Dulcissime, totam tibi subdo me,*" Ryce whispered, his blush turning positively crimson.

A warm, fuzzy feeling spread through Matt's chest, and he fought—and failed—to suppress a grin.

"You didn't tell me you understood Latin," Ryce reproached, watching his reaction.

"Let's pretend that I don't."

"You're such an asshole," Ryce said, the corners of his eyes crinkling with amusement.

"See, this is exactly what—" Matt began, but Ryce silenced him with a kiss.

Chapter Seven

Unfortunately, the saying about no good deed going unpunished was proving to be true. The sight of military personnel coming and going at all hours aboard *Lady Lisa* made Matt's skin crawl, and as they were bent on installing new equipment and upgrading the sensors, he was forced to hang with them in the engine room and the bridge instead of taking refuge in the rec room.

Val was even less keen than Matt about strangers tinkering with his baby, but he was somewhat mollified by all the fancy new fittings and trappings. Matt wasn't quite as enthusiastic for the additions, but he wasn't about to turn down expensive rig that would give him an edge over future competition when it was offered to him for free. Spacecraft maintenance was anything but cheap.

"Too bad we weren't here a month ago," Matt said quietly to Val as they watched one of the *Lennox* engineers fit new wiring on the bridge control panel. "Maybe they would've sprung for a new engine and saved us a huge pile of cash."

"You mean save Easom a huge pile of cash," Val said, watching the working engineer with a frown. His thick arms were crossed over his chest, most likely in an attempt to hold himself from shoving the man aside and doing everything himself the *right* way. "Unless you two got hitched without telling the rest of us and shared your accounts."

"I'm not the hitching type," Matt said airily, pretending to study a side panel and hide an unexpected blush.

Val harrumphed, but whether in agreement or disdain, Matt couldn't tell.

"Have you thought about what you're going to do while on shore leave?" Matt asked, mainly to change the touchy subject.

Val tore his gaze away from the exposed circuits. "I'm not going on shore leave."

"Don't start." Matt rubbed the bridge of his nose. "They wouldn't want any of *Lisa*'s crew hanging around on this run."

"You're staying," Val pointed out.

"I'm the captain. I can't leave my ship."

"Easom is staying too."

"Trust me, if there was any way I could make him sit this one out, I would," Matt said wearily. He'd had this discussion with Ryce already, and predictably but no less annoyingly, he had refused to budge.

"See if you can make Tony sit this one out, Captain," Val deadpanned, returning to watching the repairs.

"I don't care what Tony says," Matt said with a cockiness he knew was entirely unwarranted. "This is way too dangerous for you guys to tag along."

"Dangerous? With all due respect, we've all seen our fair share of dangerous. And besides, weren't you the one who thought this plan was going to be a bust in the first place? We may yet end up going the lengths of the system for nothing, and this whole thing could just prove a waste of time and fuel."

To be totally honest, Matt was secretly (and admittedly shamefully) hoping Val was right, and that despite Walker's apparent confidence, their covert search for the Alraki would prove futile. Not because Matt didn't understand the importance of the mission, but because he knew his lucky streak of surviving near brushes with death was bound to end sometime, and this was the perfect setup for the universe to pull a fast one on him.

The only thing that could dash Matt's hopes for a reprieve was that Ryce had been throwing himself into finding a way for them to track the

Alraki ship's movements across the system. Matt had hardly seen him during the last few days as Ryce spent most of his time aboard the *Lennox*, collaborating with their science officer on efforts to develop a computer program to detect the electromagnetic radiation emitted by a sporadically generated wormhole. Even a small one, as Ryce had explained to him, would emit a high level of radiation detectable by Fleet ships' sensors. By eliminating the background emissions from the working jumpgate of the Freeport 16 station, it would be (theoretically) possible to detect the signature of an opening wormhole, within the confines of the system, once the program was installed on all the ships and on planetside stationary sensor arrays.

Matt shook his head. He might not understand the physics behind it, but if Ryce had anything to do with it, it'd probably work.

"Both you and Tony deserve some time off, so why not now? Seriously, what employee turns down a bit of paid vacation?" Matt insisted in a desperate attempt to gain upper ground.

"The kind that have their boss's back because he has theirs," Val said, unperturbed.

The arrival of Commander Walker on the bridge saved Matt from having to find an answer to that.

"I'd like to speak with Captain Spears alone," the commander said in a tone that brooked no argument.

"What is it?" Matt asked when Val and the other engineer had cleared the bridge. "Your guy was just about done here."

"There's been another attack," Walker said. "A hauler carrying an ore shipment from the mining station on Waga, the Sonora-4 moon. The admiral is trying to keep a tight lid on the incident, and the local mining company is willing to cooperate for the time being, but it's only a matter of time until this news leaks out. We have to move as soon as you're finished installing everything and we have Easom's algorithm up and running across our contingent."

Matt didn't share Walker's doubts regarding Admiral Cummings's ability to strong-arm anyone with anything to lose into permanent silence but refrained from comment.

"Right," he said instead. "Well, we're all up and raring to go, as it were. So we're ready when you are."

"I'll have my team up here as soon as we get the all clear from CenCom," Walker said. "Again, I appreciate your help, Captain. I'm sure the admiral does too."

Matt shook his head. "I don't care about that. Really, I'm only doing this for Nora."

A wry smile touched Walker's lips. "I guess that makes two of us," he said, and gave Matt a curt nod before he headed for the exit.

*

When Matt saw Tony leaning against the wall next to the door to his cabin, arms crossed over her chest, he already knew what this was going to be about, and her determined expression only solidified his suspicions.

"Oh, no," he said, skidding to a halt. "Not you too."

"What?"

"I've said this to Val, and I'm gonna say it to you. I can't let you come on this run. Not this time. And trust me when I say it is a decision I make with a heavy heart because if there's anyone I'd rather watch my back, it's you. Seriously, you've gone above and beyond already, especially with the entire Griggs situation. But this time, the Fleet people call the shots, and I can't in good conscience—"

"Stop." Tony raised a hand in warning, cutting off his protests. "Val already talked to me, and we both agree we're not staying behind. I know you're captain and all, but there's no way we're taking your orders on this one. You know you need us. Val is the only one who can get *Lisa* out of a jam, and I'm the one who can get your ass out of one."

Matt sighed and rolled his eyes. "You're making it very difficult for me, Tony."

"Well, I think it's easy as pie, Captain."

"Okay, fine." He threw his hands up in defeat. "You can come."

She gave him a look that clearly indicated she didn't really need his authorization on this. Matt didn't know if he should be flattered or offended.

"Now, with all this nonsense out of the way," Tony continued. "There was another reason I wanted to talk to you. I have a favor to ask." Her expression changed, turning serious, almost grave. "I need some time off. Once we're all safely back, of course."

"Sure," he said, taken aback—more so by the sudden earnestness of her tone than by the request itself. "You're certainly due a vacation, but… Did something happen?"

"No. I don't know. I guess…" Tony took a deep breath. "I just got a call from my daughter."

That was a bit unexpected. Following Tony's conviction for embezzlement while working as a clinical trial coordinator in the IMA, her husband had divorced her and won sole custody of their only child. She didn't like talking about it, the pain and the heartbreak being still too near, so Matt wasn't aware of all the details, apart from the fact that her ex was a space mining engineer, living and working in the Kuiper Belt, and her daughter Sarah was studying in a boarding school on Mars. As far as Matt knew, they hadn't spoken to Tony in years, apart from strictly legal communications.

"Is she okay?"

Tony nodded. "Sarah is about to finish school, and she asked me to come for her graduation. It's the first time she's wanted anything to do with me since the divorce." Her eyes flickered with what looked like unshed tears. "I can't fuck this up, Matt."

"You won't." Matt patted her arm. "When's the ceremony?"

"In three weeks."

"Okay. If we aren't done with this whole chasing Alraki ships nonsense by then, I'll arrange for you to get a transport to Mars from the Freeport. And if you'd rather go there right now, that's okay too. Seriously, I'm not trying to get rid of you after everything you said, but if she needs you, then that's where you need to be."

Tony shook her head. "There's still plenty of time. I wouldn't know what to do with myself, biding my time on Mars. As you said, if the mission isn't over by then, I'll take a break, though I'd hate to be bailing on you like that."

"Don't worry about it. You need to do this. I know how important this is to you."

"Thanks, Matt," Tony said quietly. Some of the tension around her eyes and mouth eased, but she still had a slightly haunted look to her, like a soldier caught in the middle of an ambush with no ammo.

"Just do me a favor, will you?"

"Sure."

"When you go, take Val with you to Mars," Matt said. "Out of all of us, he's the one who could really use some downtime and relaxation. Taking it easy for a few days sightseeing and hiking on Olympus Mons would do him good."

Tony sighed, her shoulders sagging. "I know. I'll talk to him. If anything, I could use the emotional support on the way there."

"You'll be fine," Matt said, drawing her into a short but fierce hug. "Sarah reaching out to you is a good sign. She's doing the right thing."

I wish I could have done the same while my mother was still alive. The thought was laden with too much sorrow, and he let it float away. Second chances were among the rarest things in the universe, and he swore to himself he'd do whatever it took to help his friend have hers.

*

Matt's commlink chimed just as he was about to enter his cabin, announcing someone was requesting permission to come on board, and he hurried to answer the door. Opening the main hatch, Matt was surprised to see Grayson standing on the ramp.

"Hi," he said cautiously, letting the lieutenant inside.

"I came to make sure everything you needed was installed and in full working order," Grayson said. "The admiral agrees with Commander

Walker that you should set out as soon as possible. If everything is ready, his team will be here tomorrow."

"Tomorrow?" Matt knew they were on a tight schedule, but that was way too soon. Ryce hadn't even had the chance to test out his program properly—not that Matt doubted it would do exactly what it was supposed to.

"I know it's not ideal," Grayson said. "But with the Alraki seemingly going on a rampage, I'm afraid we don't have any choice but to hurry things along. May I take a look at your computer specs?"

"Yes, of course."

Matt led him to the bridge, which was silent and dark, the Fleet engineers having finished tearing into the ship's electronic guts for the day. Grayson glanced around curiously on their way but offered no commentary on the shabby interior.

Matt connected to the ship's computer, and Grayson wasted no time pulling up all the specs, meticulously going through every detail of the upgrades. He was too intent on what he was doing for idle conversation, so Matt watched him in silence, slumped in the copilot chair.

Despite Grayson's age, which was close to Matt's, there were touches of gray around his temples, peppering his dark hair. Tension lines around his mouth marred his otherwise handsome face. Being an aide to the Foreign Intelligence Admiral seemed to be taking its toll.

It was weird seeing Grayson after all these years, especially considering his new position. Their parting had left a bitter taste in Matt's mouth, but they'd had some good times, too, before it all went terribly wrong and Matt's life took a downward trajectory. And Grayson wasn't a bad person. He simply had the tendency to lose sight of the road while trying to reach his goals.

"I'm sorry if I was a bit of a grouch earlier." Matt didn't mention the unfortunate incident of arriving drunk to a top-secret briefing, though, of course, he was sorry for that too. "I was just so anxious about Nora, and it was all too much to take in."

"I understand," Grayson said, his attention on the console. "Don't worry about it."

"I'm happy to see you be so successful, with your career and all. I hope you have everything you wanted."

Grayson finally looked up at him, his expression strange, almost hostile, but his features smoothed into blandness in an instant.

"I did." His soft voice was in complete contrast to the unfriendly look he'd given Matt just a second before. "I got the promotion I wanted. I married a good man. We only had two years together before he died."

"I'm so sorry."

Grayson shook his head. "He had a weak heart. We always knew it was a risk, even with all the surgeries. But at least I still have my daughter, and that is a blessing I could never regret."

"You have a daughter?" Matt was unable to hide his surprise. He'd never pictured Grayson as a parent; he'd always been too career-oriented to let things like family and children interfere with that. But it seemed Matt wasn't the only one who'd had to reevaluate his life choices. Or, more likely, he hadn't known Grayson as well as he thought he had.

Grayson nodded and tapped on his commlink, pulling up a picture. It showed him and a soft-faced man with red hair and blue eyes, his hand resting on the shoulder of a girl of about seven or eight. The girl, smiling shyly into the camera, sported the same red hair and a spatter of freckles.

"Her name is Elisabeth," Grayson said.

"It's a beautiful name."

"She's Jo's biological daughter from a previous marriage. He was a much better father than I could ever hope to be. But I love her every bit as much as if she were my own. Everything I do, I do for her."

Matt glanced at Grayson. He was intent on the picture, frowning, his mouth set in a hard, angry line.

Caught a bit off-guard by this quiet display of grief, Matt fumbled for something adequate to say, but Grayson shook his head and swiped the comm screen before putting it back in his pocket.

"Everything appears to be in order," he said, nodding to the console. He rose from the chair. "I'll let the admiral know we're all ready to go."

"Good." Ryce stepped onto the bridge, crossing his arms over his chest. He wore that expression of haughty aloofness Matt had learned to recognize as his go-to mode when dealing with people he found unpleasant. "Would you like me to show you out?"

Grayson glanced sideways at Matt, raising an eyebrow, and shook his head.

"Thank you, but I think I'll manage. I'll talk to you later, Matthew."

After he departed, Ryce took the vacated pilot chair, frowning slightly.

"What did you two talk about?"

"The tech upgrades, mostly. Why?"

Ryce drummed his fingers on the control panel. He wasn't connected to the ship at the moment through his neuro-adapters, so it didn't respond to his touch.

"I find it odd that he would come to make the inspection himself. He could've left it to the engineers. You know—the people who actually know what they're doing, as opposed to administrative personnel."

"He's responsible for coordinating this entire operation. So I can understand why he'd want to make sure everything was running smoothly. Especially with the admiral and Central Command breathing down his neck," Matt said mildly. "Besides, once you get to know him, he's a pretty decent guy, or at least he used to be. You should give him a chance; maybe he'll grow on you."

"It's you growing on him that I'm worried about."

Realization dawned slowly. "Seriously? You're jealous of Grayson?"

Ryce shrugged defensively. "I'm not."

"Oh my god," Matt said, grinning. "You *are*. You're totally jealous."

The idea was so utterly ridiculous it practically begged gleeful teasing on his part. But seeing Ryce's pained expression, Matt reined in his amusement.

"You know you have nothing to fret about when it comes to Grayson and me, right?" he said in a much more sober tone.

Ryce grimaced. "You can't blame me for being a bit insecure here. Grayson's handsome and smart. You have all this history, and he's...experienced."

Matt realized his mouth was hanging open and promptly shut it again. *Experienced*? Where did that come from?

It was true Ryce was very young, and that there was over ten years of an age gap between them, but Matt was far from considering himself the wise, mature one in their relationship. With Ryce's know-it-all attitude and proficiency on nearly every subject, it was sometimes easy to forget he wasn't nearly as worldly as he appeared. For all his superior skills and intellect, he was still human, prone to the same doubts and insecurities as everyone else.

"As far as I'm concerned, that history is ancient. And besides, he's Fleet," Matt said. How else could he explain his complete and total disinterest in rekindling his romance with Grayson? *He isn't you?*

"I was Fleet."

"That's different," Matt scoffed.

"How's that different?"

Matt reached out and took Ryce's hand into his.

"I fell in love with you long before I knew—or suspected—that you were Fleet." He looked straight into Ryce's stormy gray eyes. "I didn't realize what was happening at the time, and then it was too late—career officer, criminal, it didn't matter. I had no choice but loving you. Maybe that's why I treated you like a total asshole in the beginning, coming on to you when you weren't interested. Maybe I was just afraid of this attraction being deeper than I could handle."

"You *were* quite an asshole." Ryce flashed him a reluctant smile, but now that familiar twinkle in his eyes showed he was amused. "Perhaps I shouldn't have forgiven you so easily."

"Just goes to show you're not always the astute genius everybody thinks you are."

"I thought you liked me being an astute genius."

"I do. But it's nice to know you're just as much of a fool in love as the rest of us."

"On the contrary. I think it's one of the smartest things I've done," Ryce said and leaned in to kiss him, their hands still tightly clasped together.

Chapter Eight

Matt couldn't remember the last time there were so many people aboard *Lady Lisa*. Walker's special team consisted of only half a dozen people, but the small ship felt overcrowded, with the rec room and the galley suddenly occupied at all hours; and while the rest of the crew seemed to get along nicely with the soldiers, he staunchly refused to be sociable.

It'd been three days (two and half, really, but who was counting?) since they departed the *Lennox*. Walker had set a route for Waga, the Sonora-4 moon where the last sighting of the Alraki had been reported, but it amounted to basically cruising the system until they got a positive reading on either their or some other Fleet vessel's sensors, detecting the radiation signature of an opening wormhole. The working assumption was that the Alraki frigate wouldn't be able to jump right away, so if it appeared close enough to their location for them to reach it before it recharged, they would be able to spot it before it disappeared again.

So far, the run had been uneventful, and the only thing to have crossed their path was a transport vessel on its way to the Freeport. But there really was no escaping feeling caged in with folks who were basically highly trained killing machines with an equally highly developed sense of entitlement. None of them had been rude to Matt or his crew, exactly, but none of them had bothered to hide their casual disdain for civilians either.

He itched to get a sip of something strong and bitter to calm his progressively fraying nerves, but the rec room appeared to be occupied and filled with loud voices whenever he poked his head in, and drinking alone in his cabin reeked of an ennui he wasn't keen to go back to, so he reluctantly gave up on that.

Coffee, however, was a habit Matt wasn't ready to kick. Even if he had to jostle elbows with every operative in the entire Federal Fleet in his tiny galley, he wasn't about to forgo the life-affirming hot liquid, especially after waking up to the prospect of spending yet another day of being surrounded by unwanted passengers.

Walker had agreed to let Ryce pilot the ship, having witnessed his skills firsthand flying through a mine-rigged asteroid field. Matt didn't have to tell him he could hardly wish for a better pilot, covert mission or not. But that meant Ryce was kept busy and up at all hours, while Matt was left with nothing better to do than catch up on his sleep.

One of the advantages of getting a late start to the day was that the kitchen was blissfully empty after everyone had already had their breakfast, and there was some leftover coffee simmering in the pot. However, this time, Matt's careful calculations proved to be off because two members of Walker's team still lingered in the kitchen, lounging against the counter. They were engrossed in friendly chitchat that ceased when Matt stepped inside.

"You're out of granola breakfast bars," one of them said accusingly.

The man was tall and broad-shouldered, but then they all were, to some extent. Matt caught a glimpse of a *kanji* tattoo behind his ear when the guy turned his head, but it was too small to make out without staring.

"I'm not your damn supply officer," Matt said irritably, walking up to the coffee maker and punching the buttons with a lot more force than the poor machine deserved. "Take it up with your commander."

The man—Ikeda, Matt thought his name was, the team's communications officer—exchanged a look with his friend but said nothing.

Matt sighed. "Here." He opened a side cupboard and took out a box of dry yogurt cereal. The special ops team had brought their own rations, but they'd practically been living on the less than healthy contents of the *Lisa*'s pantry, including coffee and snacks. "It's not granola, but it should fix you up."

"Thanks," the other soldier said, tossing her hair back. "Sorry we're all up in your business."

She reminded Matt a little of Tony—not so much in appearance as in the feel of poised alertness, like a tight spring ready to uncoil. As much as Matt wanted both her and Val out of harm's way on this mission, he was glad to have Tony by his side, watching out for all of them, even if it meant having to go several rounds with Walker and his higher-ups to obtain the necessary clearance for his crew.

"Not your fault, I guess," he said, relenting a little. "I'm sorry too. Not used to having so many folks around."

"Ikeda, Martin," Walker said briskly, coming into the kitchen and offering Matt a curt nod by way of greeting. "I'll be giving a preliminary status report in the rec room in sixty minutes. Easom told me the sensors picked up a strong radiation reading somewhere off the Sonora-4 moon cluster, relatively close to the last sighting. We should pass Waga in a few hours, which would take us to that general location."

"What makes you think they'll still be hanging around there waiting for us?" Matt asked when the two operatives departed, grabbing their breakfast on the go first. "Even if they can't jump right away, it doesn't mean they can't take their asses elsewhere the conventional way. As far as I remember, there are plenty of places to hide in that cluster."

"It is a long shot," Walker conceded. "But it's our best bet. I'm keeping tabs on the local media outlets in addition to receiving direct reports from Fleet Intelligence, but so far, there hadn't been any other leads."

"Whatever."

Matt wasn't about to tell Walker he was likely to end up on a wild goose chase as long as he was willing to shell out the cash. From a business standpoint, it'd be better for him if they wasted their time chasing shadows all over Sonora. But as someone who had agreed to this preposterous plan in the first place—out of a misguided sense of camaraderie with the rest of humanity—Matt sure hoped whoever was in command, whether Admiral Cummings or some other high-ranking hotshot, came up with a better long-term solution.

"You want some coffee?" he asked.

"I'd love some actually."

Walker sat at the table while Matt eked out another cup of steaming coffee from the machine. They sat together in silence, punctuated by the low distant hum of the ship's engine.

"Who's in charge of the *Lennox* now that you're away?" Matt asked, trying for polite chitchat.

To his surprise, he realized he'd grown to like Walker. Well, perhaps "like" was a strong word, but certainly respect him. Despite Walker having saved his life in the past, they were probably never going to be best buds, but Matt could appreciate the man's loyalty and blunt honesty.

"Nominally, Major Cummings's first mate," Walker said. "Though with Admiral Cummings making it his temporary headquarters, I assume he'll be the one running the show for a while."

"He's used to that," Matt muttered.

"You and the admiral seem very...different," Walker said, sipping his coffee. "I'm sure you get that a lot."

"Yeah." Now that the initial shock of running into his father had worn off, it was easier to not let the implied question nettle him. "We've never really seen eye to eye about anything. He and Nora got along great though."

As hard as it was to believe, Matt had never begrudged Nora being Thomas Cummings's favorite. He'd been aware of that fact from very early on, and he'd never tried—or wanted—to compete with her. But he'd been angry when she chose to side with their father against Matt's decision to leave the Fleet. Perhaps it shouldn't have come as such a profound surprise, but it'd felt like yet another betrayal when the whole world seemed to have turned against him.

"I could tell when he came to see her," Walker said. "I know you think he wasn't being sincere about that, but I saw how upset he was to find her in such a serious condition, even though he was trying not to let on."

"You were shaken too. You care about Nora a great deal, don't you?"

Walker shifted uncomfortably in his chair but, to his credit, didn't change the topic.

"I respect her as a fellow officer and a commander. We've served together for a long time."

"It's more than that, though, isn't it?" Matt insisted.

Walker leaned back in his chair and set his mug down, his strong jaw hardening.

"That's none of your business."

"All right." Matt threw his hands up. "I'll keep my nose out of where it doesn't belong. It's just...well, I know I haven't been a good brother to her, and my opinion is hardly relevant or wanted, but I'm glad there's someone like you in her life. In whatever capacity."

Walker's expression softened, turning almost wistful. Matt never imagined he'd conjure the word "vulnerable" when thinking about Commander John Walker, but there was definitely a flicker of some unguarded emotion in the man's eyes before he lowered them to his mug.

"I appreciate that."

"Any time. And I know it may not seem like it, but I'm here to help with whatever you need. Since we're already here and all."

Walker downed the last of his coffee and stood up.

"Be careful. I might hold you to that." He chuckled, a lot more good-naturedly than he might have a few days ago. "I should get going. Thanks for the coffee."

*

"Captain, your presence is required on the bridge." Walker's voice sounded through the alarm system speakers, startling Matt out of his afternoon nap. "We have a visual of the enemy."

"You must be fucking kidding me," Matt groaned, sitting up on his bunk. He cast about, bleary-eyed, but his cabin was darkened and empty. Perhaps he was taking this sleeping-in thing a bit too far.

He put on his shoes and burst into the corridor, still somewhat sleep addled. He nearly collided with Ryce, who must have been coming out of his own room to fetch him.

"Sorry!" Matt put his hands up. "I can't believe this is happening. It's like they were waiting for us to arrive or something."

"Let's see what's going on." Ryce looked as calm as ever, but of course, Ryce always performed better under pressure, whereas Matt tended to panic and was painfully aware of the fact. But really, he thought as they hurried down the corridor, this was a time when panic was entirely warranted.

"I've directed your ship's sensors feed to my commlink, so I'd be notified the moment something was up," Walker said, forestalling Matt's inquiries as soon as they entered the bridge. "But we need either you or Mr. Easom to connect to the computer."

Matt pointedly pushed past Walker and his second-in-command, Lieutenant Gonzales, who stood next to the main control panel, plopped into the pilot chair, and tapped the adapters on his temples. The dormant canopy screen, which also served as a window, went black before displaying the image of a distant alien vessel, its twisted shape almost lost against the darkness of the void.

Damn it. He knew Ryce's algorithm would eventually lead them to the Alraki, he just hadn't counted on it happening quite so soon, or with such unyielding precision.

"The ship's 500 klicks away," he said, frowning. "I don't think it even spotted us yet."

"Yes," Gonzales said. "The new sensors have an extended visual range."

"Their velocity is low, but their current trajectory takes them farther away from Waga and the established transport route to the moons," Ryce said, touching his own adapters. Matt hadn't looked at the computer analysis yet, but he had no doubt Ryce was right.

"Good, we're just in time, then," Walker said, his usually impassive face animated with something close to genuine excitement. "Are there any other vessels currently within range?"

"No," Matt said after consulting the sensors readings. They really were state of the art for a humble freight hauler. At least whoever had authorized this daring endeavor hadn't skimped on hardware.

"In that case, shut down the engine, and send out a distress call, Captain."

"What? Why?" Matt was so astonished he didn't balk at being issued a direct order.

"The Alraki are listening to the open human frequencies. My bet is they won't be able to resist the lure of a lone ship apparently stranded without any immediate aid forthcoming," Walker explained. "This is the whole point of posing as bait. We need them chasing us, not the other way around."

"Clever," Ryce said, turning his gaze to Walker, who shrugged. Matt couldn't tell whether he was pleased or miffed by the compliment.

"Are you sure you know what you're doing though?" Matt insisted when the two soldiers headed for the door. Deep down, he'd been so convinced they wouldn't find the Alraki ship that he'd never actually bothered to learn about the practicalities of the operation, and now he felt hopelessly out of the loop. "If they pick up the call, there's no going back."

"That's what we're counting on," Walker threw over his shoulder. "Let's do this, Captain."

*

"I have a really bad feeling about this," Matt whispered, mostly to himself.

He and Ryce were huddled in a corner of the crowded rec room, watching Commander Walker pull the schematics of a generic Alraki frigate onto the large screen on which *Lisa*'s crew usually watched movies and newsreels. Strictly speaking, Ryce and Matt weren't supposed to be privy to the more sensitive information, especially the parts pertaining to the actual extraction. But considering Ryce's background, it was nothing he hadn't seen before, and Walker had proved himself willing to bend a few rules where they were concerned, placing their cooperation above the requirements of confidentiality. Tony and Val weren't in attendance, but Matt planned on filling them in on any important details later.

"This is it, people," Walker said in his usual brisk tone. "In less than an hour, the Alraki are going to be here, and I want to make sure everyone knows exactly what they're doing. We can't afford any mistakes on this one."

He tapped his commlink, zeroing in on the blueprints on the screen, which looked more like several intertwined labyrinths coiling around one another than anything resembling a standard ship layout. But of course, Alraki standards were very different from those of humans.

"As you can see, the bridge is located here." Walker pointed at the bow portion of the second deck. "We believe the electronic components of the wormhole-generating system are located in the bow sensor compartment right below it. If we access the ship's computer, we'll also be able to download the schematics. Our hardware might not be compatible with that of the Alraki, but this adapter will allow us to connect to their system." He held up a small black box, about half the size of a commlink. "It also serves as a high-volume data storage unit."

"Is it possible to access their computer from elsewhere?" Ryce asked.

All the heads in the room turned to him, but Ryce (being Ryce) weathered their disapproving regard impassively, waiting for Walker's response.

"It's possible," Walker conceded. "As far as we were able to deduce, there are several all-access consoles in different areas around the vessel, like the engine room, the main hatch pressure chamber, and the weapons silo. There could be more that we don't know about. Why?"

"If we could hack into their computer from one of these points, there wouldn't be any need to make it all the way to the bow," Ryce said.

"One of our major objectives is getting all possible hardware modules as well as the specs," Walker said. "We don't know what this system might include or where it could be installed, but logic—even alien logic—dictates it'd be somewhere on the bridge with the rest of the controls. We must get there to accomplish the mission, which is obtaining the schematics and all available electronics, and planting the detonator where it'll have the chance to do most damage, which is either the bridge or engineering."

Walker paused, then sighed and continued, reluctantly: "We'll be using the new stealth-technology armor which will hopefully help us avoid detection. Basically, we should slip by and reach the bow unnoticed. However, this particular tactical gear is still experimental, so I'd appreciate your circumspection regarding its existence."

Ryce didn't look convinced, but he nodded curtly without adding any more commentary.

"What are you thinking?" Matt asked him quietly as Walker continued to explain the shortest route from the inner docking bay to the bridge.

"It'd be much easier to get the specs from the closest available access hub and blow up the ship from there," Ryce said just as quietly. "I realize they want to tinker with the actual hardware to cover all their bases when it comes to previously unknown technology, but traversing the length of the ship to get it amps up the risk unnecessarily, even with this new concealment technology they'd be employing. The specs should be enough for R & D without resorting to full-on reverse engineering."

Matt raised an eyebrow. "Really? I thought you'd be all for a daring foray right into the heart of danger. You seem to thrive on those."

Ryce shook his head. "Daring doesn't mean reckless. I know I sometimes give the impression of playing fast and loose with personal safety, but I always weigh the risk against the possibility of success before doing something you'd call foolhardy. This time, the ratio is off by a very wide margin."

"You don't think they can do it?"

"They can. At least, they believe so. But none of them has ever been aboard an Alraki vessel this size. There are too many points of failure for them to take into account."

"Why didn't you say so to Walker before?" Matt asked.

Ryce shrugged. "I didn't know the details of his plan until now. Besides, I might be wrong. They're special ops; they know what they're doing. As someone who's only served as a Falcon fighter pilot, with little hand-to-hand combat experience, I lack perspective."

Matt tended to disagree. Ryce's assessment only ramped up his own doubts, but he couldn't contest the parameters of the mission. At this stage, there was nothing he could do but trust Walker not to screw it up.

"Once the detonator is set in place and activated," the commander continued, "we have exactly one hour to get back on *Lady Lisa* and retreat to a safe distance. Provided we meet no resistance, this should give us a rather narrow window, so try to avoid engagement. Stealth is the key word for this operation. We can't risk shooting our way out."

A murmur of agreement rippled through the crowd. Highly trained operatives or not, no one wanted to fight the superior strength of the notoriously savage, seven-foot aliens on their home turf if it could be avoided.

"I've already requested urgent backup from the military base on Waga," Walker said. "Their fighters will attack the frigate as soon as they tow us in, creating a distraction for the Alraki personnel while we infiltrate the ship. Hopefully, they'll be too busy fending off the Falcons to pay close attention to what goes on directly under their noses.

"We have approximately forty-five minutes to rendezvous. Gear up, and hide in the secret compartments in the cargo hold that Mr. Spears will show you. We have taken a calculated risk by leaving *Lady Lisa*'s shuttle behind on the *Lennox*. With the shuttle missing, the Alraki will most likely assume the crew has chosen to evacuate and abandon their stranded ship, facing the threat of the incoming frigate, and therefore won't search it too closely. Once their first response party is gone, we'll make our move before the sweepers come to pick it clean. Mr. Spears, Mr. Easom, and their crew will be waiting for us, ready to fire up the engine as soon as we're safely back on board."

"How do we open the dock doors on our way out?" Ikeda asked from where he lounged on the sofa. His pose was almost too relaxed, but he was focused on the screen with unwavering intensity.

"We program them to open when we gain access to the ship's computer," Walker said. "Whatever we do, this step is imperative. Otherwise, we'll be trapped there when the ship explodes."

"Wonderful," Matt muttered. Ryce made a sound that was as close to a grunt as Matt had ever heard him produce.

"I don't have to remind you all how important this assignment is, and I know all of you will do your best. Godspeed, everyone. Dismissed."

"Well," Matt said, watching Walker's team file out of the room. "At least we'll have the chance to finally test how handy those secret compartments really are."

Chapter Nine

The compartments in *Lisa*'s cargo hold were a feature added by the ship's previous owner, who'd had a lot more straightforward and practical approach to smuggling than Matt ever dared to implement. They were fitted in a tight space behind one of the walls, which barely left room for sitting without brushing one's head against the low ceiling. The tightness was making the wait quite excruciating, which, in turn, was making Matt anxious—not that there wasn't plenty to be anxious about already.

It was also freezing down here since Val had never had the chance to fix the cargo air-conditioning system. Now, Matt definitely rued his decision to put that particular project on a back burner. While the special ops guys had their protective gear to keep them comfortable, the rest of them had to suffer the consequences of Matt's negligence.

Val and Tony shared an adjacent, slightly bigger cubicle. Matt could hear them shuffling inside, but otherwise, they kept pretty quiet. Walker's teammates' voices, on the other hand, rose and fell in a constant hum, traveling easily through the metal walls.

"These guys are making too much noise," Matt whispered to Ryce, who was hunkered down next to him, his back pressed against the wall. "They don't think the Alraki will be able to hear them chatting?"

"You're chatting," Ryce pointed out, far too reasonably not to be annoying.

"I'm not chatting, I'm venting," Matt said, but shut up.

Long, tense minutes passed. With the engine shut off, the silence was complete and oppressing, chatting or venting notwithstanding. Matt didn't like silence. It was all too easy to fill it with conjured images of aliens tearing into his beloved *Lisa*, leaving nothing but senseless destruction in their wake. What if they damaged the delicate electronics, rendering the ship incapacitated? Or if the search party had infrared scanners that could pick up their hiding place? There were so, so many things that could go wrong.

Ryce's steady breathing right next to him was the only thing helping Matt maintain the outward appearance of (relative) calm. It was almost shocking, in a way, to realize just how much he'd come to depend on Ryce's solid presence, how much just having him there, even when he was saying nothing at all or busy with his own projects was crucial for Matt's peace of mind. If Matt was a ship, drifting from one storm to the other, then Ryce was his anchor, keeping him moored in a safe haven.

He took a deep breath, willing the agitation to subside, but in such a situation, it was too much to hope to be able to reach genuine equanimity.

"Are you sure the aliens were headed our way?" he asked, half worried, half hopeful. "Because it takes them a hell of a long time to—"

There was a loud bang as something hit the hull on the port side, shaking the immobile ship and effectively cutting off both his ramblings and the others' loud whispers.

"Attention everybody," Walker's crisp voice sounded in Matt's earpiece, which linked him to the rest of the team. "The Alraki have deployed a magnetic grapnel and are towing us into their docking bay. The Falcon fighters are on their way. Maintain radio silence. Hold your positions until my signal."

Matt swallowed hard. Even though there was no real sense of movement, in his mind's eye *Lady Lisa* was being pulled like stunned prey into the yawing jaws of a hungry monster. It wasn't the first time he'd experienced that feeling of utter helplessness waiting to be boarded by the enemy, but he had to admit that this time, despite the preparation and meticulous planning, he was scared shitless. The Alraki terrified him on a much deeper, primal level than humans ever could, including pirates and murderous thugs. With the Alraki, there was no deluding himself into being able to talk his way out of being eviscerated.

Ryce's warm hand reaching out to clasp his surprised him. It was too dark in the cramped compartment to discern the other man's expression, but he could just make out the glint of Ryce's eyes and imagine the ghost of his smile. Matt entwined their fingers, holding on to that warmth and unwavering strength. Whatever was going to happen, at least they'd face it together—a dubious solace, considering the likelihood they'd both end up dead.

I love you, he thought, and, even though Ryce couldn't possibly know that, he squeezed Matt's fingers in reassurance.

Walker and the rest of the team must have had the ship's camera feeds displayed inside their protective helmets, but in lieu of any special gear, the jolt of the *Lisa* landing on a docking pad took Matt unawares. The ship rattled as the grapnel's hold was released, and then stilled. A muffled rumble ending in a thump indicated the frigate's bay doors closing shut. They were now trapped in the bowels of an alien ship, and the only way out was in.

*

Waiting was always the hardest part. Those dread-filled minutes of nail-biting anticipation, that feeling of helplessness when they could do absolutely nothing. Matt hated waiting with every fiber of his being. In his experience, nothing good ever came out of hanging around hoping the other shoe wouldn't drop because, inevitably, it always did. But this time, he had no choice but to wait in his little cocoon of darkness, listening to Ryce's steady heartbeats and any stray noises coming from the outside.

No sound from the upper deck quarters penetrated the reinforced walls of the cargo hold, but that didn't stop Matt from imagining the Alraki searching *Lady Lisa*, sniffing out its unfortunate crew. He hoped Walker was right about the missing shuttle fooling the aliens into thinking the humans managed to escape prior to them overtaking the ship. *Nothing to see here. Nothing to find. Just move on.*

Matt had almost managed to convince himself the aliens would forgo checking the cargo altogether when he heard the main door of the hold slide open with a characteristic hiss. The silence in his earpiece changed quality as all the members of the team and Matt's crew held their collective breath.

Heavy thumps of armored feet sounded against the metal floor, and then a series of loud clicks. Was it an actual language, or some sort of code? Either way, the aliens were conveying something to one another. He just really wanted to know what it was.

He tightened his grip on Ryce's hand, probably to the point of pain. Several sets of footsteps approached their hiding place, coming so close Matt could hear the creaks of their joints. And then they stopped.

The moment stretched long enough for Matt to begin calculating his next move, namely tackling the Alraki the second they ripped into the protective paneling. As far as survival tactics went, this was an exceptionally poor one, but it would hopefully give Ryce, Tony, and Val a fighting chance.

But Matt didn't have the opportunity to test this theory. A subtle vibration, probably generated in the much larger vessel that now contained them, ran through the entire ship. The Alraki exchanged a series of louder clicks. Matt thought he could detect an urgent, frantic note to them, but it could well have been his wild imagination playing tricks on him.

There was motion again, the heart-chilling thumps moving away as the Alraki made a quick round of the hold, rattling empty storage containers. Matt cringed at the loud clatter of metal against metal, biting his lip. Finally, after what seemed an eternity, the footsteps retreated, and the cargo hold door slammed shut again.

"Fuck my life." Matt flexed his shoulders, releasing some of the tension and waiting for his heart rate to return to a reasonable level.

"They're leaving," said Walker over the link, monitoring the camera feed. "Don't move until we're sure the coast is clear."

Matt groaned. Walker had insisted the *Lisa*'s crew all stay in the smuggling compartments right up until it was time for them to fire up the engine for take-off, in case the Alraki poked into the hauler again. While there was something undeniably appealing about sharing close quarters with Ryce, the thought of spending several more hours hiding in the metal hole made Matt's aching muscles lock up all over again.

"It's going to be okay," Ryce whispered, shifting where he was crouching next to him.

"Sure," Matt said, although he knew he wasn't fooling anybody with his false confidence.

"They're gone," Walker said. "It's go time."

The wall panels clattered as they came undone, accompanied by the stomping of people stepping out of their temporary hideouts.

"The frigate is under attack, but the fighters cannot engage for very long on their own. We're on a tight schedule here. Everybody remember the route?" Walker asked briskly.

"Yes, sir!" That was Corporal Martin's voice. Matt had learned to distinguish them by sound by this point.

"Good. File out. Captain Spears, guard the home base."

"You got it," Matt said. "Break a leg."

He waited to hear the sound of the cargo door closing once again before switching off the mic. The team's exchanges came through in his earpiece, but there was no point in distracting the guys by talking.

"Why do they say 'break a leg' anyway?" Ryce mused. "Seems counterintuitive— Wait, what are you doing?"

"Getting out of here." Matt pushed the panel and climbed out.

The cargo hold certainly looked like it'd been searched, upturned crates lying everywhere. He was afraid to think what the rest of the ship might look like after the Alraki inspection.

"Commander Walker ordered us to stay put."

"Then it's a good thing I don't take orders from Commander Walker."

"It's for our own safety," Ryce said, nevertheless following Matt out and casting his eyes about the hold. He raised an eyebrow at a container that appeared to have been flung with excessive force across the room.

"I'll feel much safer on the bridge where I can keep an eye on things as opposed to waiting for the Alraki to sniff us out."

For once, Ryce didn't argue with his logic. Knowing him, Matt supposed the imposed helplessness didn't sit well with him either.

"I don't care what Commander Walker says. I don't ever want to go back in there again," Tony said as she and Val emerged from the adjacent compartment. She wrapped her arms around herself, shivering. "And I thought hiding with you in a utility closet aboard a yacht was tough."

"I'm not a fan of tight spaces either," Matt said. "Sorry about that. Let's all stay together in the meantime, in case we need to scramble back to safety."

"They can't really do that, you know," Ryce said as they headed for the stairwell to the upper deck.

"Do what?"

"Sniff you out. The Alraki have a very poor sense of smell compared to humans."

"Is aggression a sense? Because that sure is heightened."

Ryce chuckled, but the amusement quickly died as they entered the common areas.

Unsurprisingly, the galley had been completely ransacked, the contents of the cupboards spilled onto the floor and trampled. The coffee machine looked like it'd been hit with a blunt weapon, its maintenance lights blinking red in distress.

"I swear, if those motherfuckers broke my goddamned coffee maker, I'll personally blow their ship up with everything in it," Matt stressed through his teeth.

"Don't go scaring a hedgehog with a bare ass," Val said, deadpan.

The Russian adage was both funny and true, but Matt was too pissed off at the loss of his caffeine lifeline to acknowledge it.

"They didn't have to make that much of a mess," Tony complained, taking in the chaotic state of the galley. "Look at what they did to my pantry! They don't even eat this stuff. Do they?"

"Come on. We'll deal with it later," Ryce said, pulling Matt and Tony out of the kitchen before they could start organizing.

"I can't function without coffee," Matt grumbled. He briefly considered stopping by the cabins and the rec room to assess the damage but decided against it.

"Trust me, I know. Have you met yourself in the morning before you've had a cup?"

"I try my best not to," Matt said.

"We all do," Tony said, and Val snorted. Matt turned and stuck out his tongue at her.

The bridge also bore the unmistakable signs of having been searched. Matt winced at the dented sideboards and ripped wiring, but thankfully, the control panel dutifully lit up when he tapped his adapters, establishing connection with the ship's computer. Ryce sat in the copilot seat (which he rarely occupied these days) after righting its bent axis. Val crouched in front of the damaged lower panels with an annoyed grunt and produced an ammeter out of his pocket. Tony leaned against the back wall, her hand casually resting on the gun in her hip holster.

"Let's see what's going on out there," Matt said, bringing the external camera feed on-screen.

The image showed the stark interior of the alien ship's docking bay, illuminated by strips of dim bluish-green lighting running the length of the walls and across the floor in seemingly haphazard lines. There were no other vessels around, as far as Matt could see, but darkness lingered in the corners of the oblong space, making it difficult to determine its exact size.

"There," Ryce said softly, and Matt zoomed in on the far wall toward the inner airlock.

This was the first time he was witnessing the stealth armor technology in action. It looked like an invisibility cloak more than anything else. The surfaces of the armor pieces covering the soldiers' chests, backs, and legs became highly reflective when activated, as they now were, and the silhouettes of the operatives blended into the surroundings. Even now, Matt strained to pick them out of the shadows, the flickers of movement and the light reflecting off their weapons the only indication of their passing. There was something deeply disconcerting about it, like watching a procession of ghosts, and his bad feeling intensified.

"That's nifty," he said to distract himself from superstitious nonsense.

Ryce nodded. "It won't be of much help if they run into an Alraki patrol face-to-face, but hopefully it'll be enough to avoid being spotted from a distance."

When the operatives slipped behind the sliding doors and disappeared from view, Matt switched on the communication channel again, listening in to their quiet, mostly monosyllabic exchanges. Special ops had their own codes, which sounded meaningless to Matt, but which Ryce probably understood, having served as a fighter pilot.

"Godspeed," Matt murmured even though they couldn't hear him. He turned to Ryce. "Do you reckon the Alraki might send their dock workers to strip our ship despite being on alert?"

Ryce shrugged. "They've asserted it's empty, so there's hardly any urgency, but I can't say I'm terribly familiar with their internal operations. I guess we'll know soon enough, won't we?"

Matt couldn't boast the same cool nonchalance at the prospect of holding the fort by themselves against another search party, but Ryce was right in that there was nothing they could do to prevent it. He sighed and ran a quick check on *Lisa*'s systems to make sure everything was in perfect working order for when they'd have to hightail it out of here.

He would've liked to watch the swarm of Falcons descend on the frigate and the unfolding battle, but there was no way to see beyond the dark belly of the hold. Walker had been right in that the little fighters weren't a match for a ship this size and with such firepower, but hopefully, they could give the infiltration team enough time to get in and out while the Alraki personnel's attention was directed elsewhere.

Instead, he switched back to listening in on Walker's team. Their breathing came in loud and clear over the comm, underscored by the soft shuffling of their footsteps and an irritating low hum.

"What is that?" Matt wondered, cranking up the volume.

"I think the sound, coupled with floor oscillation, serves as a ship-wide alarm," Ryce said. "I can still feel the vibrations. They haven't stopped since the Alraki were attacked."

"Stop flaunting your superior senses."

"It's not flaunting if it's true," Tony pointed out.

Matt chuckled, but the halfhearted attempts at humor quickly died down as they settled in for a long, tense wait. The quiet was punctuated only by the sounds of Val digging inside the paneling and the terse, succinct communications of Walker's team on the open channel. The rest of them stayed in place, left to guess at the team's progress as minutes trickled by, slowly building up to an hour.

How big was this ship, anyway? Yes, okay, it was big, but not nearly as spacious as the *Lennox*, for example. The operatives were taking way too long, Matt decided, checking the clock for the umpteenth time. They were supposed to have access to the visual feed of the ship's layout in their helmets, but who was to say whether all Alraki vessels followed the same design? If the ops team was lost, it would only be a matter of time until they ran into some very pissed-off aliens.

He was about to relay his concerns to Ryce when Walker's voice, clear and crisp above the hum, drew everyone's attention.

"I got a visual of the sensory array room entrance. Shapiro, Martin, Ikeda, you're going in with me. Gonzales, Blair, cover us. Go!"

Matt winced at the distinct sound of a plasma rifle being discharged. It seemed Walker had opted for the quickest way to open the doors—by blasting the control pad. Ryce frowned but refrained from comment.

"The computer interface panel is on," Ikeda reported after a few moments. "We have access to the mainframe. Pulling up schematics."

"Good. I'm plugging in the adapter."

"Yes, sir."

Seconds of tense silence trickled by as Ikeda tinkered with the alien control panel, producing sounds more resembling the Alraki communication clicks than the familiar beeping of electronics. It mixed rather eerily with Ikeda muttering to himself as he flipped through the system. But the quiet was far from complete. The humming in the background intensified, and now, even Matt could feel the slight quivering under his feet, superior senses or not.

"This can't be good," Val said, looking up from where he was busy reconnecting the wires the Alraki had torn out.

"Come on," Matt whispered, though neither Walker nor Ikeda could hear him. "What's taking them so long?"

"I think I got it," Ikeda said after what felt like a lifetime, and Matt let out a relieved breath. As annoying as these people had been, commandeering his ship, he didn't want them to get hurt. "I'm downloading the schematics. In the meantime, we'll have to disassemble this console to see what we're dealing with."

"Get to it. Shapiro, help him," Walker ordered. "The Falcon squad commander informed me that the frigate has begun an evasive maneuver. We don't want to be stuck on it in deep space. Gonzales—status."

"All clear, sir," she said. "It's getting loud here though."

She was right, as the humming had gotten noticeably more resounding.

"I don't like this at all," Ryce said, a deep furrow creasing his forehead. "Perhaps we should—"

The entire ship shook as a laser fire volley hit it somewhere disconcertingly close to the spacecraft hold. Tony let out a curse as she grabbed the doorframe to keep her balance.

"Those Falcon pilots do know we're in here, right?" Matt clutched the armrests of his seat. "Are they *trying* to get us killed?"

"Hostiles incoming!" Gonzales yelled. The last syllables were drowned out by the rapid barking of plasma rifles and snarling noises that were definitely not human. "They cut us off from the corridor!"

Matt and Ryce exchanged a startled glance, their eyes mirroring each other's horror. The lack of visual was like an itch Matt couldn't scratch, but this time, there was hardly anything he could imagine that would be worse than what was happening in reality.

"Sounds like shit's going down." Val snapped another piece of wire back in place, his movements steady despite the violent shaking. It seemed, as far as the engineer was concerned, his job was to make sure the ship was ready to go at a moment's notice, and he wouldn't let anything distract him from it.

"Damn, that was fast," Matt said. The Alraki would have discovered the infiltration team eventually, affected invisibility notwithstanding, but Matt had been holding on to the foolish hope it wouldn't be quite so early in the game.

"Retreat into the room," Walker ordered, raising his voice to be heard over the racket. A muffled grunt of pain indicated one of the soldiers had been hit. "Now!"

"Shut the door," a female voice—probably Martin's—panted, as loud blasts echoed over the comm. "I'll hold them off. Just shut the door; they're trying to push through!"

"No! Martin, get in here!"

"I can't close the door, sir. The controls are fried!"

"Rip those things out; barricade the doorway!"

Several blasts echoed in the corridor in rapid succession, and then there was screeching and the metallic bangs of falling armature. Something sizzled with the distinct crackling of damaged electronics.

"This is bad," Matt said, biting his lip. "This is so fucking bad."

Tight-lipped, Ryce switched on the audio connection. "Commander, what's going on?"

"We're trapped in the sensors room," Walker said. In the background, plasma blasts, cries, growls, and heavy thuds blended into the familiar cacophony of a violent skirmish. "We managed to partially block the entry, but it won't hold for long."

"Have you obtained the specs?"

"We're on it," Ikeda said, sounding strained, and grunted as he seemed to hoist something heavy. "I think I can get some of the relevant circuit boards, too, but their wiring is a doozy."

"Can you get out?" Ryce asked.

"They keep on coming!" Martin shouted in between gunshots, her voice rough with pain.

"No," Walker answered. There was another round of shots, and something crashed hard, eliciting a chorus of cheers that was cut short by a fusillade of blasts. "There's no other way out."

"Hold on. We're coming." Ryce disconnected the audio, cutting off Walker's protests, and rose from his chair with the air of purposeful determination. Both Val and Tony looked up at him with concern.

Matt grabbed him by the arm. "What do you mean, 'we're coming'?"

Ryce stopped and looked right at him.

"Aren't we?"

Matt swallowed hard.

It wasn't the first time he'd had to make such a decision, and it was one that no amount of regret, or repression, or drinking himself into a stupor could change. A few years ago, during that first fateful encounter with Dylan Rodgers's *Black Baza* as a navigator on a mining company barge, he'd chosen to save himself, leaving the rest of the ship's crew to die on the pirate ship as he made his escape, and the memory had haunted him worse than the vague recollections of his own torture.

The people he'd left to die had been thrown briefly in his path by the circumstances of life, just like the soldiers on Walker's team. And yet, in his heart he felt as responsible for them as for any one of his crewmates.

Was he really about to repeat his mistakes?

Could he live with himself if he did?

That whole doing-the-right-thing notion was a serious pain in the neck.

"Yeah." He glanced at Tony and Val, seeking the silent approval in their faces before meeting Ryce's gaze. "We are."

Chapter Ten

Matt adjusted his face mask and looked around the dim cavern of the hold from where he was crouching next to *Lady Lisa*'s hull. The space around them seemed empty, the Alraki probably still busy fending off the Falcon fighters, but it didn't mean they could dawdle. As loath as Matt was to leave his ship, eventually he'd have to make that first step into the belly of the beast and hope to God he wouldn't be swallowed.

"Ready?" Ryce whispered beside him, and Matt nodded. Ryce's face was half-obscured by the mask needed to adjust to the different oxygen and nitrogen levels inside the Alraki craft, but otherwise, they didn't bother with any cumbersome protective gear, especially as the artificial gravitational pull was slightly higher than the regular 1 g. The environment wasn't toxic, per se, just deeply...well, alien.

They ran across the floor, their feet bouncing softly on what felt like rubbery coating. Out in the open, the vibrations were much more pronounced but not strong enough to throw them off balance.

"Do you know where to go?" Matt whispered when they neared the tall arched doorway.

"Yes. I memorized the ship's map from Walker's briefing." Ryce scanned the corridor in both directions, a blaster gun set on maximum impact at the ready.

"Of course you did. Watch out!"

They ducked, hiding behind opposite sides of the opening as several Alraki trotted down the corridor, their bio-mech armor creaking softly. Another party followed in their footsteps after less than a minute.

"They're gonna spot us," Matt said. "There's no way we can evade them if they find us in the hallway, not without that fancy stealth armor."

"You're right. They're on high alert now that Walker's team has been compromised." Ryce peered into the corridor again. Thin veins of reddish light ran through the curved walls, illuminating it. He gestured upward with his gun. "We'll use the air ducts."

Matt looked in the direction Ryce was pointing, at an opening in the ceiling covered with a ridged grate that made him think of gills. He shuddered involuntarily.

"Do you think the ducts are big enough for us?"

"Only one way to find out." Ryce holstered his gun and stepped into the corridor, motioning for Matt to follow him. "Come on, I'll give you a boost."

Matt sighed. He didn't think it was possible to like this mission any less, but every new development seemed to prove him wrong.

Ryce knelt on the floor and laced his fingers to make a support for Matt to step on. He pushed upward as Matt hoisted himself up, shoving hard at the grate. It had the same rubbery texture as the floor and the walls as if it were a part of a giant animal rather than an intelligently designed piece of machinery, which made him squeamish about touching it. With a bit of extra pressure, the grate gave, and Matt pushed it inward, grabbed the edge of the opening, and scrambled to slither inside as Ryce lifted his feet, giving him more leverage.

"Quick, someone's coming," Ryce warned.

Matt cursed and wiggled forward. The ventilation tunnel was just wide enough for a grown man to crawl inside, but it was hardly a comfortable fit, and its round shape was vaguely reminiscent of a corroded pipe or a blood vessel. Behind him, Ryce jumped, catching onto the edge of the hole as Matt had done before him, and heaved himself inside just as the footsteps of more Alraki soldiers echoed in the corridor below them.

They both held their breath, lying still as the aliens passed underneath them. Thankfully, none of them glanced up to notice the open grate.

"Now what?" Matt whispered after the Alraki retreated to a safe distance.

"Onward and upward," Ryce said, deadpan.

Matt snorted, adjusted his mask again against the stronger flow of cold air blowing in his face, and pushed forward, putting his elbows to work.

They passed several more grates, spaced at what seemed like irregular intervals but which must have made sense for the Alraki. The advantage of the ducts not being made of metal was that the sound of their passage was much more muted and less likely to attract attention. Even so, they crawled in relative silence, with Ryce giving directions when the duct split. It was just as well because Matt didn't have the slightest idea as to their location or which way they were headed, so he was more than happy to let Ryce take the lead, going on his recollection of the frigate's layout. The ducts curved along with the corridors and the open spaces rather than running in straight lines, which made their progress more difficult, slowing them down.

Every minute they spent fumbling inside the alien ship's guts was a minute Walker and his troops were fighting for their lives, and Tony and Val were sitting ducks aboard the captured *Lisa*. Matt didn't dare switch on the communications channel so as to not be distracted by the noise. They had to pay close attention to what was going on directly below them, and the anxiety of not knowing what was happening in that sensor array room or the holding bay wore on his nerves.

"Wait," Matt said, stopping. Ryce halted behind him. The tunnel ended abruptly, meeting with a vertical shaft. "Damn it."

He peered up and down, both ends of the shaft lost in reddish gloom. The air rushed past him from below, making him squint.

"We go down," Ryce said.

"That's what worries me."

The shaft was roughly the same circumference as the horizontal duct, and the setup could hardly be any more claustrophobic. Matt wasn't afraid of tight spaces, but considering the amount of time he'd been spending in them recently, he had a feeling that was going to change by the time they were done. Matt carefully grabbed the rounded upper edge of the duct and leaned forward as far as he dared to give himself enough room to bring his legs forward. He shoved his feet against the far wall of the shaft, straining to balance himself above the gaping void in a way that would give him enough purchase going down.

"This is...not ideal."

"It shouldn't be far to go. We're just above the main bow ventilation hub." Ryce crawled forward to peek into the shaft and met Matt's eyes.

Matt sighed and began his descent, the muscles in his arms and legs quivering with the effort of holding himself in position, stretched across the vertical tube and against the powerful flow of air. He moved downward with the pace of a snail, making sure the rest of his limbs were firmly planted in place each time he slid one of them along the textured walls. When this was all over, he thought, he really should amp up his workout routine, with extra emphasis on upper body strength.

Above him, Ryce stretched himself across the shaft, mimicking Matt's movements. Matt knew he was slowing them down with his overly cautious descent, but he really didn't fancy falling, especially seeing as the red light below had intensified.

Glancing down, he noted the shaft opening into a wider space. Something was obstructing his view of the floor, but he didn't have the chance to take a better look. A shudder went through the walls around them as the ship either maneuvered sharply or sustained a direct hit. Matt let out an undignified yelp as his grip slipped, and he tumbled down the shaft, bumping his knees and elbows on the walls painfully in a vain attempt to break his fall.

"Matt!" Ryce cried out, but it was too late. Matt went crashing down, landing on something bouncy and slippery, and rolled off onto the hard floor with a grunt.

"Are you okay?"

"Ugh," Matt said, pushing himself off the floor. "I'm fine."

The fall left him a bit dazed, and he felt a bump beginning to form on the back of his head, where it hit the floor. But it seemed nothing had broken, at least, and the thought of lying about on the weirdly textured floor to catch his breath made his skin crawl.

Ryce jumped out of the duct and landed in a neat crouch right between the...things that had broken Matt's fall. They looked like netted sheets, their shapes resembling fins or petals, coming right out of the floor in haphazard patterns. They filled the chamber, trembling and swaying gently with the flow of circulating air as if they were parts of a living organism. A yellowish slime covered the nets, some of it dried. Suddenly, Matt was grateful the breathing masks filtered out all ambient odors.

Ryce picked his way around the sheets and helped him up. He gripped his shoulders tightly, raking him over with concerned eyes.

"Are you sure you're all right?"

"Yeah. Just clumsy, that's all." Matt wiped his hands on the trousers of his fatigues and looked around while his heart rate returned to normal. "What is this place?"

"A ventilation hub." Ryce gave Matt's shoulder one final squeeze and stepped back to examine their surroundings. "I think those are the air filters."

"They sure could use some cleaning."

"Apparently, humans aren't the only species with a lackadaisical approach to basic maintenance."

The alarm system oscillations were less pronounced here, but the ship occasionally shook as the battle went on outside. The Falcon fighters were putting a valiant effort into distracting the Alraki, but Matt had no doubt they were paying a heavy cost. He owed it to the pilots as well as the special ops team to get his ass in gear and hurry up.

They crossed the chamber amid the "breathing" filters, the strong currents tugging at their clothes. Ryce's short fair hair moved with the flow, Medusa-like wisps floating around his head, and Matt had to restrain himself from reaching over and touching it.

"This hub must control the air circulation for the entire bow," Ryce said as he walked up to a console that took up most of the curving wall of the chamber. He ran his hand over it, lighting up the wall-mounted screen that resembled a stretch of opaque membrane. It glowed a dull red, which didn't add much illumination to the darkened room, but was otherwise blank.

"I hope they're also slipshod about putting up a password," Matt muttered. They simply didn't have time to deal with any security layers over the alien computer data.

Ryce grimaced. "Let's see."

The console height wasn't adapted for humans, so tall as he was, Ryce had to stand on tiptoes to see the control panel. It took him a few swipe combinations to bring several lines of what appeared to be text on-screen. Matt glanced at it as he joined Ryce by the console, but his knowledge of the Alraki language was hardly sufficient to decipher the markings.

Ryce tapped something, bringing up an image of the complex network of air ducts on the membrane surface. After the initial pause, he was clearly feeling more in his element, his fingers flying above the screen as he zoomed in on a tangle of lines and flashing dots that Matt assumed indicated the locations of ventilation grates such as the one through which they'd come.

"Can you cut off the air flow to the sensor room corridor?" Matt asked, interpreting his intention.

"I don't know. I can try," Ryce said, frowning. There was something ominous in the way the red glow of the screen fell across his face, his eyes glinting eerily above the mask. "As a matter of fact, I can try sealing that corridor off altogether."

"That'll leave Walker and his people trapped. You heard him; there's no other way out."

"I'll time out the outage," Ryce said, tapping rapidly on the control panel, his arms outstretched. Across a long section of the map, the flashing dots blinked and went out.

"Wow," Matt said. "I didn't know fluency in Alraki was on the list of your accomplishments, but I can't say I'm surprised."

"I'm hardly fluent," Ryce said, his attention fixed on the console. "I can read it, but I wouldn't be able to ask any of them where the bathrooms are."

"They don't seem very tourist-friendly anyway," Matt said. "Are we good to go?"

"Yes. We have about ten minutes. It should give the team enough time."

Matt touched the adapters on his temples, switching on the communications channel that linked him to the *Lady Lisa* and Walker's team.

"Commander, can you hear me?"

"Yes," Walker answered promptly. Human voices and groans sounded in the background along with thin beeping, but thankfully, there were no gunshots. "What is going on? The chamber blast doors just slammed shut on us. I think they cut us off."

"No, that was us. Ryce and I are here to get you folks out."

"What? Captain Spears, you were both supposed to stay—"

"There's no time for rank-pulling," Matt said. "Do you have everything you wanted?"

Thankfully, Walker abandoned his admonitions and focused on more pressing business. "Yes, we got it. As to whether any of it is in working condition after dismantling, well…"

"Fleet R & D can worry about it later. Do you see an air duct opening on the ceiling anywhere?"

"Yeah," Walker said after a moment. "I see it. But that'd have to be our last resort. Some of us are in no shape to use it as an escape route."

His grim tone precluded Matt from asking why that was.

"Damn," Matt swore under his breath and turned to Ryce, who'd been listening in on their conversation. "What do we do now?"

"I guess we're going to chat up the locals," Ryce said mirthlessly.

*

By the time they reached the tiny nook Ryce had identified as a utility room off the sealed corridor, Matt decided he'd had enough of crawling through tight spaces to last him a lifetime. Granted, it could yet prove to be much shorter than anticipated.

They wiggled out of the vent, pushing the grate to the floor. Matt shook his bruised hands and took out his gun.

"How long till the air supply in the corridor comes back online?"

"Three more minutes," Ryce said, taking out his own weapon and heading to the closed narrow door. The little room was filled with crates, tall tube-shaped containers, and what appeared to be globs of gray silicon-y material that Matt couldn't imagine the use of. He gave them as wide a berth as the cramped room allowed.

He joined Ryce by the door, leaning against it to hear what was happening on the other side, but could discern nothing over the incessant vibration of the floor.

"Aren't they getting sick of this by now?" he murmured, checking to make sure his gun was set to maximum impact. It remained to be seen what a handgun could do against the notorious Alraki bio-mech armor, even at this intensity (though Matt was resentful of the fact he'd actually have to test it).

"I guess their code red isn't over yet, what with the Falcons attacking and intruders barricading themselves in the most sensitive part of their ship."

"And it's about to get louder. Walker, are you ready?" Matt said, opening the channel again.

"As ready as we're gonna be," the commander replied.

"All right then." Matt took a deep breath and nodded to Ryce.

"Three, two, one... Go!"

Ryce punched the control window, and the door swooshed open, revealing a dimly lit corridor. They both rushed into it, firing their guns at the Alraki gathered at the far side, near the now closed entrance to the sensor room. Matt didn't stop to take better stock of their numbers, but there were at least a dozen of them. Their reaction, when they wheeled around to face their fire, was sluggish, most likely due to the air circulation having been cut off, and that was the only thing that kept Matt and Ryce from being torn to shreds within seconds. The Alraki lunged toward them, but then the doors to the sensors room slid open, and Walker burst through leading the charge, his team's plasma rifles blazing. The hallway filled with howling and shrill cries, shots going off in all directions. The numbers' ratio wasn't in the humans' favor, but with their opponents still dazed and startled, they managed to press their advantage.

"Clear the exit!" Walker shouted over the racket, and Matt rushed to the mouth of the corridor while Ryce covered him, his handgun banging loudly.

"Clear!" Matt yelled after casting a cursory glance at the perpendicular corridor. Ryce's back pressed to his, and he was momentarily distracted by the feel of his strong muscles flexing with every shot.

Looking back, he saw the last of the Alraki go down. The team members picked their way around the fallen bodies, some of which were still twitching. The team's invisibility armor threw Matt off a bit, especially when movement blurred out of the corner of his eye where he wasn't expecting anyone to be, but up close, he could distinguish them all clearly. Ikeda and Shapiro held up Martin, who was bleeding from a deep gash on her neck right beneath her helmet, and Blair limped heavily on his left leg. Gonzales was nowhere to be seen.

"Where's—" Matt began.

"Dead," Walker clipped, joining them. His reflective suit was smeared with blood, both human and Alraki, judging by the colors, but otherwise, he seemed unharmed. He carried a bulging backpack which Matt assumed contained parts of the alien apparatus. Somehow, he'd thought there'd be more stuff to tote, but he was hardly an expert on laser tech—or whatever the thing was supposed to be.

"The docking bay is that way," Walker said, pointing right with his rifle. "Whatever we do, we must be off this ship in under half an hour."

"Why?"

"I've planted a bomb in the sensor array, as per my orders."

"Are you fucking kidding me?" Matt winced at the shrill note in his own voice and lowered the volume. "Hasn't this mission gotten botched enough without risking us all exploding?"

"We can't let them know what our ultimate target was," Walker said. "With a bit of luck, Alraki HQ will think the Falcon fighters managed to take their frigate down. It's not like they can hop over here to investigate. This will help us cover our tracks."

"Unless it kills us!"

"Then I suggest you get a move on before that happens."

Matt didn't need to be told twice. If avoiding capture by enraged Alraki wasn't enough of an incentive to hurry, the imminent risk of being blown to pieces certainly was. They ran down the empty hallway, Ryce taking the lead and Walker bringing up the rear, on the lookout for any signs of their enemy giving chase.

The corridors, illuminated by the same eerily glowing veins, curved and diverged, seemingly at random. Sometimes, they'd hear approaching footsteps and clicking sounds, but successfully dodged pursuit by ducking into another hallway or hiding around the corner of an intersection until the noises dwindled into the distance. Even with all these mad dashes, it seemed to Matt they were moving too slowly, their awkward group shuffling too audible in the empty spaces.

Matt had almost gotten used to the vibrating floor, but every now and again, the ship shook with impact, and every time, his heart plummeted, anticipating an explosion. The clock seemed to have sped up, and for once in his life, Matt wouldn't have minded having a little more time on his hands.

Finally, they reached an oval-shaped atrium, a connecting point for several corridors and two translucent shafts built into the walls, which appeared to be elevators.

"Our dock is there," Ryce said, pointing to the dimness beneath one of the archways.

Matt opened his mouth to say something (like thanking all gods in existence), but a laser beam swooshing past his head effectively silenced him.

"Get down!" Walker shouted, rounding on their attackers. About half a dozen Alraki were advancing on them from behind, armed with laser guns, and—invisible armor or not—there were still plenty of potential targets for them to zero in on. Another blast seared the wall next to where Ikeda and Shapiro had paused, midway between holding up Martin and reaching for their weapons.

"Leave me; I'm slowing you down," Martin panted, but thankfully, her teammates didn't heed her. Instead, they dragged her off in the direction Ryce had indicated as leading to the dock bay. The rest of them returned fire, taking cover behind the curve of the walls.

Walker unslung his backpack and shoved it at Matt, who staggered under the unexpected weight of it.

"Take it. The schematics, the adapter, everything is in there. Make sure Admiral Cummings gets it. I'll cover your retreat."

"No! What's up with everybody wanting to be a goddamned hero?! I'm not leaving you here." Matt tightened his grip on the bag and leaned closer to Walker, dropping his voice to a whisper. "If you die, do you realize what it'd do to Nora?"

"I'm doing this *for* Nora!" Walker growled, his eyes flashing behind the transparent visor of his helmet before he turned back to fire on their attackers.

"We don't have time for this conversation! You can nobly sacrifice yourself for her some other day; now get your ass back on the *Lisa*!"

"Someone still has to open the cargo doors," Walker threw over his shoulder. His rifle fired off in rapid succession, and he didn't bother taking precise aim as more Alraki joined their comrades, advancing on them over the bodies of their fallen. "Otherwise, the *Lisa* will still be trapped here."

"I'll do it," Ryce said, lowering his handgun. "I know how to tap into their computer. The rest of you, just get to the ship."

"What? No! What is *with* you all today?" Matt demanded.

But he didn't get a response as gunfire and the crackling of lasers filled the tiny space, and everyone ducked, scrambling for cover. Blair, who was holding the defense by Walker's side, let out a muffled cry and toppled backward as a beam hit him square in the chest. The operatives' body armor was enough to withstand a blaster shot but not a high-power laser at close range.

Wasting no time, Ryce dove into an adjacent hallway. Without sparing a second to consider what he was doing, Matt tore after him, clutching the bag to his chest, just as another volley hit the floor where they'd just stood.

"Spears, what are you doing? You have everything we took! Spears!" Walker called after him with growing frustration, but Matt didn't stop.

The wormhole technology, the strategic advantage, this whole fucking war could go to hell. The only thing he cared about was making sure Ryce got out of here alive.

Chapter Eleven

"You were not supposed to tag along," Ryce snapped as Matt caught up with him.

"If you think I'm letting you run off on your own, you're out of your goddamn mind." Matt slung the heavy bag on his shoulder, wincing as something sharp inside dug into his back. "Where are we going, anyway?"

"The main dock computer terminal. We can open the bay doors from there."

"Do we have enough time to make it back to the *Lisa*?"

Ryce threw him a glance, his gray eyes hard. "We'll find out soon enough."

"This is not very encouraging!"

Ryce didn't answer. Matt cursed under his breath and opened a direct link to the bridge.

"Tony, do you copy?"

"Yes," she said promptly, "we're here."

"It's all systems go. Fire up the engine. Commander Walker and his team will be there in a few minutes."

"Walker? What about you and Ryce?" Her voice rose in pitch. "Where are you?"

"We're coming," Matt barked, struggling to control his ragged breathing and hoping to all hell he wasn't lying. "Just get her ready!"

They ran, following the curve of the corridor, the wobbling floor making Matt lose his footing a few times. Then Ryce took a sharp turn, and a huge cavern of a hangar opened up before them. The same reddish light splashed across the walls, illuminating rows of small alien spacecraft, their shapes reminiscent of scorpions poised to attack. The frigate didn't carry strike fighters aboard—this type of battleship relied on its agility and fire power in combat, but it still employed a wide array of shuttles and recon vessels.

Matt paused, flinching instinctively, but the hangar seemed to be empty. Ryce led the way inside, creeping along the wall. A long narrow console protruded from the floor in one of the corners, creating an enclosed area for controls and surveillance screens. They headed toward it, crouching in the shadows. Matt half expected a response squad to come charging at them the second Ryce touched the control panel, but the hangar remained quiet.

Ryce grabbed what appeared to be a crate from a pile next to one of the docked maintenance pods and climbed on top of it to reach the control console comfortably. This one had a tabletop monitor instead of a wall screen, and Ryce leaned above it, trying to decipher the alien writing.

Matt glanced at his comm, his heart plummeting as he took in the time. They had about five minutes before the imminent explosion. Their run through the alien spaceship had taken them longer than anticipated.

"Damn it." Matt bit his lip and touched his adapters while Ryce tapped furiously on the console. "Walker, status!"

"We've just reached the *Lisa*," Walker answered promptly. "Those of us who could make it. But the clock is ticking, and the Alraki are firing on us. Where are you?"

"I swear, if these fuckers damage my ship—" Matt took a deep breath. "Make sure she's ready to go and prepare for takeoff."

"If you don't get here with the schematics in the next two minutes..."

"We'll be there," Matt said and disconnected before looking up at Ryce. "Right?"

Loud noises from the hallway leading to the hangar staved off whatever response Ryce was about to offer. Matt raised his gun, stepping forward, his heart hammering loudly enough to be heard all the way across the dock. Ryce remained intent on the jumble of glowing characters floating across the screen.

"Now would be a good time to punch it!" Matt shouted, but it was already too late for the two of them. The Alraki coming up the corridor effectively cut off their only escape route and would be on them in a matter of seconds. The only thing they could do now was make sure the others got away before the bomb went off. He reached for his adapters to notify Tony and hear her chew him out one last time.

"Got it," Ryce said, straightening above the console. "The cargo doors in *Lisa*'s dock are opening. The main airlock will shut and open automatically, but they have to go now." He tapped his adapters before Matt had the chance to touch his. "Commander, you're clear to leave."

"What about you?"

"Don't worry about us, just go!"

Matt gripped the blaster gun with both hands and took a deep breath, taking aim at the entrance. The thunder of approaching footsteps resonated in his chest. Something cold and nauseating rose up in his throat, but he didn't have time to analyze it.

"Ryce," he said, doing his best to keep his voice (and his hands) from wavering. "Whatever happens, I just want you to know that I love—"

"Me too, but let's save it for later." Ryce jumped off the crate, grabbed Matt's arm above the elbow, and dragged him in tow, retreating farther into the hanger. A deep low rumble gave warning as the huge bay doors leading to the airlock at the mouth of the chamber began to slide open.

"What are you doing?"

"Come on, in here!"

They ran toward the closest spacecraft, which turned out to be one of the smaller, single-flyer recon jets. It was much larger than an average

Falcon fighter jet, but then again, the Alraki were much larger than an average human. The fuselage coiled in on itself without any visible point of entry, but Ryce ducked under its massive tail and pressed something on the side of it. A long narrow panel opened downward, creating a ramp. Ryce and Matt dove inside just as laser shots pierced the air around them, bouncing off the slick walls and the body of the jet. Matt absently wondered what they were made of to make them so resistant to lasers.

"Can you even fly this thing?" he asked instead, moving aside as Ryce hit the controls to shut the hatch.

"Of course."

"Have you? Like, ever?"

"No."

"Oh, this is just great." Matt's heart still pounded, but at least now he could draw a breath again without feeling like he was going to throw up. With Walker's bomb about to detonate, their relative safety would be short-lived unless they hauled ass, Ryce's experience (or lack thereof) notwithstanding.

Ryce sat down in the pilot's chair—a huge, spiky thing, more resembling a half-hatched cocoon—and tapped the control panel, lighting it up. There was no glass, but the opaque membrane of the dome turned translucent, revealing the red-tinted darkness outside. The Alraki didn't use adapters to create a link between the pilot's mind to a ship's computer, relying instead on several sticks of varying sizes for manual steering. Matt couldn't tell if that made Ryce's task easier or not.

"With full manual control I have limited access to the craft's capabilities," Ryce said, echoing Matt's thoughts. "Some of the more advanced features—"

"Fuck advanced features. Just get us out of here!"

"Copy that."

The jet didn't have a navigator's chair, and Matt crouched on the floor behind the only seat after holstering his gun. He unslung the backpack and huddled around it, holding on to it as the space jet's thrusters came to life. The spacecraft lunged forward like a startled animal, made a sharp turn around the row of its mates, and sped toward the exit under the barrage of Alraki lasers.

"Come on, come on, *come on*," Matt whispered, and the jet reached the airlock before the Alraki could override Ryce's programming.

A low but resounding bang rippled through the hangar. The jet shot into the wide airlock, the hangar doors slamming behind it just as a massive explosion shook the frigate. Matt cowered instinctively, his heart jumping to his throat at the deafening roar, punctuated by the keening wail of ripping metal. For a split second, he worried that the external doors would jam, and they'd be smeared all over them with the impact, but then the black void gaped around the ship, and they hurtled into open space.

Angry red writing flashed across the screen, and the jet shook, its thrusters straining as Ryce struggled to keep the spacecraft on a steady trajectory. Despite his efforts, the shock wave sent it into a tailspin, and Matt grabbed the wall with one hand while cradling the bag and its precious cargo with the other.

"Hold on!" Ryce shouted. He alternated between pulling the different control sticks at an almost superhuman speed, but having only two hands, unlike the Alraki, there was only so much he could do.

"I'm trying!" Matt winced as he bumped his head painfully against the ridged wall and hunkered down even more. "Don't worry about me, just get away!"

"Let's see what this thing can do." Ryce swiped the panel, shutting down the alarm notification, and gripped the two larger sticks, abandoning the others and leaning on them with a grunt, pushing them as far forward as they would go. The engine revved, its angry roar drowning the reverberating booms coming from the alien ship, and the jet sped up, veering away from the debris being blasted into space all around them.

"I can't access the rear cameras," Ryce said. "We'll have to make do with the front view."

Easing up the pressure, Ryce swerved gently to the side, and the image of the burning frigate filled half the domed screen as they sailed past it. With most of its bow gone and pieces of armature protruding from the gaping holes like broken bones, it resembled a fatally wounded whale in the throes of agony.

Matt looked up, unable to tear his eyes away from the terrible sight unfolding in front of them, and let out a deep breath. It was hard to believe they'd been minutes—no, seconds—away from being trapped in that blazing inferno.

"We're clear." Ryce relaxed a little, his shoulders sagging, but maintained a firm hold on the controls, scanning their immediate surroundings for any incoming threats. "Are you all right?"

"Yeah, I'm fine." Matt sat up, readjusting his mask, which had been jostled by his tossing about in the cramped space. There'd be some bruises, but he much preferred them to the alternative. "Do you see *Lady Lisa*?"

"Negative." Ryce tapped on some symbols on the control panel and frowned. "Either the sensors were damaged by the blast, or I can't access them, much like the peripheral cameras. It's impossible to run a scan, and I can't lock onto a visual. Basically, we have to make do with what we see right in front of us."

"Shit." Matt hauled himself upright, grabbing the back of Ryce's chair for support, and touched his adapters again.

"Walker, do you read me? Where are you? Walker?"

Eons seemed to pass before an answer came through.

"We're okay. The *Lisa* got out."

"Oh, thank god." Matt slumped in relief. "You have no idea how happy I am to hear you."

"The sentiment is mutual, I assure you. How did you guys make it out?"

"We stole an Alraki vessel. Did you call off the Falcons in time?" Ryce asked.

"Yes. They were all safely away when the bomb exploded. We're headed to the moon base. Their heavier craft are on their way to capture the remains of the Alraki frigate. I'll notify Admiral Cummings of the success of the mission."

"If that's what you want to call it," Matt muttered.

There was a tense pause. "I would do anything to bring Gonzales and Blair back," Walker said finally. "But I can't. Every person on my team is cognizant of the risks we're taking, me included. Sometimes there's just no beating the odds. There's only completing the mission."

"I know," Matt said, regretting his words as soon as they left his mouth. It seemed easier to fall back to his asshole mode with vestiges of panic still coursing through his system, but it was no excuse. If it were him in Walker's place right now, he'd be too broken up to function. "I'm sorry. That wasn't fair. You did your best, and yeah, it was a success. We got what we came here to find."

"Do you still have it with you?"

"Yes." Matt glanced down at the backpack lying at his feet. "We have it."

"Good. We'll rendezvous at the base. Mr. Easom has the coordinates."

"ETA in approximately sixty minutes," Ryce said. "Just make sure no one fires at us by mistake when the Fleet shows up, Commander."

"Will do. See you there. Great work, everybody," Walker said before disconnecting.

For a while, they enjoyed the relative silence, watching the cloud of debris surrounding the incapacitated ship expand.

"I've always wanted to fly an alien vessel," Ryce said, running a caressing hand over the controls. "To see how it feels. If it's really that different. I just wish I could have done it under different circumstances."

"Yeah." Matt could understand the curiosity, but the experience didn't move him in quite the same way. "Is it? Different?"

"Not as much as I thought it would be. Well, apart from the obvious inconvenience when it comes to size. Are you sure you're okay?" Ryce turned in his seat to face him. "You look...queasy."

"Being rattled around in a tin can will do that to you. But I'm really fine."

He was indeed queasy, but mostly just giddy with relief. There was no rush quite like emerging alive out of a hopeless situation, but Matt would've preferred to never experience it again. He leaned down to hug Ryce, molding himself awkwardly against his body in that enormous chair, and buried his face in the crook of his neck.

"I should kill you for that stunt you pulled back there," he whispered, closing his eyes. The masks they wore were the only reason he was talking instead of kissing his boyfriend silly. "If you'd ended up dead..."

"You'd end up dead too," Ryce said, ruffling Matt's hair and pulling him closer. "I should be no less mad at you for dashing off after me. You endangered the outcome of the mission, running off with that thing."

"Fuck the mission," Matt said fiercely. "You're the most important thing to me. You know that, right?"

"I know." Ryce's hands tightened on his shoulders. "Believe it or not, I don't have a death wish. I knew I could help everybody out and still make it on time."

"Knew?"

"Well. I was reasonably sure."

"Wiseass," Matt said, smiling into his mask.

An alarm message bleeped on the screen, and the jet shook, gently at first, and then more and more violently, conveying an emergency much as its parent frigate had. Matt jumped to his feet, and Ryce grabbed ahold of the control sticks again, pulling the jet aside sharply just in time to evade a laser-cannon blast.

"What the hell?! Who's firing on us?"

"I don't know. Trying to get a visual here." Ryce held a stick in one hand, the other hovering over the panel.

"I thought Walker called off the Falcons," Matt said, digging his fingers into the rubbery surface of the chair to stay upright as the jet tilted and dived.

"I don't think it's a Falcon." The vessel shook, barely avoiding another hit. Ryce hissed and grabbed both sticks, abandoning his efforts at manipulating the sensors. "That's far too much firepower."

"This is supposed to be one of the quietest corners of the sector, not the fucking Sawyer Strait! Is it another Alraki ship? How would they know we're not one of theirs?"

"I don't know. I'm trying to maneuver so we can turn around and get a direct view of who we're dealing with, but it's not—hold tight!"

Another laser beam grazed the jet, hitting one of its winglike protrusions. Unfortunately, while the hull could apparently easily weather laser-gun charges, a ship-sized cannon was another matter. Matt lost his balance with the force of the impact, bumping into a wall with his shoulder and then crashing to the floor. He grunted in pain, clutching his hurt shoulder. Bouncing about like a rubber ball in an empty cage was getting really old, but any thought of his own discomfort evaporated as the jet spun out of control. Matt flattened himself on the floor, risking a glance upward. Ryce threw himself over the console, struggling to maintain a hold on the sticks.

"Whoever that was, they stopped firing at us," he said through gritted teeth.

"That's 'cause they already shot us!" Matt shouted back. "How bad is it?"

"Pretty bad." Ryce pulled back roughly, steadying the jet, but Matt could tell by its violent shaking that Ryce was right in his succinct assessment. "One of the thrusters is busted, and we're losing pressure fast."

"Damn it." This kind of damage necessitated an immediate return to the mother ship's maintenance hangar—impossible in their case, just as staying any longer in open space with their jet decompressing would be. "We have to land somewhere. With actual atmosphere. Can this thing hold till we get to Waga?"

"It's not like we have much choice, seeing as the integrity of the hull is compromised." Ryce's knuckles turned white as he held the controls in a death grip, but the spacecraft still swayed like a fishing boat in a storm on high seas. "Landing is our only option. I'm shutting down all auxiliary systems and directing all power to the remaining thruster. Hopefully, it'll be enough to reach the moon before the ship starts falling apart."

"How about reaching that Fleet base?"

"We could try. I remember the coordinates, but we're only flying on direct visual here. Our chances of finding the exact location without the sensors are pretty slim."

The jet keened, picking up speed, its shuddering intensifying. At least it kept to a more or less straight course, but with life support shut off, it was getting significantly colder by the minute. Matt could imagine the air leaking out in a steady stream—not that it was much use for them anyway.

"How long before we run out of oxygen?" he asked, touching his mask. It wasn't an easy question to ask, but even he had to admit it was better to be prepared than taken unawares by a sudden inability to draw breath.

"We still have a good few hours with the portable generators," Ryce said, his attention divided between the dome screen and the console. "Don't worry about it. Even if we don't make it to the base proper, the garrison will be able to pick us up pretty fast."

Being stranded without an air supply was a good reason to be worried, in Matt's opinion, but Ryce didn't need the added pressure of his agitation right now.

"I'll call Walker and let him know what's up." Matt switched on the communications channel again. "Commander?"

The faint crackling of static accentuated the ensuing silence.

"Walker, do you copy? It's Captain Spears. Walker?"

Matt switched the channel to the direct line to the bridge. Surely, they would all be there? Tony wouldn't leave the bridge until Matt and

Ryce were safely back on board; they would have to drag her away kicking and screaming for her to relinquish her responsibilities as first mate.

"Tony? Tony, come in! Val? Anybody?"

He raised his voice over the stirrings of panic that threatened to seize his throat. Why weren't they responding?

He tried again, with no success, and then again, and again. There was no answer.

Chapter Twelve

Matt turned to Ryce, his heart hammering with awful premonition.

"You don't suppose whoever fired on us—" he began, his voice strangely hollow.

"No," Ryce said firmly, glancing sideways at him while still hanging on to the steering sticks. "It had to have been one of the Fleet vessels, mistaking us for an enemy craft. That's the only logical explanation. The *Lisa* is fine. Something must be scrambling communications from your adapters, that's all. Nothing seems to be working like it's supposed to on this thing."

Matt let out a long breath. "Yeah. Yeah, sure."

"See if you can get ahold of someone on your comm," Ryce said, turning back to the screen. "Mission control would want to know what's going on. Those things in your bag are their first priority, and they're currently with us, not *Lady Lisa*."

"Okay."

Matt flexed his hands to stop them from trembling and fished his commlink out of the inner pocket of the flight suit, forgoing trying to use his adapters to establish connection. He scrolled through his contacts until he came upon Grayson's name. As awkward as their interactions had been, talking to him was preferable to trying to explain to Admiral Cummings how they'd ended up in a malfunctioning Alraki spacecraft, in need of extraction along with his precious alien tech.

He hit the contact, praying that whatever mysterious forces had suddenly prevented him from talking with his crew would relent enough for the call to the admiral's aide to come through.

"Yes?" Grayson's imperious voice was heavily distorted by digital interference, and there was no video, but Matt had rarely been happier to hear someone being snooty to him over the commlink.

"Grayson! Thank God," he said, not bothering hiding his relief. "It's Matt. We made it out of the frigate before it blew up, but Mr. Easom and I were separated from the rest of the team and our crew after commandeering an Alraki spacecraft. The schematics and the hardware are with us. It's a long story, but we've sustained significant damage, and—"

"Where are you right now?" Grayson responded curtly.

"We're on our way to the Waga moon," Matt said. "But I'm not sure we'll be able to arrive at the base in this thing after someone used us for target practice." As if to emphasize his words, the high-pitched wail of the thrusters hit an especially jarring note.

"I'll arrange a transport to come for you," Grayson said. "Send me your exact coordinates when you land."

"Great," Matt said. "Thank you."

"I'd advise you to maintain complete radio silence as you wait for pickup. The Fleet is shutting off the Waga quadrant as a no-fly zone for now, and it's best if you don't add any more confusion to the mix. No more chatting on your comm, please."

Matt made a face, but he knew it'd be useless to argue. "Fine. In that case, could you contact Walker and make sure everybody aboard the *Lisa* is okay? We can't seem to get through to them. The bridge isn't answering."

"It'll take care of it." Static over the channel distorted Grayson's voice. "Commander Walker is most likely under the same instructions from mission control regarding keeping the frequencies clear. That's why they're not responding to your calls. That's how the chain of command works."

"Sure," Matt said, rolling his eyes. It wasn't as if he expected anything from Grayson other than being treated like a nuisance, let alone that he'd care about Matt's precarious situation or his concern for his crew. Frankly, he didn't mind being talked down to, as long as Grayson lived up to his apparent efficiency in handling difficult situations. "We'll be nice and quiet. Unless, of course, we crash, in which case—"

"Is there anything else?"

This time, Matt definitely didn't imagine the exasperation in Grayson's voice.

Suppressing a flash of resentment, Matt debated within himself whether he should ask Grayson to deliver a message to his father. He didn't know where the unexpected urge had come from. Maybe it was that he'd narrowly escaped a very close call, or maybe it was the childish, deep-seated desire to appease his dad. A tiny voice inside clamored, *Look, Ryce and I, we did it, we got you everything you wanted! Aren't you proud of me, for once in your life?*

But Matt knew better than to say anything. It would be pointless; there was nothing he could ever say or do to win his father's approval, not when the admiral had made his opinion of Matt perfectly clear on several occasions, both privately and in public.

"No," he said, rubbing the bridge of his nose tiredly above the mask. "Nothing else."

"Let me know the minute you land, and sit tight," Grayson instructed.

"Roger that," Matt said, but Grayson had already disconnected.

Matt sighed and turned to Ryce. "I wish he'd give us a real update on *Lady Lisa*. He sounded for all the world like I was his deadbeat uncle, trying to borrow a grand till Tuesday."

"It seems the two of you still have some unresolved issues," Ryce observed.

"I don't need a therapy session; all I want is for him to make sure we all return safely aboard my ship."

The engine was making a strange noise, an irregular rattle now clearly audible above the continuous wailing. The ambient temperature was dropping rapidly now that the life-support systems had been shut off. Like all humanoids, Alraki were warm-blooded creatures and operated in roughly the same range of basic physiological conditions as humans, differences in their breathable atmosphere notwithstanding. Without atmosphere control, it was quickly becoming cold—much more so than it had been in *Lisa*'s cargo hold. Matt hugged himself and rubbed his shoulders, shivering.

"How long till we get there?" he asked, leaning against Ryce's chair again.

"Estimated arrival in about twenty minutes. If our working thruster holds for that long."

Unfortunately, it was a concern Matt shared. He wasn't a combat pilot or an engineer, but he'd piloted his own spaceship long enough to know when things weren't running smoothly—and when they were about to stop running altogether.

Waga slowly came into full view on the domed screen, its rocky face, pocked with craters filled with pools of liquid methane, clearly visible for the thin atmosphere. It was an inhospitable little world, but the lack of seismic activity and its proximity to the mining operations on other Sonora-4 moons made it a perfect location for a minor military outpost.

The jet finally stumbled into lower orbit and began its descent, gliding over the craggy surface below.

"The Fleet base shouldn't be far from here, if I recall the location correctly," Ryce said. "If we only maintain cruising altitude—"

Something snapped with the sickening crack of dried bone. The ear-piercing squeal of the remaining thruster ended abruptly, giving way to ringing silence. For a split second, it seemed as if time stood still, suspended in uncertainty, and then the jet dived, losing the battle against the moon's gravity.

"Oh, shit!" Matt clutched the control panel as the spacecraft skewed right sharply and spun as it plummeted. "Ryce!"

"I'm trying to restart it! Here, help me!" Ryce thrust one of the sticks at Matt while frantically tapping on the controls, Alraki script flashing and receding across the on-screen image in quick succession.

Matt grabbed the stick, trying to pull up from the dizzying downward spiral. His palms were suddenly slick with sweat, despite the cold.

"Can you get it working again?" he gritted through his teeth, digging his feet into the floor to keep his balance.

"I can't connect with their computer directly like we're used to, and manual control is...challenging," Ryce said, his attention riveted to whatever he was clicking on the console.

Matt sucked in a breath. If Ryce thought the situation was "challenging," then there was a really good chance of them not surviving it. Like, close to a hundred-percent chance.

The ground was rapidly approaching, the blue-gray sandy plain stretching before them like an endless sea. This wasn't how Matt imagined he'd go, though he supposed one way was no better than another. It would appear his father wouldn't have that chance to be proud of him after all.

"Hey, remember that thing I started telling you in the hanger? Can I say it now, seeing as we're about to crash and all?" Somehow, he even managed to stop his voice from shaking.

"You know, your fatalistic outlook is one of the few things I *don't* like about you," Ryce said, hunched over the console.

"I don't think it counts as an outlook if you're actually about to die!"

"I won't let you die," Ryce said with a ferocity that took Matt aback, though he still wasn't looking at him. "Not if there's anything I can do about it. I won't, so save it. Tell me...after."

There won't be any "after" in about five minutes! Matt wanted to scream. But Ryce clearly didn't want to hear it, so he swallowed hard and shut up. He kept pulling on the stick, though the jet wasn't responding to his efforts. He didn't want the desolate landscape to be the last thing he saw; instead, he focused on Ryce's profile and his eyes above the rim of his breathing mask, flashing like angry stars. It was the most beautiful sight in the world, and one Matt wished he'd never laid eyes on—not if it meant Ryce was about to die here right along with him. Whatever twist of fate had brought them here, to this moment, Matt was pretty sure he was the one to blame for it being their last.

He drew a ragged breath, bracing himself for imminent impact, just as Ryce hit something hard on the control. It took Matt a second to realize there was something different in the way the jet was shaking, and then the engine roared, almost deafening him after the near silence.

"Now, Matt!" Ryce shouted, drawing Matt out of his stupor, and he tightened his grip on the stick, pulling it with every ounce of strength he had. The revived thruster revved, and the jet zoomed sharply, coming out of the nosedive. Matt almost lost his balance as the craft tilted, but held on to dear life, fighting the warring gravitational forces.

Ryce grabbed the other large stick and fought to right the jet. Matt stepped back, letting him take over the controls, and crouched behind the pilot chair again, breathing hard. Their velocity was still too high, with not enough time to slow down. Even with a working thruster, the landing was going to be rough.

The jet flew over the rocky landmass, skimming just above the surface. Ryce managed to avoid colliding into the low hills, trying to keep the jet up in the air for as long as possible, but they were still going too fast.

"Here it comes," Ryce said, again calm and collected, guiding the alien spacecraft downward for all the world as if it were a regular old shuttle.

Matt opened his mouth to offer a witty comeback, but then the jet hit the ground, bouncing off like a rubber ball, and all thought of running his mouth evaporated. Metal furrowed into rubble with awful screeching, and then the jet skidded to a stop, the engine winding down.

"We have touchdown," Ryce said into the ensuing silence, gently pushing the sticks back into neutral position and then slumping in the oversized chair.

Matt rose carefully to his feet. The walls continued to vibrate, and a new set of bruises was forming all over his body, but they were both alive and their vessel relatively intact. He would have called it a miracle, except it was Ryce's skill and moxie he had to thank for that, not some esoteric luck. He let out a long, adrenaline-laced breath.

"So." Matt hoped his voice matched his intent and not his state. "What else don't you like about me?"

There was a moment of stunned silence, and then Ryce snorted. It was probably the most inelegant noise Matt had ever heard him make.

"How much time have you got?" he said wryly, and Matt playfully slapped him on the shoulder.

"Probably not enough," Matt said, sobering, and touched his mask. "We're going to run out of oxygen at some point. Or freeze. The surface temperature here is pretty low. I better tell Grayson where we are. What are our coordinates?"

He shot Grayson a quick message with the information Ryce gave him, stressing the urgency.

"Sure hope whoever is coming to pick us up hauls their ass," Matt said, looking at the screen. The view outside looked particularly bleak—craggy terrain crisscrossed by deep fissures filled with ice against the dark sky. Wisps of oily black smoke rose from the busted thruster, mixing with the veil of dust raised by their near crash. With no sign of human presence in sight, it was a depressing place to end up in.

Cast in deep shadow, the only illumination in the cockpit came from the dim glow of icy ground outside. Ryce switched off the engine, which was still rumbling brokenly in the background, and rose from the chair, sighing and rubbing the back of his neck.

"I must say, this has been a rather perturbing experience."

"No shit. Did you get your fix flying an alien spacecraft?"

"Yes, and I hope to never have to do it again. At least not until after I've had proper training in their pilot interface."

Matt raised an eyebrow. "Are you admitting you weren't adequately prepared for the job?" he asked jokingly.

"I'd rather not incriminate myself by admitting anything." Ryce got out from behind the console. With both of them standing, the cockpit was cramped, even considering its impressive size. "But yes, some in-depth instruction on the Alraki mode of flight and a few extra sets of hands would've been helpful. I'd love to take a better look at this thing if we ever manage to deliver it to the Fleet though. It's so different from how human fighters or recon vessels operate. They even have their own jumpgate laser-excitation technology installed on this thing. The Fleet never bothers with it on spacecraft of this class."

"Sounds fascinating. What now?" Matt asked, shivering. With the rush of panic receding, the cold and worry were starting to creep in again. Unexpected survival came with its own set of problems, like a dwindling oxygen supply, nonfunctioning life-support systems, and complete ignorance regarding the fate of his friends and his ship.

"Now we wait." Ryce wrapped his arms around Matt, sharing warmth. Both their hearts still raced, beating in unison. "You're sure Lieutenant Lee got the message, right?"

"Yeah." Matt leaned into Ryce, holding him tight, finally letting himself close his eyes. Something continued to pulsate steadily inside the control panel, alerting the pilot (somewhat redundantly) of the extensive array of malfunctions, and Matt's heartbeats eased and steadied, falling in rhythm with the vibrations.

"I'm sorry," Ryce said softly. "For acting like a jealous jerk about him."

"You know you have nothing to be jealous of, right? It ended between us a long time ago. We're both completely different people now."

"I know. But you get why him popping back into your life had me worried?"

"Yes." Matt snuggled closer, breathing in the scent of him, sweat mixed with metal and burned rubber. "If any of your exes unexpectedly showed up and tried to boss us around, I would have blown a fuse."

"It's a good thing I don't have exes."

"If I'm lucky, you won't have any." It came out sounding more sinister than intended, so Matt hastened to amend: "That is, I meant—"

"I know what you meant," Ryce said. Matt heard the smile in his voice. "I hope so too."

"Can I say it now? That thing you told me not to say at the frigate hangar?"

"Yes. Please, say it."

"I love you."

"I love you too." Ryce ran his hand through Matt's hair, ruffling it even more than it already was. "So much it—"

"Hurts?"

"No." Ryce sighed again, wearily. "You're the person who has the power to hurt me the most in this world, Matt, but I know you wouldn't. It doesn't hurt, but it scares me. Doesn't it frighten you sometimes, knowing how much another person's happiness rests on your actions?"

It wasn't the way Matt would have put it, but he couldn't deny that Ryce was right. Not just frightening—terrifying. But knowing he could also be the cause of happiness for the person he loved was the most beautiful feeling in the world. It was what he wanted to do for the rest of his life.

He looked up at Ryce, ready to tell him that, but Ryce turned away, his attention drawn to the screen.

"What is that?"

The air outside shimmered with the heat emitted from powerful thrusters, and dust particles rose in a new flurry, partially obscuring the view of something big silhouetted against the dark sky.

"It's a ship." Ryce turned sharply to Matt, his eyes wide. Neither the possibility of being eviscerated by angry Alraki nor the very close danger of crashing and burning had caused him to look this shaken, and that made Matt scared like nothing else. "A black ship."

Chapter Thirteen

"We have to get out of here," Matt said, his throat suddenly as dry as the icy desert around them. The sense of deja vu was so strong he was sure he must be dreaming, caught up in one of his usual nightmares.

"I don't think we can," Ryce said tersely as they watched the ship descend. "We don't have any spacesuits. Even if the masks would prevent us from suffocating, we'd freeze in a matter of minutes if we go outside."

"So we just wait here until they board us? No way. We gotta do something."

How could this be happening? Dylan Rodgers was behind bars, in a maximum-security prison on charges of piracy, aggravated assault, and murder. His ship, the *Black Baza*, had been impounded by the authorities. Either someone was playing a joke on them, or... Matt didn't know what it was. His usually vivid imagination utterly failed him this time, refusing to supply any logical scenario that would end in them coming face-to-face with his archenemy on some godforsaken Sonora moon.

Matt got out his commlink again and tapped on Grayson's contact, but this time, there was no answer.

"This is not the time to ignore me, Grayson!" Matt shouted at the comm in frustration. "Damn it!"

Ryce lit up the control panel, frowning at the writing on the screen.

"Can you get it up in the air again?" Matt asked, frantically going through his contacts to find somebody who could be of any help in a we're-about-to-be-abducted kind of emergency.

He knew it was a long shot. Without a second thruster to support it, the spacecraft most likely wouldn't be able to reach escape velocity, even if they were able to take off. And nobody in the entire fucking galaxy was answering his calls!

"No," Ryce said, confirming his fears. "This thing needs a complete overhaul before it can fly again."

"Fuck!" Matt hit the control panel in frustration and turned his attention back to his commlink. "I can't reach anybody. None of my calls go through. Commlink, adapters to bridge... No one's answering. Not Tony, not Val, not Nora. Hell, I dialed my father. It's like—"

"They're jamming our communications." Ryce whipped out his own comm and quickly scrolled through his contacts, frowning.

"Fuck this." Matt said fiercely. He shoved his comm back in his pocket and took the blaster gun out of its holster.

"What are you doing?"

"Getting ready to offer whoever comes through the hatch a warm welcome." Matt turned toward the exit as if expecting the pirates to come bursting in at any moment, though their ship still hovered somewhere above.

"You can't shoot your way out of this."

"I know!" Matt's voice came dangerously close to cracking, and he swallowed before continuing. "But what else is there to do? If we surrender, do you understand what will happen to us? We may as well have stayed on that frigate. At least the Alraki just kill you on the spot, no questions asked. They don't care. Dylan Rodgers fucking *cares*." Matt ran his other hand through his hair, wincing as his fingers swept over a tiny gash in his scalp. "He cares enough to have chased me all the way here into the heart of Federation space. How...how can I protect you against that kind of hatred?"

"You can't." Ryce slid out of the pilot chair and joined him near the hatch, laying a hand on Matt's arm. "But that doesn't mean we should just give in. Listen to me. There's nothing we can do here, but falling on your metaphorical sword isn't the answer. If we stay focused, we can figure something out to get ourselves out of his mess. And we will, all right?" His voice, usually so calm and level, rose in urgency. "Please, trust me on this, Matt. *Dum spiro spero.*"

Above the rim of his mask, Ryce's eyes shone in the fickle lighting, their impossible beauty a reminder of everything they stood to lose.

Matt took a long, unsteady breath. He still had a choice—a quick, easy death, either by his enemy's weapon or by his own, or a future in which suffering was the only certainty. But Ryce was asking Matt to trust him, and he couldn't deny Ryce anything, least of all his faith in him.

"Okay," he said, lowering his gun. "Though you using Latin on me is a dirty trick."

Half of Ryce's face was obscured, but Matt could sense his crooked smile.

"Now we—" Matt began, but then the jet shook, and they both staggered, clutching each other to keep their balance as the ship lifted, pulled upward by some unseen force as if plucked by a giant's hand.

"They're using a magnetic grapnel to reel us in," Ryce said, glancing back to the canopy screen. "This way, they won't even have to land."

"Great." Matt cast about, his gaze landing on the backpack lying forgotten, half tucked behind the pilot chair. He let go of Ryce and dived for it.

"Help me," he said, pushing hard at the rubbery wall casing, trying to pry out a panel. "Rodgers might kill us both, but I'll be damned if he's getting the jump tech. He'd be completely unstoppable."

Ryce crouched beside him and opened the bag while Matt clawed at the walls. He fished out the adapter Walker (or, more likely, Ikeda, as the communications officer) had used to plug into the Alraki system and download the blueprints, and connected it to his own comm. He brought the raw data on-screen and scrolled through it, staring intently at the small screen, his lips moving silently.

Matt stopped what he was doing, watching him warily. Finally, Ryce nodded to himself and disconnected the device. Slipping the comm back into his pocket, he stood up, threw the adapter on the floor, and stomped on it, hard. The little box cracked, and the electronic circuits crunched under Ryce's heel as he continued to grind it into the floor.

Matt gaped behind his mask and looked up at him.

"The hell are you doing? That was—"

"The only copy of the wormhole-generating system schematics. And now, it's all here." He pointed to his temple. "Where the pirates can't get to it, unless we use it as a bargaining chip to stall for time."

"Tony said you had balls of steel, and she wasn't wrong." Matt stared at Ryce with something close to awe. By now he knew just how extraordinary Ryce's cognitive abilities were, and he had no doubt his partner had managed to commit every single detail of those files to his memory. They were as safely intact in his brain as they'd be inside a computer server. "Now what about the rest of it?"

"Let's stash it, like you said."

The wall casing wouldn't budge, but together, they managed to remove a part of the flooring under the console, exposing a nest of wiring that looked not so different from the electronics of a regular human ship, apart from size. It was a tight fit, but Matt shoved the backpack inside and snapped the panel shut.

"I have a sense of deja vu," Ryce said, echoing Matt's earlier thoughts, and sat back on his haunches.

"Feels more like a nightmare," Matt said, slumping against the wall and closing his eyes for a moment. "Maybe I'm in my cabin on the *Lisa*, dreaming, with you lying beside me, and all this will go away once I wake up. Then you'll hold me, and make love to me, and it'll all be okay again."

"Want me to pinch you?" Ryce asked, huddling closer.

"Oh, I think there'll be plenty of pinching going around in a little while."

Part of the pirate ship hull loomed on-screen like a black shadow as the ground fell farther and farther away. Their cabin interior dimmed, and the sound of heavy cargo hold doors slamming shut reverberated through the jet and their bones. The small spacecraft dropped on its shock absorbers, wobbled for a few seconds, and then stood still.

"This is it," Matt whispered into the silence. His heart seemed to stop beating for a second, making him almost choke on the bile that rose in his throat, and then it ratcheted up, going off at the speed of a racing pod.

Ryce drew him into a quick, tight embrace, their masks clashing.

"We'll get through this," he said in the same low voice. "Trust me, okay?"

Matt only nodded, not trusting himself to speak, tightening his grip on the other man just as someone began banging loudly on the outer hatch.

*

The interior of the *Black Baza* looked exactly like Matt remembered, down to the scuffed metal flooring and the dim lighting along the long narrow corridors. By now, he had the route from the docking bay to the torture chamber memorized. He didn't need the armed guards leading Ryce and him into the bowels of the ship like some mock versions of mythical ferrymen escorting their charges into the underworld.

It felt surreal, being here again. However Rodgers had managed to escape from a federal prison and get his ship back, and whatever his plans for the future, Matt was pretty certain it would be his last time seeing both the *Black Baza* and its captain. It was the length of his stay aboard that was yet to be determined.

The pirates had divested them of their oxygen masks, commlinks, and weapons, and bound their hands behind their backs. Neither of them had offered any resistance. If their goal was to stay alive for as long as possible, there was no point in wasting strength and energy getting beaten up right off the bat.

Ever since the pirates pulled them out of the Alraki craft, Matt had been racking his brain, trying to come up with any solution. Deep down, he knew it was hopeless, at least where he was concerned. Once Rodgers had him in his clutches again, there would be no getting out. But Ryce was a different matter.

Matt had no doubt Rodgers would take great pleasure in hurting Ryce just to see him squirm. If the pirate knew where to find them, he had to have known they were lovers. There could be no feigning indifference this time, so Matt had to come up with some other tactic to divert Rodgers's attention elsewhere even if it was the last thing he did—which, all things considered, it likely would be.

Matt had almost succeeded in fooling himself into believing he held any rein over his panic, right until the familiar smell of the torture chamber (a distinct blend of blood, urine, and disinfectant) hit his nostrils. All traces of rational thinking fled as the door slid open before them, and they were pushed inside and shoved down on their knees, the barrels of plasma rifles pressed against the backs of their heads.

Matt clenched his jaws so tightly his teeth hurt. Beside him, Ryce remained silent and motionless, his tension a palpable thing. There was no way Matt could retain the same level of outward calm, his breathing shallow and his hands trembling. He wished he could wipe them on his fatigues.

Heavy, unhurried footsteps approached them from across the room, and Matt risked looking up despite the cold metal chafing at his nape. A dark figure loomed above him, a monster out of his nightmares and a memory that haunted his waking hours.

Dylan Rodgers crouched, just out of reach even though Matt's hands were tied. He regarded Matt serenely, as someone would an antique vase in a curio shop, and then backhanded him across the face with enough force to leave a stinging imprint on his skin.

This was no way to treat a priceless object.

"That's for getting me arrested," Rodgers said, his deep voice booming in the cavernous space. "Not that it did you much good."

He hadn't changed much from the last time Matt had seen him. Rodgers boasted the same bulky build and thick mane of dark hair, the same electronic patch over his left eye. Only the flight adapters on his temples were a different model, one Matt hadn't seen before. It was sad that he could spot the differences in all these little details, really.

Fate, Matt mused, was a real bitch. It seemed he was destined to die at Rodgers's hands, and no matter how many times he eluded him, he'd always known it would come to this. He just hadn't expected Ryce to partake in it.

Matt gingerly ran his tongue over his lips, testing for any damage. Rodgers had hit him hard, but not hard enough to actually draw blood. Which only meant he was saving all the fun for later. Matt had to do something before that happened.

Like keeping Rodgers preoccupied with him instead of turning his attention to his boyfriend.

"I'm flattered," Matt said with all the bravado he could muster. Admittedly, it wasn't a lot, and the effect was probably spoiled by the stench of fear Rodgers could undoubtedly pick up on. "Coming all this way just for me? I must really tickle your fancy."

Ryce sucked in his breath sharply. Matt couldn't tell if it was due to him brazenly goading a psychopath, or because of his extra-cheesy choice of words.

"You should be," Rodgers said, unfazed. "Took some work tracking you down. It's a good thing you can't resist pissing off the wrong people wherever you go. They're only too happy to tell me all about your business."

"How did you get out of prison?" Ryce spoke up. "There could be no bail with the type of charges laid out against you."

"I told you I had friends in the right places," Rodgers said, addressing Matt instead of answering Ryce directly. "But you were never one to listen."

He grabbed Matt by his hair, pulling his head back so Matt had no choice but to stare up at him.

"I'm going to take my time with you, you little shit. An eye for eye, right?" Rodgers tapped his eyepatch. "I'll save that one to the last."

"Don't tell me you're still mad about that? All the cool pirates wear one," Matt said.

He fully expected Rodgers to lose it right there, and for a second, it looked like he would. His nostrils flared, and his lips pulled back in a snarl, but his features stilled into calmness just as quickly. The uncharacteristic display of restraint sent a quiver of unease down to Matt's roiling stomach.

"As much as I want to see you squeal, business comes first." Rodgers released Matt abruptly, nearly sending him tumbling over. "Where's the jumpgate device you stole from the Alraki ship?"

Matt involuntarily glanced at Ryce. His face was a rigid mask, but Matt could tell he, too, wasn't surprised at the question. It was highly classified information, but since Rodgers had been able to pinpoint their location with supernatural accuracy, it stood to reason he also knew the purpose for which they were there. And unless the pirate had a crystal ball or direct access to the super-protected Foreign Intelligence computers, the odds were someone, somewhere, had spilled the beans on the operation.

"I don't know what you're talking about," Matt said, aware his knee-jerk reaction had given him away.

"Do you really think I'd be risking my neck coming into this Feds-infested sector just to nail your scrawny ass to the wall?" Rodgers voice dripped with contempt. "I've got bigger fish to fry. Getting my hands on you is just a bonus."

Matt wanted to wisecrack about Rodgers's apparent fixation with touching him, but words utterly failed him.

"I know you must have hidden it somewhere on that jet," Rodgers continued. "My men are searching it as we speak. I'll tear that thing apart if I have to, but I think we can speed things up with some incentive."

Matt shook his head in helpless negation, fear coiling under his breastbone, but Rodgers was already signaling one of the crewmen gathered along the far wall. The man nodded and slid open a different door, admitting a small group of people—all handcuffed and escorted by half a dozen armed guards.

Matt froze, his jaw slackening.

"*No*," someone said in a broken voice, and Matt realized with a peculiar detachment that it was his.

"Get your hands off me!" Tony glared defiantly at the guard who'd shoved her inside. Her own hands were bound behind her back in magnetic cuffs, but other than that, she was unharmed, as was Val, who followed in her wake, prodded by another guard.

Walker looked the worst for wear. It seemed the Fleet operative hadn't surrendered without a fight, and the pirates were only too happy to continue what the Alraki had started. His left eye had swollen shut, and his torn ear still bled profusely, his neck and shoulder spattered red. The pirates had stripped him of his weapons and protective gear, and he was dressed only in a dark undershirt and tight-fitting pants.

The rest of his team weren't brought in. Matt fervently hoped that meant they were detained elsewhere rather than dead.

"As you can see, I have your ship and all your little buddies right here," Rodgers said. "Want to tell me what I want to know now, or do you want to see them bleed first?"

"Spears, don't," Walker warned, glaring at the pirate, though the effect of his authoritative tone was somewhat spoiled by how battered his face was. "You won't get away with this, Rodgers. I don't know how you managed to break out of federal prison, but you can't kidnap civilians and Fleet officers in the middle of a military operation and expect to get away with it. Every battleship in this sector will be on your ass within hours."

"You don't need to break out of prison if you can be legally released," Rodgers said. "That's what friends are for."

He nodded to the guard again, who opened the door. A man in Fleet uniform stepped inside, this time without pirate escort, and Matt couldn't hold back a gasp when he saw who it was.

Chapter Fourteen

Grayson looked around the room, taking in the bound captives. His eyes rested on Matt and Ryce, still kneeling in front of Rodgers, and his mouth tightened, though he otherwise remained impassive.

"You? What are you doing here? Did my father—" Matt halted, his tongue suddenly refusing to cooperate.

"Admiral Cummings has nothing to do with this," Grayson said. "He doesn't know I'm here."

"I can't believe it! You spying little shit," Walker spat out. "Whatever happens to us, the admiral will have your hide for selling us out."

One of the guards holding him hit him in the kidneys with the butt of his gun. Walker groaned with pain, his indignation effectively silenced.

Grayson ignored him, turning his attention to Rodgers. "I've scrambled their commlinks using the remote access I installed on them, but a ship this size is harder to conceal, considering our proximity to the Waga moon base and the degree of alert. The local command center has already begun an active search for the Phaeton vessel and the Alraki jet. We should leave this area before they have the chance to discover us. I told you you should have let me use a shuttle to pick them up rather than come in with the *Baza*."

"The hell is going on?" Matt whispered to Ryce, looking between his ex-boyfriend and the pirate. "They were in on this together this whole time?" Fear gave way to temporary shock as he struggled to reevaluate the events of the past week in light of this new information.

"Why?" Ryce demanded of Grayson, his voice level but with an undercurrent of fury. "You know this qualifies as treason. Is what he's paying you really worth it?"

"He's not paying me!" Grayson snapped, his calm finally cracking. His fierce, hate-filled gaze seemed to include all of them. "He has my daughter."

"What?" Matt said. "Elisabeth? But how—"

"That's enough blabbering." Rodgers snapped his fingers at one of the guards. "Take him to the bridge and tell Payne to set course to Sonora-2."

"I want to see Elisabeth."

Grayson drew himself to his full height and crossed his arms over his chest. If looks could kill, Rodgers would definitely have been in a pickle, but it seemed all Grayson could do was glare at him impotently.

"I don't give a flying fuck what you want," Rodgers said. "Shut your hole and wait your turn unless you're eager to join your buddy."

The guard grabbed Grayson's upper arm, none too gently, and pulled him toward the door. For one split second, Matt was sure Grayson was going to balk despite the warning, to disastrous consequences. But then Rodgers's commlink chimed, breaking the tension.

"What?" he barked into the comm.

"Sir, there's a Federation vessel following. An F-class corvette," a female voice said. "It's hailing us. Your orders?"

"Fucking shit," Rodgers said and spat on the floor, then squinted at Grayson. "Is this your doing?"

Grayson shook his head. He looked just as surprised by this new development as everyone else, but Rodgers was clearly not buying it.

"You better not try to double-cross me, officer," he said, lowering his voice to a much more dangerous register.

"I warned you about coming here yourself." Unfazed, Grayson sneered in return. "With your big-ass black ship, you might as well send a 'wanted' alert to every Fleet vessel in the sector."

"Well, we're here. Get rid of them."

"I can't order a Fleet battleship around. I'm a goddamned lieutenant, not the actual admiral!"

"If you want to convince me of how useless you are to me, you're doing a damn fine job."

Grayson visibly swallowed, seeming to tone down his outrage.

"You can, and you will," Rodgers repeated. "And you'll do it right now."

He gestured to the guard again, who pushed Grayson out of the room, despite the man's protests. The door slammed shut behind them, and at the same time, Rodgers grabbed Matt by the hair again, pulling painfully.

Matt hissed through his teeth. Damn it, he really should have cut his hair sooner.

"Unfortunately, he's right," Rodgers said, giving Matt a shake that rattled his teeth. "Our first priority is getting the Feds off our tail, so we'll have to speed things along and leave the fun stuff for later. You either tell me where you hid that alien contraption, or they all go into the airlock. Can't have all this useless ballast on board."

Matt hesitated. His mind stalled, already unsettled by the way his circumstances had tumbled downhill with the speed of a rolling boulder.

The pause was enough to spur Rodgers into action. He let go of Matt's hair and pointed to Ryce, addressing the armed pirate standing above him.

"Start with this one."

"No!" Matt cried as the pirate yanked Ryce to his feet. The guard behind him pressed the barrel of a gun between his shoulder blades in warning, but Matt ignored it. "Leave him alone."

"Wanna save his uptight ass? Make it worth my while." Rodgers smirked.

Matt took a deep breath and closed his eyes for a second, bracing himself for what was to come.

"He's your son."

The entire room went quiet, the only sound Walker's labored breathing through his bruised ribs. Matt avoided looking at Ryce, so whatever expression the revelation elicited from him remained a mystery, which, all things considered, was for the best.

"The hell kind of crap are you trying to pull?" Rodgers asked finally, his dark, bushy eyebrows drawn together, the smirk slipping off his face.

"It's true," Matt insisted. There was no stopping at this point, so he pressed on. "Twenty-three years ago, you raided an Onorean ship in the Gemma sector. You ended up raping one of the female researchers aboard, and he's the result."

Tony gasped, her eyes going wide with shock. Val looked between Ryce and Rodgers, his stony expression changing ever so slightly as recognition dawned.

"Guess the ace-pilot-thing runs in the family, huh?" Matt went on, his cheery tone ringing all kinds of false.

"Matt." Ryce's voice was so choked up Matt almost didn't recognize it.

"I'm sorry," Matt said softly, lowering his gaze to the dirty floor, the faded rust-colored stains blurring.

"I don't give a shit who he is," Rodgers snapped and made an impatient gesture to the guard who held Ryce. "Unless he has the Alraki device in his pocket, he's gonna—"

"I *do* have it."

Everybody, including Matt, turned sharply to Ryce. Something dark and dangerous lurked in the depths of his stormy eyes, but otherwise, his face was once again a mask of unshakable calm.

"I've destroyed the files the special ops team obtained from the Alraki ship." Ryce held his head high as if he wasn't admitting to a crime that could potentially land him in jail for the rest of his life, his gaze fixed on Rodgers. "But I've memorized all the data, and can recreate it from memory to—with enough resources—construct a working prototype. The surveillance jet we've commandeered should be enough to provide spare parts to adapt the electronics."

Rodgers's eye narrowed as he regarded Ryce. Matt held his breath, afraid to make a sound that might tip the scale in the wrong direction, but, apparently, Ryce didn't have any such qualms.

"I'm ready to make a deal if you're done with your psychotic little games," he said with his usual unnerving aplomb. "So how about it?"

"Easom, if you're gonna sell us out the way Lieutenant Lee did, I swear to God—" Walker began angrily, but a well-aimed blow to the head made him crumple to the floor in an ungainly heap. Tony sucked in a breath as he fell right at her feet, but another guard tugged sharply at her bonds, preventing her instinctive move to help him.

Ignoring the minor scuffle, Rodgers sized Ryce up, and Matt bit his lip. Wherever Ryce was going with this, he would play along.

"Yeah, let's deal," Rodgers said. "But if you try anything funny, smartass, all your friends are dead." He nodded to the guard again. "Take him to the docking bay. You have permission to shoot if he so much as farts without warning." He turned to Matt. "Sorry to cut the party short. But don't worry; we'll continue later, once we reach the home base. Got big plans for you, Spears."

With a final smirk, Rodgers followed Ryce and the guard out of the chamber, letting the heavy door slide closed after them with a thud.

*

In Matt's experience, the pirates didn't keep prisoners aboard long enough for it to warrant special accommodations. As far as he knew, he'd been the only one to require a more prolonged stay, and that was only because he'd managed to piss off Captain Rodgers enough to garner his personal attention. The few days spent in captivity aboard the *Black Baza* were forever etched into his brain, though he couldn't recall the details with any clarity. Those were reserved for his nightmares, with their all too vivid images of pain and torture.

Matt and his crew were all ushered into a cramped cell right off the main dock, which took up most of the lower cargo hold and now more than likely housed both *Lady Lisa* and the captured Alraki recon jet. These would be their temporary accommodations until the *Baza* landed on Charon, the tiny moon of Sonora-2 where the pirates had set up their local base of operations after Rodgers's prison break. Matt suspected that Grayson's daughter, Elisabeth, was being held hostage there as well. And she might not be the only one, depending on how many pawns Rodgers currently had in action.

Walker, still unconscious, had been taken elsewhere. The remnants of his special ops team were being kept in a different cell, with heavier security measures in place. For whatever reason, the pirates hadn't disposed of them right away, but Matt would hate to venture a guess as to how long they'd be kept alive once the ship arrived at its destination.

"I hope the commander is okay," Tony said as she lowered herself carefully to the floor in the far corner. "That was sure to leave a nasty bruise, and he'd be lucky to not have a concussion."

"Some people can't keep their mouth shut when someone with a big gun is standing right next to them," Matt muttered.

The cell was too small to pace in, so he leaned his shoulder against the wall, tugging uselessly at his magnetic cuffs. His arms were beginning to ache from being bound in that awkward position, and it was only going to grow worse.

"You've done plenty of talking there as well, Captain," Tony remarked.

She cast about the cell, but it was completely bare of any furnishings or facilities. The only opening, aside from the locked door, was a narrow-grated drain along the far wall, which was probably intended to be used as a toilet and to clean up any possible bloody messes.

"Is it true what you said about Easom?" Val asked, sitting down beside Tony. "Rodgers is his biological father?"

Matt sighed, bumping his head against the metal wall. "Yes. Well, I don't know with absolute certainty, but I have a pretty good hunch. I never meant for him to find out. Not like this."

"What do you think he's going to do?"

"I have no idea, and, frankly, I'm a little afraid to speculate."

Matt closed his eyes. He should have been relieved they'd all narrowly escaped torture, or worse, but in their precarious situation, any relief felt premature.

"He knows what he's doing," Val said with conviction.

"How can you be so sure?"

"He's saved our collective asses more than once." Val absently rubbed the thin scar around his index finger. "I trust the kid to pull through."

As grateful as Matt was to him for making those arguments, he wished he could support them. Usually, Ryce kept a tight rein over his emotions, but when compromised, he was capable of doing things that would otherwise be categorized as "stupid," wherein "stupid" meant reckless and dangerous.

Ryce had asked Matt to trust him, but Matt had been the one to break his trust, first by withholding an awful truth, and then by throwing it out there without warning or permission. What if by doing so he'd managed to emotionally compromise Ryce enough to...he didn't know what, exactly. But the sure thing was that, in this case, he wouldn't be the only one paying the price for it.

"How the hell did you end up here?" Matt asked, mostly to keep his thoughts from running around in frantic circles. "I was sure you guys were already safe inside the Waga base."

Tony made a face. "Almost as soon as we were out of the Alraki ship, the *Lisa*'s main computer shut down. That was just after Walker had talked to you. Val did everything he could think of, but he couldn't get it back on. The commander tried contacting the base and the *Lennox*, but all communications were cut. We couldn't even reach you on the commlink."

Matt scoffed. "Grayson must have been remotely controlling the computer through the spyware he installed on our commlinks when we had that briefing with the admiral. Fucking damn it. I knew we shouldn't have trusted him. I fucking *knew* it."

"Whatever it was, with the engine and every other system shut off, we were like a sitting duck when the *Baza* showed up," Tony continued. "I must say, being boarded twice in one day is a bit much, even for us."

"They didn't actually damage the ship, did they?"

Val shook his head. "Apart from incapacitating the computer, no. But they could have easily blown the crap out of us. I guess Rodgers wanted us all alive as bargaining chips, though the soldiers gave them a hell of a time."

"Are they okay?"

"They were alive last we saw them," Tony said. "I don't know what happened to them later though. They wouldn't let us talk to Walker when they brought us to see you."

"Killing a Federation officer is a serious offense," Val said. "Much less four of them. That'd be Rodgers pretty much declaring war on the Fleet."

"I seriously doubt it factors into his considerations anymore," Matt said bitterly. "With an operational jump tech, he'll be able to do whatever the hell he wants. And then maybe Fleet Lieutenant Grayson Lee will get him off those charges as well. Just after he arranges safe passage for a fucking pirate ship with kidnapped civilians on board through the heart of Federation space."

It seemed unlikely Grayson possessed the authority needed to turn away a federal corvette sent to investigate suspicious activity, but Matt had learned long ago not to underestimate the capability of a desperate man.

"I know what he did was terrible, but did he really have a choice? God knows that if a murderous criminal ever threatened my kid, I'd probably do the same." Tony shook her head.

"We always have a choice," Matt said, but his heart wasn't in it. Deep down, no matter how furious he was with Grayson, he couldn't really blame him for wanting to protect someone he loved—even if he'd gone about it in a completely wrong way. Like Ryce was doing right now.

At least now he didn't have to wonder about Rodgers's miraculous resurgence. With Grayson being the proverbial mole with all the resources of the admiral's office at his disposal, forging a high-clearance warrant for the release of a known criminal was risky, but not impossible. Admiral Cummings's name and authority held a lot of sway throughout the Fleet, even when used without the admiral's knowledge.

What would hurt his father more—the breach of trust by an exemplary officer, or the fact that it led to the loss of his son? It was a petty thought, but Matt couldn't help but wish that his death might elicit some of the paternal feelings his life never had.

"We have to do something," Tony said, distracting Matt from his sulking.

"Like what?" he asked. "Draw sticks to decide who tackles the jailer and gets shot first?"

The earlier adrenaline surge had abated, and how he was feeling every single one of the bruises blossoming across his face and chest, and it wasn't helping his mood any. These fuckers could at least have offered him a last drink before making him wait for death.

"Well, we can't just sit here doing nothing," Tony said irritably. "I doubt we'll get better chances of escape down moonside. Most of these small Sonora moons are barely terraformed."

"If they managed to overpower a team of highly trained operatives, I don't see what the three of us can do against them now."

"First of all, half of that team was seriously injured. And besides, you've escaped from this ship before. How did you do it?"

"Truthfully? I just got lucky." Matt winced as his fingers touched scraped skin under the cuffs. "I saw an opportunity, and I took it."

"What happened?" Val asked, sitting up from where he was slouching. "You never talked about this before."

There were several excellent reasons Matt had refrained from discussing his time in captivity with his friends. For one, some of his memories were fuzzy from the damage incurred when Rodgers had cut his flight adapters out of his skull with a knife. For another, the memories he did retain only made him want to repress them with copious amounts of alcohol. The recurring nightmares were enough; he didn't need to rehash them in broad daylight.

But they were most likely about to die anyway. Maybe letting go of some of that pain and shame would bring him closure before the end.

"We were alone in the torture chamber, Rodgers and I," Matt said. The words were heavy, dropping out of his mouth like lead, and his palms suddenly became sweaty. "I remember lying on the floor, only partially bound. I guess they weren't considering me a threat at that point, and, well, it made...doing certain things to me easier."

Tony and Val exchanged a quick glance, but, thankfully, neither of them said anything.

"He was holding a knife to me. Then a subordinate called him on the commlink, and his attention slipped for a moment. I barely understood where I was, but I knew I had to take that chance. Wherever the strength came from, neither of us expected it. I grabbed his hand and shoved that knife into his face as hard as I could. And then I ran like hell before anyone had the chance to respond to his screaming and before my legs gave out."

"Whoa." Tony's eyes were huge in her face. "No wonder he hates your guts. You really took his eye out."

Matt nodded. "I don't remember much after that. It all comes in bits and pieces, and there are gaps in time I can't fill. All I know is I somehow managed to steal a lifeboat from the docking bay and fly it on manual until a passing freight barge picked me up."

He shook his head, trying to dislodge the cloying traces of panic. "I don't think we'll get this kind of break again. Rodgers would be a fool if he doesn't keep the lifeboats password-locked now."

But even as he admitted defeat, Matt's thoughts kept circling back to Ryce. Maybe he had a plan and maybe he didn't, but there was no way in hell Matt would stand by while Ryce went through the same thing that had happened to him.

Ryce had been right about thing—there was still hope while they breathed. And if Matt had only one breath left, he was going to spend it trying to save his partner and his friends and the folks from Walker's team whom he barely knew yet couldn't abandon.

Chapter Fifteen

After a while, the guards brought them a few plastic water bottles and a handful of protein bars, uncuffing them so they could eat. Tony cast Matt a meaningful glance, but he shook his head minutely, having glimpsed more guards in the corridor. With just the three of them, unarmed and unsure of the whereabouts of the others, the odds were stacked against them. In the current situation, Matt preferred to wait and err on the side of caution until a better opportunity presented itself—the obvious risks notwithstanding. Tony made a face but kept still until the door was shut again.

"That was a missed opportunity," she said when the pirates were out of earshot. With a sigh, she flexed her cramped arms and unwrapped her protein bar.

"We couldn't have taken on all of them," Matt said. "And I'd rather not try anything reckless right now. Ryce had asked me to have faith in him, and that's what I'm doing. If he's got a plan, we might be putting it— and him—in danger."

Tony looked at Val, who shrugged silently. She sighed again.

"I know you believe in him, Captain, and so do I, but...what if he fails? And even if he doesn't, we might still all end up dead anyway."

"We won't." Matt scooted closer and put his hand on her arm. He glanced at Val, including him in their little sacred coven of improbable hope. "We won't. We'll all do whatever we need to do to get out of here, right? You still have Sarah's graduation to get to, hot stuff. I ain't gonna let anyone screw that up."

She nodded and gave him a tight smile, but her heart clearly wasn't in it.

"Anyway, this is a good sign," Matt said, driving his point further to alleviate some of her obvious misery. "They would hardly bother keeping us fed if they planned to dispose of us right away."

"Let's hope whatever they are planning isn't worse," Val remarked.

He didn't sound too optimistic, and Matt tended to agree with him, despite his best intentions to cheer his friends up. He hadn't eaten in what seemed like ages, but the gooey bar stuck in his throat when he swallowed it. Minutes turned into hours, and there was nothing he could reasonably do but fret.

The *Baza* was a fast ship, but getting to the environs of Sonora-2 while avoiding the regular transportation routes would take time. It was a vast sector, and, even with the high alert of the Federal Fleet forces in the area, the pirates stood a good chance of slipping by undetected as long as they gave the larger outposts a wide berth. It had worked for the rogue Alraki frigate, and there wasn't any reason it wouldn't work for the *Baza*, whose captain was much more familiar with the local routes.

Eventually, they all dozed off, huddled in the corners of the cell. Matt was sure his anxiety would prevent him from falling asleep, but after what felt like days and days of being in nonstop fight-or-flight mode, his body seemed to need the rest, even if his mind claimed otherwise.

He was woken up by a tremor all around him, which indicated the ship had activated its close-range thrusters and was about to land. Tony and Val came awake as well, pushing themselves to sit upright, bleary-eyed.

The pirates didn't bother blindfolding them. However, Matt didn't see much of the secret base as they were taken off the ship and escorted into their new cell, which was more like being in an actual prison than the previous one. As far as he could tell, most of the base was nestled under a temporary environmental dome, similar to the kinds used during construction of permanent colonies. Matt was able to get a sense there wasn't a lot of personnel on the premises. That was somewhat encouraging—right until they were separated and taken to different holding cells.

The only positive thing about the days of solitary confinement that followed was that he wasn't being tortured to death. But after a while, Matt was willing to get beat up if it meant knowing what was going on with Ryce and his friends. The guards brought him his daily food rations, but none of them were willing to talk to him, or be goaded by insults.

As a result, he slept poorly, haunted by anxiety and physical discomfort. The cell was equipped with a cot and a toilet, and not much else. Though Matt was accustomed to cramped accommodations aboard a spaceship, it wasn't long before the setup seriously wore on his already frayed nerves.

That was why he was more relieved than frightened when, on the seventh day of his incarceration, the door to his cell opened, and two guards cuffed him again before taking him out.

*

Black Baza was docked outside the dome on a patch of relatively even ground amid the rocky landscape, where it loomed like a giant monster, blending with the black sky above as they approached the main hatch with their transport.

Seeing as he was the only prisoner escorted there, Matt didn't try to resist despite fully expecting to be taken back to the torture chamber. Instead, however, the guards marched him all the way to the bridge. Two of them ushered Matt inside, while the rest departed.

It hadn't changed since the last time he saw it all those months ago during their altercation in the Colanta system. The bridge felt crowded with about half a dozen people, including crewmen and the armed guards, sharing the same space. But Matt's gaze was immediately drawn to Ryce, who sat on the floor next to a half-disassembled control panel, holding a screwdriver and what looked like a plasmonic circuit board. Various spare parts and wires were strewn haphazardly on the floor around him, like the guts of some unlucky biomechanical animal. Matt had a solid basic understanding of the inner mechanics of a spaceship, but even he had no idea what some of them were for.

At Matt's entrance, Ryce looked up, his expression carefully blank. His face and hands were smudged with grease, but otherwise, he didn't appear to be hurt.

Something loosened in Matt's chest as if a tight spring inside him had suddenly uncoiled. It wasn't until this moment that he realized how afraid he'd been of the possibility of never seeing Ryce again, and the thought left him weak in the knees.

"Good, your boyfriend's here," Rodgers said, sprawled in the captain's chair that dominated the bridge. He glanced at Matt briefly before turning his attention back to Ryce. "Just a little incentive to make sure things are running smoothly. I catch a whiff of any shit going down, and he gets it."

As if to emphasize his words, one of the guards who'd escorted Matt from the holding cell shoved him from behind with his rifle. Matt stumbled forward and then shot the man a dirty look over his shoulder, but with his attention riveted on Ryce, his heart wasn't in it.

Matt knew better than to question Ryce's actions out loud, even though the notion of him willingly installing the jump technology on a pirate ship made his stomach turn. Whatever game Ryce was running, Matt was going to back him up. He just wished he didn't feel as if he'd already lost.

Ryce threw him a pointed look as the guard led Matt down toward the command chair but turned back to the disassembled control panel before Matt could decipher its meaning. Ryce started to screw the circuit board back inside.

"I can't guarantee the first try will be successful," Ryce said, making a vague gesture with the screwdriver. "This isn't magic. I'm using a lot of components from the Alraki craft to make everything stick, and their wiring wasn't designed to be compatible with ours."

"I don't care. You're supposed to be the brainiac, right? Figure it out."

Clearly, those two hadn't wasted any time on father-son bonding. But at the very least, Ryce hadn't been hurt, and for now, his exceptional skills were keeping him relatively safe.

"I did," Ryce shot back, once again seemingly unconcerned with angering a cold-blooded murderer. "The Alraki have adapted the existing laser-excitation system used to activate the Mnirian jumpgates to create similar space-folding patterns without the need for the physical gate infrastructure. As genius as it is, at its base, it's simple. It means that any ship equipped with this capability—which means pretty much all of them—can be potentially adapted to jump through space independently. But it still has to be done right in order for the technology to work."

"Spare me the physics lecture," Rodgers said. "You've been at it long enough, and I'm all out of patience. You had your deadline. How about I take one of Spears's fingers for every extra ten minutes it takes you to get this thing up and running."

"Yes, sure, let's rush the process that could result in creating a wormhole in the immediate vicinity of your ship," Matt said. "Nothing bad would come of that." He flexed his bound hands behind his back, hoping his sarcasm was enough to disguise his dismay.

"I can add a finger for every time you open your mouth," Rodgers suggested.

Matt wisely didn't respond, focusing instead on Ryce's neat and precise movements. It was too bad he hadn't asked for Val's help doing whatever it was he was doing. With the three of them there, maybe they could've come up with some way to sabotage the *Black Baza* long enough for the Fleet to find them.

And maybe Ryce was doing that right this moment. Matt held his breath at the thought. It certainly made much more sense than equipping one of the most ruthless pirates in the known galaxy with the most coveted technology known to man in hopes he'd do the decent thing and let them all go afterward. The chances of that happening ran about as high as the temperature outside the walls.

"The deal was no one is tortured until I am done, and I'm not quite done yet," Ryce said evenly as he tucked the scattered pieces of circuitry back inside the panel. "Besides, mutilation is uncalled for. Believe me, I have a pretty good idea of what's at stake. I have to run a few more scans to make sure everything is connected properly, and then we can test it to see if it actually works."

"Good. Payne, systems check for the new hardware."

The pilot nodded and stepped to the panel to bring the specs on-screen. Ryce stood up, wiping his grease-stained hands on his pants. He didn't spare another look for Matt, who was growing more confused and agitated.

"The system has detected the hardware, sir," Payne said, her fingers hovering above the touch panel. "Applying a compatibility test for the jump activation sequence."

The hell? This wasn't supposed to be working. Despite the imminent risk of losing a body part, Matt opened his mouth to issue a protest, but the doors to the bridge slid open, admitting a very pissed off–looking Grayson, also accompanied by an armed guard.

At Rodgers's signal, the guard retreated.

"What is going on here?" Grayson demanded. His gaze swept the bridge, and he frowned, noting both Ryce and Matt's presence.

Ryce straightened. "Lieutenant Lee is to be included in the deal."

"The fuck he is. All I agreed to was his mutt. The dashing lieutenant knows too much to let him go."

"What deal? What are you talking about?" Matt asked, forgetting the imminent risk of losing his digits.

"We agreed that if I succeed in making the jump, Captain Rodgers lets everyone go on *Lady Lisa*. Well, certain people excluded," Ryce said levelly.

"You mean...Elisabeth will be safe?" Grayson asked, looking between him and Rodgers, while Matt tried his best to digest this new information.

"Nobody leaves this ship until I make sure this alien crap you promised me does what it's supposed to," Rodgers said. "And if it does, the lieutenant here is gonna make sure we won't run into any trouble where we're going."

"Ryce," Matt said urgently, turning to him. "You can't seriously believe he'll uphold his end of the bargain. Whatever he's promised you, he's gonna—"

"I'm getting fucking tired of all of your shit," Rodgers announced, addressing no one in particular. "Easom, make the jump."

"But, sir," Payne said, turning to her captain. "The computer hasn't finished the compatibility testing. If the circuitry connection fails—"

"This quadrant is swarming with Feds," Rodgers said. "Charon might be bumfuck nowhere, but it won't take them long to find it if they're already looking. I don't have time to follow experimental testing protocols. Easom here knows what happens if this shit doesn't work, so get to it."

"First, I want to see them, like we discussed," Ryce said, crossing his arms over his chest.

Matt was sure Rodgers was going to balk at that request, but the pirate nodded to Payne, and she brought the feed from the docking bay on-screen.

The overhead camera zoomed in on a large group of people standing next to the ramp leading up to the main hatch of *Lady Lisa*. Matt picked out Val and Tony, who had her arm around the shoulders of a redheaded girl in a green T-shirt. Grayson's hitched breath told him this was Elisabeth. She clung to Tony but seemed otherwise unharmed, glaring defiantly at the guards holding them at gunpoint.

A little over to the side was the remainder of Walker's team—Ikeda, Martin, Shapiro, and the commander himself. Martin, though limping and leaning on Ikeda for support, was cuffed along with the rest of the operatives.

"See? All ready to go," Rodgers said.

Ryce nodded. "And the Alraki jet?"

"Stashed in your ship's cargo hold, like you asked. Though I can't see why you'd bother. The state it's in, can't be worth much."

"The Fleet could still have a use for it. Any enemy vessel may provide valuable intel for our forces."

Rodgers shrugged. "Whatever. All your terms are met. Now make the jump. If I lose my patience, somebody'll start losing body parts."

Ryce took the not-so-subtle hint and stepped up to the control panel. Reluctantly, the pilot surrendered her seat to him, but stayed close, hovering over Ryce's shoulder.

Ryce's fingers fluttered over the panel, and the string of numbers on the screen sped down as the view switched to the bow front cameras. Matt held his breath as the ship decelerated, the muted perpetual hum of the engines changing pitch ever so slightly.

"Let's see what we can do here," Ryce murmured, bringing up the jumpgate activation interface that replaced the live camera feed. The laser-excitation technology was a requirement on every spacecraft larger than a shuttle, allowing for independent activation of the existing stationary jumpgates—a precaution that prevented any ship from ending up stranded in a star system without a Freeport station to regulate interstellar traffic. Matt didn't recognize the coordinates Ryce put in, but they didn't elicit any reaction from the pilot, so he assumed it was something they'd discussed before.

His hope that Ryce was planning on stranding the pirate ship in some godforsaken corner of the galaxy was effectively dashed. Not that he *wanted* it to happen, but surely Ryce had some plan of action in mind that wouldn't result in Rodgers's complete and utter triumph.

He risked a glance at Grayson. His lips were pressed in a thin line and his jaw clamped shut so hard he must be grinding his teeth. Instead of watching the screen, his eyes darted between Ryce and Rodgers, and despite his visible rage, his gaze was calculating.

"Everybody ready?" Ryce asked with his usual calm. "Here goes nothing."

He tapped the control panel, and Matt flinched, closing his eyes. He imagined all that energy being directed inward, to the patchwork assemblage of human and alien hardware nestled deep inside the electronic guts of the spacecraft, instead of being projected outward to an enormous stationary jumpgate. The *Baza* lunged, and for one awful moment Matt was sure it was going to explode.

With his hands bound tightly behind his back, he struggled to keep his balance as he was hit with the familiar bout of disorientation, of falling in all directions at once. Light flashed, bright even behind closed eyelids, leaving colorful dots dancing in the darkness that followed.

Matt stumbled, but his escorting guard held him back, and for once, Matt was grateful for the strong grip on his shoulder. He sucked in a breath and risked opening his eyes, encouraged by the fact that he was still in one piece instead of disintegrated into a cloud of atoms.

The image on the screen was drastically different, the reds and purples of a giant gas planet lazily swirling beneath them, the unique pattern of the vibrant clouds instantly recognizable as Gemel-6, the largest known exoplanet in Federation space.

Chapter Sixteen

"Fuck," Matt breathed, forgetting he was supposed to be silent. Thankfully, everyone else was just as shaken that they'd jumped to another star system dozens of light years away, and so paid him little heed.

The pilot let out a long breath and glanced back at Rodgers, who leaned forward in his chair, studying the image on the screen. Unlike the others, he seemed unaffected by the very real possibility they might have all been torn to pieces by the uncontrollable forces that folded space itself. He nodded at her, and she retook her seat, pushing Ryce out of the way.

"The axillary laser-system batteries are depleted," Payne said after tapping her flight adapters again. "There's not enough energy to make another jump. We'll have to find someplace to recharge."

"That won't be a problem," Rodgers said. "I know people in this system who'd hook us up with new axillary batteries and everything else we need."

"Your turn," Ryce said, looking up at Rodgers. "Have them board the *Lisa* and leave."

"In a minute. Gotta say, kid, it looks like you know what you're doing after all. I could find some uses for you yet. If you play your cards right, I might even let your other buddy off the hook as well. Not this little piece of shit, obviously"—he nodded to Matt—"but the good lieutenant."

Matt's breath hitched, and he curled his hands into fists behind his back, his fingernails digging painfully into skin. Perhaps his desperate wish to keep Ryce safe at all costs, including breaking his trust, could be granted after all—no thanks to him. And that was a good thing, right? He didn't know whether Rodgers's promises could be believed, but maybe, just maybe, the pirate was willing to make some concessions to avail himself of Ryce's skills? If he did, it would be an easy trade-off, as far as Matt was concerned.

As if sensing his distress, Ryce looked up at him. His lips parted, and his features contorted briefly. For a second, it looked like he was about to say something, but then he composed himself again and turned back to Rodgers.

"I did what I had to to save my friends. Because I owe it to them. Lieutenant Lee doesn't really fall under that category. But I also don't think there are any other options available to me at this point, other than the obvious. So... Yeah, I accept. I'm sorry, Matt. I really am. But we all have to look out for ourselves here, right?"

Off to the side, Grayson scoffed.

Matt said nothing. The taste of Ryce's kisses still lingered on his lips. His tender professions of love, whispered between them in the dark of the bedroom and inside the bowels of an enemy ship, were forever seared into Matt's soul. He could recite every time they'd saved each other's lives and comforted each other when no one or nothing else could. He remembered the barely contained fury in Ryce's voice when he told Matt he wasn't going to let him die.

In short, Matt knew better than to fall for an act intended for the pirates' benefit. But he still couldn't guess at what Ryce's endgame was, and that made him uneasy—mostly because he was clueless as to what was expected of him.

Maybe the embargo Rodgers had imposed on him talking wasn't such a bad thing in this situation.

"Sounds like you have your priorities straight," Rodgers said. "But let's make sure."

He rose from the chair and descended the shallow steps onto the main floor of the bridge, toward the pilot's station where Ryce was standing.

"Here." He took a blaster gun out of his hip holster and thrust it at Ryce with enough force to make him stagger and almost bump into the barrel of the raised plasma rifle held by the guard standing behind him.

"Shoot this bastard"—Rodgers gestured to Matt—"and I'll know you can be trusted. If you don't... Well, I don't really need either of you anymore, do I?"

Matt's mouth suddenly tasted like ashes. Ryce's jaw worked, and he turned toward him, holding the gun loosely in his hand. Matt could tell by the look in his eyes that this particular development hadn't factored into his stalling tactics, whatever they were.

"What happened to all that fun you promised we'd be having together?" Matt said, turning to Rodgers.

There was definitely a note of fear in his voice that belied the flippancy, but he didn't care how he sounded, or if he pushed the line a little too far. Getting kicked in the teeth was better than witnessing this fucked-up game of cat and mouse.

"No time for that now," Rodgers said, not taking his eye off Ryce. "You deserve so much worse that being executed by your own boyfriend, but that's what we'll have to be content with. At least it'll be quicker than anything I'd come up with. Count yourself lucky, prick."

Matt lowered his gaze to the gun in Ryce's hand. By the way he was holding the weapon, it weighed more than the entire spaceship. Rodgers wasn't joking, though; the blast charge was set to full capacity. A single shot fired from this distance would be enough to kill him, even if it missed his heart.

Matt swallowed. His thoughts raced, tripping over one another, and he couldn't focus on any of them long enough for coherency.

"Look," Ryce told Rodgers in a flat voice, visibly getting himself under control. "I don't know what beef you have with Spears, and I don't care. But I'm not here to do your dirty work. Find someone else to shoot him. Or, better yet, use him for something other than torturing me. His father is the Head of Central Foreign Intelligence. He can—"

"Spare me the fucking soap opera. I don't care whose brats you all are. Lee got me everything I wanted from Admiral Cummings; the only thing I want from Spears is to see him die."

Rodgers yanked Ryce's arm up, pointed the gun at Matt's face, and stepped back.

Time seemed to slow down. Matt raised his gaze from the bottomless barrel of the blaster gun, and Ryce's eyes, stormy-gray and wide with shock, filled his vision.

How lucky I am that this is the last thing I get to see. The thought flitted through his brain, bringing with it all-encompassing serenity. He smiled, filled with a sense of peace he'd thought he could never achieve. Ryce would never hurt him of his own free will, however broken their relationship was by secrets and betrayal. But this time, Ryce had no choice, and frankly, Matt knew he deserved it.

"It's okay," he whispered. "I'm ready."

"Last chance to save yourself, ace," Rodgers egged. "You've got three seconds. One, two—"

Ryce's eyes narrowed. In one fluid motion, he spun on his heel and fired, aiming at Rodgers's head.

The gunshot went off in disconcerting proximity to Matt's ear, nearly deafening him. For a second, the world froze as he struggled to breathe and then snapped back into motion like a rubber band pulled too taut.

As with most things, Ryce was an excellent shot. There was no chance in hell he'd miss, especially at point-blank range. And yet, Rodgers remained standing on his feet, inexplicably but unmistakably alive.

Ryce sucked in a breath and took a half step back, lowering the gun. Rodgers smirked.

"You really think I'm stupid enough to hand you a loaded weapon? I knew you shitheads couldn't be trusted." He nodded to the guards. "Take them both out. I'm gonna want to see Spears's face when I torture this whelp. Let the boys have a go at him first."

Matt could have told Rodgers that tricking Ryce by banking on his desperation wasn't the smartest move. Ryce performed best under acute pressure. Facing certain death—both his own and his loved ones'—was bound to spur him into action, even if he didn't have a solid chance of winning.

Ryce shifted his grip on the gun and whipped it across the face of the guard who moved to cuff him from behind. The force of the blow was enough to knock the man unconscious, and he toppled to the floor, blood spraying out of his broken nose. Rodgers snarled, and the guard who had escorted Matt rushed to tackle Ryce, but then another shot rang out.

Rodgers staggered, clutching his shoulder. Taking advantage of the distraction, Ryce spun around and ducked, lightning-fast, out of the guard's reach.

"Matt, get down!" Grayson shouted, and Matt dropped to his knees without thinking before he had the chance to process what was going on, hunching his shoulders as he wildly cast about the bridge.

Grayson stood above the prostrate body of the guard he'd knocked out while everyone's attention had been riveted to the drama Ryce was enacting. Blood trickled down the side of the lieutenant's face from a gash on his temple, but he held the guard's plasma rifle firmly, swinging it in a wide arc as he strove to ward off all potential threats at once.

"Get him!" Rodgers bellowed, and it was as if Matt's consciousness split between the past and the present. The images of Rodgers, one with his hand on his face from a long time ago, and one of him currently clutching his shoulder, screaming for his men, overlapped, making Matt dizzy with the slew of memories.

Payne jumped out of her chair, reaching for her own weapon, but a plasma shot from Grayson's rifle, aimed for her leg, brought her down with a grunt of pain.

Ryce threw away his useless gun and grabbed the other guard by the arm, twisting it viciously behind his back. The man grunted, then cried out as Ryce slammed his arm over his knee, breaking it at the elbow. Ryce kicked him to the floor and took hold of his rifle, pointing it at

Rodgers. All Matt could do was watch him through a daze, still hunched over on the floor with his hands stuck awkwardly behind his back.

"Don't kill him!" Grayson cried out. "The *Lisa* is still in the hold with all her passengers. We still might need him to bust everyone out of here."

Ryce paused, holding Rodgers at gunpoint. The pirate growled, his stance and flared nostrils reminding Matt of an enraged bull. His left hand was clasped tightly around his right forearm, the coarse fabric of his sleeve seared by the blast. The last guard standing, the one who'd escorted Matt, had his gun trained on Ryce, but hesitated under Grayson's glare and the barrel of his rifle.

Matt blinked, willing his stupor away. He couldn't afford to freeze up. This was here and now. This was the reality, not some lucid memory or a shredded nightmare, and this time, there were people counting on him, people he loved. He couldn't let them down.

"Okay, nobody freaking shoots anybody!" He heaved himself upright with supreme effort, doing his best to ignore the nervous tremor that ran through his limbs. "Anymore, that is. Grayson, close off the bridge before more folks with guns come bursting in."

Grayson backed to the door, watching Rodgers, Payne, and the guard warily, and hit the controls, locking the entrance to the bridge.

"If you think you're getting out of here alive, you all have another thing coming." Rodgers's face was distorted by pain, but the calculating look was back in his eye as his gaze slid between the three of them.

Matt ignored him and turned to the guard who had his weapon trained on Ryce.

"Drop it," he ordered, "or the brave lieutenant here shoots your captain. He doesn't need his legs or his arms to talk."

The man hesitated, the odds all at once skewed in the wrong direction. He glanced at Rodgers, but this time, the pirate remained silent. Slowly, the guard lowered his rifle and bent over to put it on the floor.

Ryce switched the setting on his rifle and shot the guard without any warning, rendering him temporarily unconscious. Matt winced in (somewhat misplaced) sympathy, imagining the headache the guy was going to wake up to. After amping up the rifle charge to full capacity again, Ryce crouched to relieve the guard of his commlink.

"Put your comm on the control panel and step away. Sit down and don't move," Matt ordered Payne, who lowered herself to the floor with her hands raised.

Matt drew a shuddered breath, looking around him. Everyone was staring at him with various degrees of expectancy.

Now, if only he knew what to do.

"Give the order to get the prisoners aboard *Lady Lisa* and release the ship," Grayson said, taking a step toward Rodgers, rifle raised. "Right now, or I swear to God—"

"Or what?" Rodgers sneered. "You're gonna shoot me? You'll have to do a lot better than that if you ever wanna to see your damn kid alive. Don't get your hopes up."

He was still breathing heavily through the pain, but he seemed to have regained control of his faculties with surprising agility. No doubt a course of action was already forming in his brain, despite him being the only one of his crew currently standing in the room, while Matt still drew a blank.

No, that wasn't true. He'd once managed to get off this very same ship while half out of it with pain and disorientation, his flight adapters brutally cut of out of his head and the entire crew chasing him. He was more than capable of doing it with his partner and his friends backing him up.

"Okay," he said. "Our best chance is to get to the *Lisa* as quickly as possible, before the rest of the crew gets wind of what's happened here." He started for the control panel. "Now, if someone could get these fucking handcuffs off me so I can—"

"No. Nobody leaves the bridge." Grayson still pointed his rifle at Rodgers, but his posture had changed infinitesimally, as if he was readying to pounce.

"Are you fucking kidding me?" Matt said, halting midway to the panel.

"I can't risk having Elisabeth aboard even for another minute. The *Lisa* is ready to go; all he has to do is give the order, and she'll be in the clear. I can't let you mess up her release."

"What about you? And the rest of us?" Matt gestured vaguely between himself and Ryce.

"We could steal a lifeboat," Grayson said, "like you did the first time. Or find another solution. I don't care. All I want is to make sure my daughter is safely out of these monsters' clutches. If that means none of us makes it, I consider it a fair trade."

It was Ryce's turn to scoff at him, but Matt forestalled anything he was about to say.

"Look, I get it. This is your daughter, your family. You'd do anything for her. Hell, you've *done* everything you could, consequences be damned. But this man"—he nodded at Ryce—"is *my* family, the one I'll do anything to protect. I'm not leaving him stranded on a fucking pirate ship if there's any possibility of him getting out. So I suggest you get your shit together before somebody out there figures out what's going down on the bridge when they fail to contact their captain."

Grayson didn't respond, but Matt knew enough of the telltale signs to see he was wavering. He'd acted on impulse before, taking a shot at Rodgers with no clear plan in mind, and now he was just as lost in the situation as they were, trying to make the best out of a particularly raw deal.

"We're gonna free Elisabeth, okay?" Matt pressed on. "I promise, Grayson. We're all on the same side, and we've got to work together, and we're not leaving anybody behind—not you, not me, and not Ryce. Are you with me?"

"Listen to your friend and be a good team player," Rodgers said.

"Grayson, come on," Matt pleaded, ignoring Rodgers's mocking.

Grayson's gaze flicked between them, but at last he deflated and lowered his rifle.

"Okay, fine. What's the plan?"

"Get everybody out of the way," Matt said, indicating Rodgers, Payne, and the fallen guards with a nod of his head. "I'll see what I can do from here."

With two Fleet officers in the room, perhaps he wasn't the best person to run the show, but for some reason, they seemed to trust his judgment. He'd better prove them right before their small window of opportunity closed.

Chapter Seventeen

Matt barely waited for his hands to be released before he ran to the control panel while Ryce and Grayson bound Payne and the unconscious guards with their own handcuffs. Matt was sure Rodgers was going to put up a fight, but he offered no resistance as Grayson pushed him back into the captain's chair and cuffed his good arm to the armrest. The uncharacteristic display of docility was anything but reassuring, but Matt was going to take whatever he could get.

With the immediate threats successfully neutralized, he plopped into the pilot seat and tapped his adapters to activate a mental link with the ship's computer—which promptly proved impossible.

"What's the override code?" he asked Payne after a few futile attempts to convince the system to play nice and let him take over.

"Get bent," she said with disdain.

"Maybe later. Seriously, can we *not* do this right now? I don't have time to kneecap anybody for information."

"Here. You can use her comm to gain access." Pulling the barrel of his rifle to the side, Ryce approached the panel and handed Matt the device. Behind them, Grayson had planted himself squarely in front of Rodgers's chair, scowling like a pissed-off watchdog.

"Thank you," Matt said distractedly and busied himself with searching for the correct override sequence.

"Matt," Ryce said quietly.

"What?"

"You meant that, didn't you? What you said to Lieutenant Lee. About me being your family?"

Matt looked up from where he was scrolling through Payne's personal data.

"Of course. Of course you are. You always will be."

Ryce's face was pinched and his gray eyes shone as if he was about to cry. Matt had never seen him look like that, not even when he was being chased by angry aliens, threatened by ruthless crime lords, or facing torture and possibly death at the hands of notorious pirates. As dangerous as all these men and creatures were, none of them had the power to wound Ryce's soul the way Matt could.

"I'm sorry," Ryce said, his voice closer to a whisper.

"What for?"

"The things I said to Rodgers, about abandoning you. You know I didn't really mean any of that, right? I was only trying to stall. The plan was to gain his trust and then to find a way to help you, Val, and Tony escape."

The sudden lump in Matt's throat had nothing to do with the copious amounts of adrenaline currently coursing through his body.

"Don't be silly," he said, a little gruffly. "I didn't buy any of that crap for a second. Not after everything—well, you know what I mean. And if anyone should be apologizing, it's me. For keeping this"—he nodded to Rodgers—"a secret."

Ryce smiled wryly. "We never learn, do we?"

"I hope we never do."

"Can you do all that lovey-dovey stuff later?" Grayson interjected dryly. "You can discuss your relationship on your damn time."

Ryce rolled his eyes again but stepped back, allowing Matt to concentrate on getting everything he needed to connect to the ship's computer.

"I'm in," Matt said after touching his adapters, and then shoved the pilot's comm into his back pocket in case they might need it later.

It felt as if it had been ages since he'd tapped into another ship. *Lady Lisa* was easy and familiar; every time that mental link of mind and machine was created between them, it was like talking to an old friend. The connection with the *Black Baza* felt entirely different. It was probably just Matt's imagination running off with him, but he could sense the ship's hostility toward him as if he were a careless intruder poking around inside her brain.

"Can you access the cameras?" Ryce asked.

"Yeah."

Matt brought up the security cameras' split-view feed on-screen. The captives were still gathered in the docking bay, sitting, with the guards standing in a loose circle around them. They'd been there for a long time, and as far as Matt could tell, some of the men were beginning to get restless, though no one dared abandon their post or call on the captain for further directions.

The corridors and the stairways leading up to the bridge were empty save for the occasional crew member scurrying along on their business. It seemed no one had yet noticed their captain's suspicious unavailability or the fact that the bridge had been locked shut.

Matt's anxiety slid down a notch. They didn't have much time, but there was still a chance to make a move before all hell broke loose.

He poked around the system and quickly found the control hub he needed.

"Order your men to escort the prisoners aboard *Lady Lisa*," he said, turning to Rodgers. "That was your original agreement with Ryce, right? Might as well stick to it."

"Yeah? Or what?" Rodgers sneered.

"Or we'll find out how dashing you'll look with two eye patches."

At Matt's signal, Grayson unlocked the cuff binding Rodgers's hand to the armrest. Without answering, the pirate heaved himself from the chair and approached the control panel. Both Ryce and Grayson followed him with the barrels of their rifles.

"Don't try anything, or I swear to God..." Matt wasn't inclined to finish his thought.

Rodgers touched the controls, connecting to the dock audio systems. "Get the prisoners to the ship and exit the hold," he said, raising his voice just a bit.

On the camera feed, the guards looked up, some in surprise, but scurried to obey the order, hauling the sitting captives upright and ushering them up the ramp toward *Lisa*'s main hatch.

"Happy now?" Rodgers said to Matt.

He didn't sound angry, and the uneasy feeling that had been gnawing at Matt's stomach intensified. Dylan Rodgers was a lot of things, but he wasn't a coward, and he definitely wasn't predictable. He was playing them somehow, or at least trying to, and Matt was damned if he had it figured out.

"Okay, here's the plan. We tie everybody up, seal the bridge, and head over to the docks." Matt did his best to sound brisk and efficient rather than freaked out. "Hopefully, there won't be any nasty surprises waiting for us along the way, but as far as I can tell, the coast should be clear—as long as we go now."

"Fine. But he's coming with us," Grayson said, waving at Rodgers.

"What? We can't take a hostage—"

"Tied up or not, I'm not taking the chance of him getting free and having his men shoot up your ship. And if I kill him now, it'll be one of his mates. We need him as collateral," Grayson said. "Frankly, I'd like nothing more than to see him dead, but bringing him to justice is the next best thing."

"Okay, fine!" Matt threw up his hands in defeat. The thought of Rodgers setting foot on the deck of his precious *Lisa* made his skin crawl, but he wasn't about to have another argument with Grayson, especially when the man had a point. "Can't do worse to my ship than the Alraki, right?"

*

"You better notify the Fleet as soon as we clear the docks," Grayson said as they hurried down the corridor. "It'll take them time either to arrive or to send backup."

Ryce led, scanning the way ahead with his rifle at the ready. Matt and Grayson followed, with Rodgers walking between them with his hands tied behind his back. They'd left Payne and the guards bound on the bridge, and Matt had placed it on lockdown using the access codes. He purposefully didn't shut down his adapters, maintaining a link to the ship's computer while they made their way to the docking bay, in case they needed a quick access to the mainframe.

"Can't you contact them yourself?" Matt asked absently, too busy watching their prisoner and glancing behind them every so often.

As painful and incapacitating the injury to Rodgers's arm must have been, Matt never expected it to actually subdue him. From the moment they'd left the bridge, the pirate hadn't said a word or made a move to extricate himself from their grasp, and this quiet compliance was so unlike Rodgers that Matt's mind prickled with premonition. His nerves were already pulled as taut as they could possibly go, and now Grayson was heedlessly harping on them.

"I don't think they'll be predisposed to listen to anything I have to say anymore, under the circumstances," Grayson said dryly.

"If you think the admiral will listen to anything *I* have to say, you really haven't been paying attention."

"That's not true," Grayson said quietly. "I've been the closest person to Admiral Cummings for the last three years. He may not show it, but he was deeply hurt by your...estrangement. He still loves you, Matt."

There were few topics that managed to make Matt feel more uncomfortable than that of his soured family relations—even without the unwanted audience.

He opened his mouth, intending to firmly nip this line of conversation in the bud, but then the familiar sound of a laser rifle going off echoed through the corridor.

"Ryce!" Matt yelled. But Ryce was already ducking and returning fire at the two men currently shooting at them from around the bend that led to the main pressure chamber at the mouth of the dock.

The split second of distraction proved enough to spur their prisoner into action. With a low grunt, Rodgers lunged at Matt, slamming him into the wall. The gun flew out of Matt's hand with the impact and clattered to the floor. Instinctively, he made to swoop for it, but Rodgers, his hands still tied behind his back, drove his knee into Matt's groin with enough force to send entire galaxies full of stars dancing in front of his eyes.

"Fucking damn it!" Matt wheezed, doubling over in pain.

Thankfully, Grayson grabbed Rodgers by the shoulder from behind and roughly wrenched him away before he could kick Matt again.

"Cease fire, or I'll blow his fucking head off!" Grayson shouted, pressing the barrel of his gun against Rodgers's nape.

"Like hell you will," Rodgers growled and then hissed as Grayson viciously twisted his injured arm.

His crewmen didn't heed Grayson's warning, continuing to fire. Matt suspected the only thing throwing their aim was them trying not to hit their captive captain in the process. Otherwise it would have been like shooting fish in a barrel—or in a narrow service passageway, as it were.

But they all underestimated Ryce, who was now free, armed, and unencumbered by the need for caution. Head held low, he sprinted down the corridor and charged right at their assailants, all the while firing his own weapon and dodging the blasts aimed his way with an almost supernatural agility. If Matt had been able concentrate on anything other than the acute pain radiating through his lower abdomen, he would have paused to admire the sheer grace of Ryce's movements and the accuracy with which his final shots took the guards down.

The two men toppled to the floor, the barking of their weapons still echoing through the tight space. Ryce stopped to check on both of them before glancing back over his shoulder.

"Are you okay?" he asked worriedly.

"Ngh," Matt managed to squeeze out, unsure whether in affirmation or negation. With an effort, he peeled himself off the floor and picked up his gun with all the dexterity of an arthritic old man.

"Come on," Grayson urged, shoving Rodgers in front of him.

"Does this mean they're onto us?" Matt asked, catching up with Ryce.

"If not, they're about to be. There!"

They passed the entrance to the pressure chamber and burst into the main docking bay. Ryce pointed to the farther end where *Lady Lisa* was tucked in a corner.

Matt's heart leapt at the sight of his ship. Her robust hull, designed to be practical rather than pleasing to the eye, could hardly be called lovely, but right now, she was the most beautiful thing Matt had ever beheld—save, perhaps, Ryce's face.

She looked to be whole enough, though the signs of speeding away from an exploding Alraki vessel were etched into her exterior in the form of tiny impact indentations and burn marks. The engines were silent, but the main hatch was still open, as if in invitation. Unless this was some elaborate trap Rodgers had somehow managed to conceive on the go, Tony, Val, Elisabeth, and the remainders of Walker's team were waiting for them inside. They had to be.

Aside from the Phaeton hauler, the capacious bay held a few shuttles and tiny maintenance vessels but was otherwise empty of either guards or other personnel. The only crewmen on shift after the prison guards had departed the area were probably the unlucky fellows who'd tried to stop them in the hallway. It was a window of opportunity they could not afford to squander.

"Seal the pressure chamber," Matt told Ryce. "We don't want any more guests crashing the party before we split."

Ryce nodded and hung back, tapping at the control pad. The heavy doors slid shut, effectively cutting them off from the rest of the ship.

Abandoning caution, Matt ran toward *Lady Lisa*, with Ryce following closely behind. The pathway to salvation was so tantalizingly close. Just a few more steps, and he'd be—

A stifled cry from behind stopped him in his tracks. Matt wheeled around in time to see Grayson locked in a death grip with his prisoner, who seemed to have somehow disposed of the magnetic cuffs that bound his hands. Grayson, caught unawares, dropped his gun, and it clattered to the floor, echoing through the hold like thunder. Spinning around with a nimbleness unexpected of someone with such a brutish appearance, Rodgers grabbed Grayson in a chokehold, squeezing the man's throat with the crook of his uninjured arm. Grayson wheezed and clawed at his arm, his face going an alarming shade of red, and tried to kick the pirate's legs. He went still when Rodgers whipped a knife out of his boot and pressed the sharp tip against his temple.

"Stand where you are," the pirate warned them, his voice a hoarse growl laced with pain.

Matt could feel the tension in Ryce's body, even though he was standing a few feet away. His finger was curled on the trigger, but he hesitated. With Rodgers using Grayson as a live shield, it was a risky shot, even for someone as good as Ryce.

"Don't even think about it, punk," Rodgers warned him, "or your buddy here gets it."

He pushed the tip of the knife into Grayson's skin, his damaged hand shaking slightly with the exertion. A drop of blood welled at the puncture, and Matt held his breath involuntarily. The memory of a knife (most likely the same one) tearing into his own temples, severing the neuroconnections that fused his brain with the flight adapters flashed before his eyes, threatening to overwhelm him.

But Grayson wasn't a pilot. There was no metal and delicate wiring standing between his brain and the blade. Just a little more pressure, and he'd be dead.

"Rodgers, don't—" Matt began, but he didn't get a chance to see how well he'd manage yet another standoff.

The sound of a plasma rifle cocking to full charge echoed behind them.

"Drop the knife," Tony said, stepping from behind a docked service shuttle, the heavy weapon in her hands trained on Rodgers's back. Stains marred her gray fatigues, and her long braid was in disarray, errant strands of hair sticking out of it. Relief flooded Matt's already overwrought senses.

Rodgers tensed, his grip going harder despite his injury. Blood trickled down Grayson's cheek, and he gulped, his Adam's apple bobbing in his exposed throat.

"You shoot me, you kill us both," Rodgers warned, angling his body behind Grayson's.

"After everything he put us through, I might not care," Tony quipped, but she hesitated a moment too long.

Rodgers's lips curved in a smirk, and he raised his knife-wielding hand to tap the adapter on his temple.

Pain blazed inside Matt's head, blossoming like an angry red flower. He went down on his knees, crying out in agony. It was as if someone held his skull in a vise, with his adapters the points of pressure, and squeezed and squeezed and squeezed and—

He was dimly aware of the metal floor beneath his palms, of Ryce kneeling beside him, holding his shoulders, of his own hoarse gasps.

"Matt?" Tony's voice came as if from underwater, but he detected the note of fear in it even through the haze of pain. "The hell did you do to him?!"

"This is *my* fucking ship," Rodgers said, addressing Matt rather than answering Tony. His voice boomed in the space, colored with anger and contempt. "You thought you could hijack it from under me by linking your adapters and walking away without bothering to log out? *I* designed the *Baza* and these things that link me to her." He gestured to his flight adapters with the blade. "She does what *I* tell her, wherever I am."

Alarms blared, and emergency strip lights flashed red around the walls and the high ceiling. A low rumble sounded from the far end of the hold, and movement reverberated into Matt's hands through the floor, the shrill noise adding another layer of suffering to his torment.

"What's going on?" Tony demanded, looking around frantically.

"The cargo airlock doors." Ryce's grip on Matt's shoulder loosened as he glanced behind him, and Matt whimpered at the loss. "He's opening them."

Chapter Eighteen

"Are you insane?" Grayson panted. He flailed in the pirate's chokehold, but Rodgers, both taller and significantly heavier with muscle, held him fast. "If you open the airlock, we're all going to be sucked into space!"

"Your friends better get a fucking move-on then." Rodgers took a step back, and then another, forcing Grayson to retreat with him.

The huge steel doors of the main cargo bay airlock began to slide apart. The outer hatch behind them still remained sealed as the spacecraft safety features prevented the two sets of doors from being open at the same time even on manual override.

At first, Matt couldn't understand what Rodgers intended to do. The searing pain between his temples wasn't at all conducive to normal cognitive processes, let alone complicated predictions. But then the floor shook, and all the docked vessels around them slid a few inches toward the slowly opening doors.

"He deactivated the docking pads!" Ryce exclaimed. "There's nothing holding these spacecrafts in place. We have to get on the *Lisa* right now!"

As if in response, *Lisa*'s thrusters revved to life, the sound as welcome as it was ear-piercing, but Matt was having difficulty focusing on it, the corners of his vision blurring and darkening. The pain edged dangerously close to a critical level short of him blacking out. Rodgers was right; he'd been a fool to be so careless as to link to a ship that wasn't his own. It looked as if Rodgers had modified his flight adapters to work on a much broader range to bypass anyone trying to tamper with his systems, and to disrupt an already formed link via remote access, without using the main controls. Matt didn't know it was possible, but the last few weeks had been full of unpleasant revelations. It hadn't been his first fuckup; all he could do was hope it wouldn't be his last.

His hand shook so badly that his fingers slipped on his adapter. But at last, he was able to touch it, disabling the useless, but still-open connection with the ship's mainframe.

The pain vanished as if by magic. The sudden letup in sensation left Matt reeling, struggling to breathe and take in anything past the ringing in his ears.

Matt grunted and pushed himself up, first onto his knees and then his feet, swaying like a newborn colt. The tremors coming from the deactivated pads did nothing to stabilize him in his current state of extreme disorientation, but, thankfully, Ryce was right there to steady him and pull him toward the *Lisa*.

Banking on Matt's crew's state of confusion, Rodgers had managed to reach the doors of the inner pressure chamber with his struggling captive in tow. He held on to the emergency handle, lowering the knife to do so, and that was when Grayson made a dash for it, dropping down and twisting Rodgers's arm in an attempt to free himself from the pirate's grip.

Rodgers cursed and let go of him but stabbed at Grayson's back with the long blade of his knife before he could scramble away. Grayson cried out and stumbled to the floor, his shirt drenching with blood at an alarming rate.

"No!" Matt yelled. "Grayson, fucking damn it!"

Grayson's moan was almost lost in the resounding bang of the airlock doors sliding to a fully open position, but he heaved himself forward, clutching at the floor with his fingers. Behind him, Rodgers lifted his head and met Matt's gaze. The electronic glow of his eye patch against the backdrop of the frantically flashing alarm lights gave him a particularly sinister appearance, transforming his face into the devilish mask from Matt's nightmares.

"Looks like you got your ship back after all, Spears!" he shouted, his booming voice echoing in the hold above the metallic screeching of the spacecraft, including the *Lisa*, skidding across the floor toward the gaping mouth of the airlock. "Enjoy it while it's all in one piece!"

Without waiting for Matt's response, Rodgers dived inside the pressure chamber, disappearing from view. The airlock doors trembled again and began to close.

"Get him, please," Matt panted, and waved feebly toward Grayson, who left bloody smears in his wake as he crawled across the floor.

Thankfully, Ryce didn't waste time arguing. He nodded curtly and rushed toward Grayson, with Tony following suit, as Matt clung to the edge of the *Lisa*'s ramp as if trying to slow her down before she hit the still-closed hatch toward which she was gliding.

Ryce and Tony carried Grayson between them to the ramp just as the airlock doors shut behind them with such force they had to crouch and hold on to one another to avoid being knocked down on their faces. The airlock was plunged in darkness, illuminated only by a few red emergency lights that marked the corners of the main hatch.

It wasn't hard to deduce what was going to happen next.

"Come on, we have to go!" Matt urged when the three of them reached *Lisa*'s hatch. As if to emphasize his words, the red lights flashed, issuing a depressurization warning.

Matt dove inside after Ryce, Tony, and Grayson, and slammed the lock, shutting *Lisa*'s door just as the outer airlock hatch opened into the void.

Something small but heavy—most likely a maintenance pod—crashed into the hull as everything tumbled into space, rattling the *Lisa* and making them all wince. Matt caught himself before falling again when the engine kicked into high gear and the ship surged forward.

"Who's manning the bridge?"

"Walker," Tony said and added, "We have to bring him to the infirmary right now." She nodded at Grayson, who was now slumped between them, whimpering with his eyes shut. "I think the bastard damaged his kidney."

Grayson was bleeding too profusely for Matt to object to the urgency, and they started down the corridor to the infirmary.

"Elisabeth," Grayson managed to push out through clenched teeth. "Where is she?"

"She's okay. She's waiting in the rec room," Tony said as she and Ryce lowered Grayson onto the bed, but her attention was focused entirely on the need to stem the bleeding and stabilize her patient. She wasn't a trained medic by any means, and it was anyone's guess as to whether her haphazardly acquired skills were going to be enough to handle a life-threatening injury.

Matt shut his eyes and leaned against the wall, taking a few deep breaths to calm his racing heart. It didn't quite work, but he was sort of keeping it together, and it was enough for now.

When he opened his eyes, his gaze rested on the rifle slung over Tony's shoulder. It was a ridiculous detail to latch on to, just a tiny brushstroke in a picture comprised of Grayson's soft moans, the thick smell of blood, and the stickiness on Matt's fingers. He wiped them on his pants, not looking down to check whether it was blood or sweat.

"Where did you get that gun?" he asked without any inflection.

"I have one stashed in the hold compartment. It's a smuggler's ship," she added, not looking up from where she was pressing swathes of gauze to Grayson's wound. "It might as well live up to its legacy."

Grayson's eyelids fluttered, and he opened his eyes again.

"Matt," he whispered but faltered. His face, already ashen gray, twisted.

"Not now." Matt pushed himself off the wall. "First we need to get away from the *Baza* and notify Central Command of the secret base of theirs. Tony, can you manage here on your own?"

"Yes, go. I'll call for help if I need an extra pair of hands. And after all is done, I'm expecting to see you in the infirmary too," Tony said, her tone brooking no argument.

"Yes, yes. I'll be back when I can. We're talk later," Matt told Grayson, who gave him a tight nod before letting his head fall back on the pillow, too wracked with pain to do anything else.

"This isn't over, is it?" Matt said to Ryce when they were alone in the corridor.

Ryce shook his head. He looked like Matt felt, which was weary beyond words.

"I wouldn't count on it, no."

They ran toward the bridge, though perhaps "hobbled" was the correct word where Matt was concerned.

As Tony had said, Walker was there manning the bridge, as was Val. A makeshift bandage wrapped the soldier's head, and smudges of dirt and dried blood still covered Val, but they were both alive.

"Am I happy to see you," Matt said earnestly, drinking in the sight.

Val cracked a rare smile, his pale eyes crinkling with even rarer open joy, and slapped Matt on the shoulder, making him stagger a little.

Walker nodded, though his expression was more tense than happy, and shifted his attention back to the trajectory calculations on-screen. Matt supposed he couldn't blame him for that. "It's good to see you too, Captain."

"I can't believe we all made it back in one piece," Val said. "You've got some luck, Captain. I was sure this time he'd gut you like a fish and throw the rest of us out the airlock." He raked Matt over with a concerned gaze. "Are you okay? You look—"

"I've been worse," Matt said, though he certainly didn't feel like it. His head was no longer about to explode by sheer force of Rodgers's will, but he was still dizzy, the recollection of the pain enough to churn his stomach even before taking all his other hurts and aches into account. As much as he resented the fact that Rodgers had once again emerged victorious and in possession of the most important technological advancement of the last century, he knew he should count his blessings— the lives of the people closest to him being chief among them.

"Guess they got everything they wanted," Walker said, bitterness underlying his words. He rubbed his face tiredly.

Matt could relate to the feeling of utter failure. After all, he'd had plenty of experience with it throughout his life, while he bet Walker was not used to being so utterly defeated, not to mention having other people paying the price for it. Matt wanted to say something comforting—an urge he would've ignored in the past. But Walker had grown on him. Hell, even his team of vexingly superior killer soldiers had grown on him, and he was genuinely sorry to see that not all of them would have the chance to go home.

"We still got the specs," he said. Anything more personal would have to wait until they were alone. "It's all there in Ryce's head. Right?"

Ryce made an affirmative sound.

"Would you like to take the controls, Captain?" Walker hadn't said "can you," but the question was evident in his tone.

Matt glanced at Ryce, but to his surprise, the other man shook his head minutely.

Perhaps Ryce was much more worn out than he let on. Matt squared his shoulders, preparing himself for the challenge, and nodded at Walker. He wasn't in the best shape for piloting, but his adapters and years-long familiarity with the *Lisa* made him far more attuned to the ship than someone who could only fly it on manual.

"Ain't no way Rodgers is about to let us off the hook this easily," Matt said. "He's a tenacious motherfucker. We might have taken him by surprise on the bridge, but he had control of his ship the entire time. He only shoved us outside because it was the fastest way to gain the upper hand, knowing he'd get us later." Matt replaced Walker in the pilot seat. "Did they activate the magnetic grapnel?"

He allowed himself a brief moment to luxuriate in the feel of the shabby upholstery, the familiar creak as he lowered his weight into the chair.

"No. Honestly, I don't think they'll bother this time," Walker said, sitting in the copilot seat.

As if on cue, a laser blast exploded on-screen, the charge grazing the starboard hull. Proximity alerts flashed across the screen, followed by a system damage report, and a ship-wide alarm sounded in the background.

Oddly, it served to ground Matt rather than spiral him further into anxiety. Maybe some of Ryce's grace-under-pressure attitude was rubbing off on him. Besides, *Lady Lisa* was the fastest ship in the sector. Not this particular one, granted, since they'd jumped out of Sonora to who knew where, but still. Matt wasn't familiar with the capabilities of the *Black Baza*, but he sure wasn't going to make it easy for them.

"Let's give these fuckers a run for their money," he said, tapping his adapters. His *Lisa* responded readily, like a loyal soldier answering a call to arms, and leapt forward, avoiding yet another blast by a disconcertingly narrow margin.

With the *Baza* so heavily armed, it wasn't a fair fight by any means, and, admittedly, Matt wasn't anywhere as good as Ryce when it came to space battles. But he'd watched him enough to take a page or two from his book, though he much preferred that his partner be the one currently calling the shots, doing what he did best.

The ship picked up speed effortlessly and swerved, evading yet another blast. Matt split his attention between watching the peripheral camera feeds and steering the ship, so at first, he failed to notice the system notification popping up at the corner of the screen.

"Matt, look," Ryce said quietly over his shoulder.

"What the actual fuck?"

Matt brought up the system report, but it was already too late. The notification beeped and flashed an alarm as the engine stalled and shut down. The sudden lack of its perpetual soft hum translated into a deep, heavy silence so unnerving it made Matt's hair stand on end.

Lady Lisa continued to sail forward by the force of inertia while Matt futilely tried every command to restart the engine. Their current situation amounted to them being the proverbial sitting duck, just waiting to be taken out by the swiftly approaching hunter.

"The hell is wrong with it?" Matt cried in frustration, failing to glean anything useful from the status report the computer unhelpfully presented.

"I'm on it," Val said.

"Have Ikeda and Shapiro help you with whatever you need!" Walker yelled after him as the engineer ran out, heading down to the engine room.

As tenuous as Matt's hope of evading the *Baza* had been before, now it was practically nonexistent. With their shuttle left behind on the *Lennox* at the beginning of the mission and their interstellar communications channels still disabled, they were now trapped with no means of escape.

"Is the Alraki jet docked inside the cargo hold, like I asked?" Ryce asked Walker.

Both the commander and Matt looked up at him in surprise. The inquiry was so untimely and irrelevant that Matt was sure he'd misheard.

"Yes," Walker said cautiously. "I saw the *Baza* crew hauling it inside when we were brought into the dock. Why?"

Another laser blast hit the ship at the top sail. Matt clutched the armrests as everything around them rattled.

"Shit, they're going to blow us to pieces soon," he said. "Walker, can you contact a Fleet outpost in this system?"

"I've tried. The communications are still jammed," the commander said, tight-lipped.

"Lieutenant Lee can tell you how to remove the block," Matt said, thinking fast. "He's in the infirmary. If we contact—wait, where are you going?"

The last bit was directed at Ryce, who headed for the exit.

Ryce turned to Matt, his gray eyes smoldering with something so dark Matt had a sudden urge to shrink back in the pilot chair. "I had a feeling Rodgers was going to do something like this."

"You think he tampered with our engine?"

Ryce nodded. "That's why he was so quick to agree to release all the prisoners and to allow us to escape. He knew we wouldn't get far, even if it meant he wouldn't have the pleasure of torturing us in person. He'd still have his revenge on you, no matter what."

Matt half rose from his chair. He wasn't surprised to hear any of it, really; he'd suspected as much when Rodgers had been so uncharacteristically cooperative under duress. What scared him more was the grim determination etched into every line of Ryce's face.

Another blast shook the ship, and they both flinched as they stared at each other.

"Captain Spears, now isn't the time!" Walker said exasperatedly, but Matt ignored him.

"What are you going to do?" he asked Ryce.

"Whatever I have to do to stop him."

"Is that why you were asking about the jet? It's in pieces!"

Ryce shook his head. "I had an entire week to work on it while I was figuring out how to install the jump apparatus on the *Baza*. They weren't watching me too closely as long as I kept busy. A lot can be done in a week with proper incentive."

"Okay, fine, I forgot you're a genius. But you can't take on an entire ship with a recon jet!"

"I'm sorry. The commander is right; we don't have time to argue."

Ryce turned and sprinted down the corridor without waiting for Matt's response.

"No, get back here!" Matt yelled, but Ryce was already well out of earshot.

He swore so graphically that even Walker cringed, but Matt couldn't stand there gaping after his wayward boyfriend. With another string of expletives, he threw himself back into the pilot seat.

With the *Lisa* drifting in the void, there wasn't much he could do except for watching the swiftly approaching black pirate ship on the aft camera. They'd stopped firing, most likely to conserve ammunition until they were close enough to deliver the final blow. After all, it wasn't as if *Lady Lisa* was going anywhere.

Matt's back pocket buzzed, startling him. He'd forgotten all about taking Payne's commlink with him, and now someone was calling him on it—not from a regular number, but over an interstellar channel he didn't recognize.

"That's an Alraki frequency," Walker said, craning his neck to peek at the comm over Matt's shoulder. "Do you think it's—"

Matt answered the call so fast he nearly dropped the comm.

"Ryce! Is everything all right?"

"Yes." Ryce's voice came over a bit distorted, with annoying static crackling in the background, but there was no mistaking his usual confident tone. "The Alraki vessel is in working order. Open the cargo doors."

Matt hesitated. His every instinct screamed at him to protect Ryce at all costs, but he couldn't keep him locked inside. As a trained combat pilot, Ryce knew what he was doing. At least, that was what Matt told himself, but he still couldn't bring himself to open the cargo hold.

"Matt, please!"

"Fucking damn it," Matt muttered under his breath, and triggered an emergency release. Another alert ran across the screen, adding to the long list of system notifications vying for his immediate response: *Cargo bay doors open. Warning. Cargo bay doors open.*

He flipped through the camera feeds and zoomed in on the image of the Alraki jet coming out of a dive beneath the *Lisa*'s keel.

"I'll engage the *Baza* so you can head straight for the Gemel-6 Federal military base," Ryce said over the comm, even more distorted now.

"Be careful," Matt pleaded.

There was a palpable hesitation in the short pause that followed.

"Matt…I have to tell you something."

Matt glanced at the canopy screen again, at the rapidly nearing pirate ship. "What?"

"Fixing the jet wasn't the only thing I did without Rodgers's knowledge while we were held on Charon. I assembled and installed a copy of the same wormhole-generating technology on it as I did on the *Baza*."

"You did *what*?"

"I wish I had more time to explain. I can only hope it works just as well, and that I'll be able to use it."

"Use it how?" Matt asked, already knowing the answer. He dug his fingers into the armrests, ignoring the concerned look on Walker's face. He was dimly aware of someone—he thought it was Val—entering the bridge, but whatever the engineer had to say, it had to wait, because right now Matt couldn't spare any thought for anyone interrupting, for whatever reason.

"If I don't stop Rodgers, he'll destroy the *Lisa* with everyone on board," Ryce said. His voice was becoming more and more tinny with every passing second as the jet sped toward the black ship, as if already being gradually wiped out from existence. "When it comes down to it, it's either me or your ship and your friends."

"No." Matt shook his head in stubborn negation as if this was an argument he still had any hope of winning. "No. I can't make that choice."

"I know." Ryce's voice softened despite the distortion. "Now you don't have to. I love you, Matt."

"No, don't tell me that! Don't you dare tell me that! Not until you get your ass back here. Ryce!"

The communication cut off, leaving him gaping at the image on the screen. The *Baza* angled slightly, aiming for that decisive shot at the slowly drifting *Lisa*, but the Alraki jet, so small against the massive silhouette of the ship, darted to the front, set on a collision course.

"Please, don't," Matt whispered, helplessly riveted to the tiny moving dot, black against black. "Please."

Laser blasts tore the darkness, this time aimed at the jet, but Ryce glided between them, seemingly effortlessly. The *Baza* began to swerve, but it was already too late.

Matt had never had the chance to see what a "portable" wormhole looked like before. He'd traveled through his fair share of jumpgates, of course, but those were huge, immutable structures reminiscent of detached corners, set in place millennia ago by a civilization advanced beyond human imagination. This time, there was no framework to contain the effusion of pure energy that shot out from beneath the jet's weirdly coiled bow. It was similar to a high-power laser beam, but so bright Matt and his companions had to shield their eyes against it.

The wide beam hit the middle of the *Baza*, going right through it. Matt thought he could discern a circle of utter blackness at the center of the beam, growing wider and wider, like a hole being violently torn through the fabric of space, with the pirate ship being no more than a stain on it. The Alraki jet tumbled toward it, pulled by enormous unseen forces, just as the larger ship exploded around the quivering wormhole. The shock wave struck *Lisa* a moment later, sending her wobbling. The glowing beam went out abruptly, replaced by a scattering of burning chunks of metal.

"No, no, *no!*" His broken wail bounced against the walls. Matt unstrapped his seat belt and lunged at the control panel as if he could hurl himself outside by sheer force of will. The ship lurched and shook, confused by the involuntary commands coming from his adapters, and yet another alarm message flashed across the screen.

"Stop it!"

Walker sprang to his feet while Val grabbed Matt from behind, pinning him against his massive body, restraining his arms in a viselike grip. Matt flailed wildly, clutching at Val's hands. The hot tears streaming down his face and his screams felt distant, as if happening to someone else far away from here. *Lady Lisa* shook again and tilted to the side as they all scrambled to keep from sprawling on the floor.

"Captain, please!" Val begged him, his voice strained and tinged with the accent that only surfaced when he was too upset to control it.

His grip tightened, on the verge of crushing Matt's already battered body, as Val struggled to contain his thrashing.

Matt barely registered Walker calling for someone, his words indistinct but urgent; then the sound of running footsteps came from behind. The alarm blocked the part of the screen where the cloud of debris now rotated, so he focused on the stars at the edges. They flickered, distorted by his tears, distant and mocking in their indifferent beauty.

How dared they go on shining when Ryce was dead? How could the galaxy not stop spinning for being bereft of him? Matt threw his head back and howled.

"Hold him!" Tony's voice instructed tersely, and then something cold and sharp bit into Matt's arm. He shied away, but Val and Walker held him fast.

"*No*," he repeated, his voice nothing but a hoarse whisper, and then everything went black.

Chapter Nineteen

When Matt opened his eyes again, he was almost blinded by the glaring white light. Someone's face hovered above him, the features distorted and fluid to his muddled gaze.

"Ryce?" he whispered, blinking rapidly.

If he was dying, he wouldn't mind. He had nothing left to live for anyway.

The shadow above him coalesced into Tony's face. She leaned above him, her lips pursed tightly, her eyes puffy and red. Matt couldn't hold back a sob of disappointment.

Taking further stock, he realized he was lying on a cot in the infirmary. An oximeter on his index finger connected to a monitor, but he was otherwise unrestrained. His head, however, still felt fuzzy, the sensation too much like a bad hangover.

He swallowed, wincing at the soreness in his throat. It appeared he'd screamed himself hoarse. He couldn't bring himself to care.

"I'm sorry, Captain." Tony took half a step back. "I had to sedate you. You were hysterical. We were afraid you might hurt yourself or damage the ship."

Matt didn't have it in him to be angry with her. She was right; he'd completely lost it. In any other circumstances, he'd be mortified by his behavior in front of his crew. Now, it mattered as little as the physical discomfort of the aftermath.

"How long was I out?" he asked, keeping his voice low.

"About four hours. The communications channels are back online." She tapped on the monitor, checking the readings of his pulse and temperature. "Lieutenant Lee contacted the admiral's office, and Commander Walker sent his own report to CenCom. Both Nora and Admiral Cummings were notified of what happened. The *Lennox* is on her way, coming through the local jumpgate. The guys from the Gemel-6 military base are sending reinforcements to clean up the mess and help us with repairs. They all should be here soon."

Matt knew Tony well enough to realize she was trying to pull off brisk nonchalance for his benefit. It wasn't working as well as she probably hoped it would.

"So everybody is okay?" he asked. "I mean, except for..."

The words were thin and brittle in his mouth, and he trailed off before his voice broke on them.

"Yeah." Tony's expression softened. "Lieutenant Lee was badly injured, but I believe he'll pull through if he gets all the medical assistance he needs. His daughter is with him now."

"You'll...look after her, won't you?"

"Of course. I like her. The poor thing is so brave. I could tell she gave her kidnappers a lot of grief, but thankfully, she wasn't hurt. Mostly, she was just bored while she was there, and worried about her dad."

Matt closed his eyes. Neither of them spoke for a while, with only the monitor beeping sedately in the background.

"He's gone, isn't he?" he said finally without inflection. "Really gone."

"I'm sorry, Matt," Tony said quietly, placing a warm hand over his forearm. "The scanners picked up no traces of life signs. It appears no one survived the explosion. I'm so sorry."

Her voice trembled with repressed tears, but it failed to elicit the same reaction from Matt. It seemed like all his emotion had been spent in that first violent outburst, and now he was left empty and devoid of any semblance of feeling. His soul had been ripped out of him; the open wound filled him with so much pain it didn't leave any room for sadness, sorrow, or anger.

There were only two ways to escape that kind of agony—drinking himself senseless, or dying. It no longer mattered which one it'd be, but he wasn't prepared to do either, not just yet. His crew, his passengers, and his ship were still his responsibility, and he would see this whole thing through. Just...not right now.

"Drug me again," he told Tony in a thick voice, opening his eyes.

"Matt—"

"Just do it. Please."

She must have seen something in his gaze because she nodded, tight-lipped, and reached for the syringe.

*

The temptation of oblivion, even a few hours' worth, had never been so strong or so welcome, but eventually there came a time when Matt had to wake up and function. Perhaps "function" was too big a word, but he did everything that was expected of him, going through the motions when the rescue crew arrived from the Fleet base on Gemel-6.

While they waited for the *Lennox* to arrive, Commander Walker opted to have the local medical team board the *Lisa* to tend to the wounded instead of taking advantage of the planetside facilities. Matt didn't dispute this decision. The mission had ultimately failed, with the destruction of the prototype-carrying Alraki frigate a small consolation for the alien technology having been lost, but secrecy still had to be maintained until full debriefing.

Matt couldn't bring himself to care either way. With Val slowly working to fix the sabotaged engine, he kept to the bridge, ostensibly to be available if he needed him to run full-system diagnostics, but really to be alone. The others must have sensed his mood because no one bothered him while he was there, sitting in the pilot chair that had been Ryce's spot, staring numbly at the screen where Fleet vessels scurried among the slowly spreading debris that had once been a pirate ship.

Rodgers was dead. Matt's ship was intact, and his friends were safe. He could enjoy a whole new life without having to look over his shoulder or suspect sinister connections wherever he went. And Ryce was the one who'd paid for it all.

Matt would never again see him raise his chin with that disdainfully arrogant expression. He'd never see his tentative smile, hear his breathless voice utter his name in moments of shared pleasure, never feel the warm, gentle touch of his fingers on his skin. He'd had his life handed back to him, but now it was devoid of all meaning without Ryce in it.

For a second, Matt couldn't breathe. He lowered his head between his arms and rocked back and forth. A whimper tore out of him despite his best efforts to contain it. His eyes stung, but no tears came. A shudder ran through him, a death rattle of a withering heart.

Fuck it. Walker could handle it all on his own. There was no way Matt could hold himself together for much longer without a stiff drink or five.

The sound of shuffling feet came from behind him, and he swiveled around in the chair, ready to tell the intruder off, but the angry words died on his tongue.

A girl stood at the entrance to the bridge. Her red hair was plaited in a tight neat braid, undoubtedly Tony's doing. Her denim trousers and green T-shirt looked worse for wear after what had amounted to weeks in captivity, but otherwise, she seemed well enough, with a healthy tinge to her cheeks. Her round face had a softness to it reminiscent of her birth father, Grayson's late husband.

Seeing Matt's expression, she threw her arms around herself but didn't shy away. She didn't say anything, simply gazed at him with those big eyes of hers, framed with dark lashes.

Matt ran a hand over his face and cleared his throat, composing himself.

"Did you …uh…want anything?"

He had no idea how to speak to children, and her intent stare made him uncomfortable.

"I wanted to say I'm sorry for what my dad did," she said solemnly. "I know that pirate caught up with you because he helped him."

Matt sighed and gestured to the copilot chair. Elisabeth scrambled to get inside it and sat crossed-legged, appearing smaller than she was.

"You don't have to apologize. I'm just glad you're okay, kid." Matt turned to the screen where the tiny pieces of the *Black Baza* floated in the distance. After a long pause, he shook his head. "If anything, I should be apologizing to *you*. If it weren't for my beef with Captain Rodgers, he'd never have extorted your dad like that. It would've been better for everyone if I'd never escaped him in the first place," he added quietly.

Elisabeth cocked her head to one side, considering his words with far more gravity than they probably warranted.

"I'm sorry about your boyfriend too," she said. "Tony told me he was the one who took down the pirate ship. Is that true?"

"Yeah," Matt managed to push out, though his throat constricted at the mention of Ryce, the memory of his jet plunging into the epicenter of the explosion ripping a new layer of denial from the gaping wound inside of him. "He saved us all."

Elisabeth studied him. Her expression reminded him a bit of Nora, so serious and levelheaded. He'd never been this insightful growing up.

"You know my other dad died."

"Yeah. Grayson told me."

"At first, I cried all the time. I just missed him so much. I still do. But when the bad guys kidnapped me and locked me up, I imagined he was with me, watching over me. I pretended he could hear me when I was scared. He wasn't really there, but it made me feel a bit less lonely, you know? Maybe...it'd help if you think about your boyfriend this way too."

Matt swallowed around a burn in his throat.

"Yeah," he said thickly, trying to smile. "Maybe it would."

Elisabeth nodded and hopped off the chair. "I'll see if my dad needs me. See you around."

"See you," Matt said and watched her sprint off down the main corridor.

*

It was apparent the Alraki hadn't had the chance to trash his cabin because all the mess was his own. It remained exactly as he'd left it, apart from the slightly musty smell he hadn't noticed before.

He really needed to shower and change, but instead of attending to the pressing matters of his personal hygiene, Matt dug out a half-empty bottle of whiskey he kept stashed under his bunk and sat down heavily on the mattress.

He pictured the smoky, amber taste in his mouth, but instead, his brain supplied him with very different memories—the fresh scent of Ryce's soap after he'd had a shower, the taste of his lips. Ryce wasn't here next to him, would never be close enough again to stop Matt from making foolish decisions.

Matt carefully placed the bottle on the side table and lay back on the bed, stinky clothes and all. He closed his eyes and buried his face in the pillow. It was probably just his fancy running away with him, but under the dusty staleness, he caught a whiff of that elusive smell he'd learned to associate with his lover. For Matt, Ryce would always smell of starlight.

He drew a ragged breath, and it was as if something snapped inside him. Hot tears burned his eyes, and he let them flow onto the pillow that muffled his sobs until there was nothing but darkness.

*

Matt's commlink chimed, and he opened his eyes, blinking. Soft murkiness shrouded his room, the lines of the furniture and fixtures limned in the faint greenish glow from the night lighting.

His mouth was dry as the desert, and it felt as if someone had stuffed shards of glass under his eyelids while he slept. His head throbbed in that steady, wearisome way it usually did after a particularly long bender, but a glance at the bottle standing on the side table confirmed he hadn't touched the booze.

The commlink beeped again, and Matt groaned. His indisposition wasn't the reason he was tempted to ignore it and go back to sleep, but as with the sedatives, he was bound to resurface eventually anyway.

He fished the comm out of his pocket and squinted groggily at the screen before answering it.

"What?" he asked in a gravelly voice.

"Thought you should know the *Lennox* is here." Tony sounded half sympathetic, half disapproving, and he felt a twinge of guilt, however dull, at letting her shoulder all the pressing tasks by herself.

"Fuck. How long was I asleep?" he asked. They hadn't anticipated the destroyer getting here for a while, even though he supposed its arrival would be given precedence at the Gemel system jumpgate.

"Thirteen hours, give or take. I judged it best not to disturb you right now."

Matt swore again and swung his feet to the floor.

"They're sending in a shuttle to pick up everybody—Walker's team and Grayson and Elisabeth. They asked you to go too. I told them you'd be there, but if you're not up to it..."

"I'll go." Matt sighed and pinched the bridge of his nose. "I just need a few minutes to freshen up."

Not unexpectedly, the world hadn't stopped while Matt was struggling to deal with his life shattering. He should have been bothered, or at least peeved by the thought of facing his father and Nora, answering their questions and most likely incurring the blame for the dismal way the mission had ended, but it left him strangely unmoved. It seemed he'd lost his capacity for exasperation.

It took him much longer than a few minutes to shower and change into a clean set of clothes. It felt good to wash the dirt and the grime of the last week off his skin and hair. The bruises had mostly faded to green and yellow, so even if his face was still mottled with them, he looked somewhat presentable.

"Just get it all over it," he told his reflection in the bathroom mirror. "Toughen the fuck up."

His haunted expression seemed to mock him, making the words ring hollow. Despite having slept for more than half a day, he was still exhausted, the weariness etched into every muscle, bone, and sinew. The image blurred as tears welled in his eyes again, but he blinked them away and took a deep breath. He could do this and let himself grieve later.

The shuttle from the *Lennox* was already docked at the sail when he arrived, and paramedics were transporting Grayson, strapped to a gurney. One of them had her arm around Elisabeth's shoulders, and the girl waved at Matt before following the gurney inside.

He waved back and waited for Walker to come up. The commander appeared to be much better, though his head was still bandaged.

"There'll be a debriefing with the admiral as soon as we get to the *Lennox*. I got the impression there was something urgent he wanted to present."

"The hell is so urgent, if everything we got from the Alraki is gone?" Matt muttered. "And they sure took their sweet time getting here. The Gemel system jumpgate isn't that far from this location."

Walker shrugged with the resigned air of someone used to the brass making inexplicable decisions, and patted Matt on the shoulder. Despite having had some time to rest, the commander looked tired, or perhaps despondent.

"Let's go," he said and gestured to the shuttle hatch. "Whatever it is, it'll be over soon."

Matt didn't have a chance to say his goodbyes to Elisabeth as she and her father were taken to the infirmary immediately upon their arrival at the *Lennox*'s docking bay. He shook hands with the surviving members of the special ops team—Ikeda, Shapiro, and Martin—before they too departed for a more thorough medical examination than Tony could have conducted, and, no doubt, to be questioned.

To his surprise, Matt was sorry to see them go. They would never be friends, but they'd achieved a level of mutual respect that came as a result of risking their lives for one another.

Major Cummings's office greeted them with the same holographic star map sprawled over the long conference table. The admiral and Nora, both looking impeccable, were seated at the far end, but Matt's eyes immediately snapped to the only other person in the room.

He opened his mouth, but no words came. Walker touched his shoulder again, and it was the only thing keeping Matt from staggering and sinking to the floor.

Ryce rose from his chair.

"Hey," he said with a self-conscious smile.

Chapter Twenty

For one awful moment Matt was sure he was still asleep in his bed on the *Lisa*, trapped in one of his nightmares. At any time, the image would shift, and Matt would find himself strapped and bound inside a torture chamber, or worse, forced to helplessly watch the pirate ship explode while taking his boyfriend out with it, over and over again in a hellish loop.

Walker's hand was a welcome weight on his shoulder, grounding him. It was warm and solid, this probably wasn't a dream, and yet...

Matt took a step forward and halted, his heart hammering.

"Is this real? Are you...real?" He barely recognized his own voice.

Ryce's face pinched. He crossed the distance between them in a few long strides and pulled Matt into a tight embrace.

"Yes," he whispered, his lips brushing against Matt's cheek. "It's me. And I'm not going anywhere."

Matt clutched Ryce in his arms, holding on to him like a lifeline. Ryce was miraculously, gloriously alive, and it was the only thing that mattered.

He closed his eyes and breathed in, filling that empty, aching place in his chest with starlight.

"I thought you were dead," he said. "I thought—"

His voice broke, and he fell silent while they stood there, holding each other so close their heartbeats mingled.

"How is this possible?" Walker asked behind them. "What happened?"

"I'll let Mr. Easom tell you everything," the admiral said. "Please be seated, gentlemen."

Tearing himself away from Ryce was one of the hardest things Matt had ever had to do, but he sat next to him at the table. He was just as curious as Walker to hear what had happened at that awful moment the *Baza* exploded, even if it was lower on his priorities list than kissing Ryce silly with relief.

Across the table, Nora gave him a sympathetic look. She was still pale and gaunt, breathing through a nasal cannula attached to a portable medical oxygen generator, but she no longer appeared frail, and her green eyes sparkled with their usual lively intelligence. He nodded at her, unable to keep back a grin when he saw her expression light up as Walker took a seat beside her. It seemed he wasn't the only one who was lucky to have avoided the heartbreak of losing the person they were in love with.

Admiral Cummings gestured to Ryce, who steepled his fingers on the tabletop. Now that Matt had a chance to look at him more closely, he could see fresh scrapes and bruises on his hands and face but, thankfully, nothing that indicated a more serious injury.

"I have already told the admiral and the major about my deal with Captain Rodgers to install the Alraki jump technology on his ship," he began in that level, calm voice of his. Every syllable was like a drop of balm on Matt's soul, fusing its shattered pieces back together. "However, under the pretense of salvaging parts and electronic components from the Alraki jet, I was secretly working on installing an alternative array on the jet itself. I knew Rodgers couldn't be trusted to keep his word about releasing prisoners who could expose his base of operations and his new advantage to the authorities. In any case, it was unlikely he'd let either Mr. Spears or myself go regardless of any arrangement. This vessel could be our only chance to escape and survive. As it happens, I was right about that, though perhaps not in the way I initially imagined."

"You only had a week to do it," Nora said. "It's amazing you managed to pull it off."

"Unfortunately, Rodgers was right about the effect of the correct incentive," Ryce said, glancing sideways at Matt. "This challenge put all my abilities to the test, but failure was not an option. The Alraki have built-in laser-excitation arrays on all their fighter and recon jets, which worked in my favor. I was able to add the new capability on the existing framework according to the information we retrieved from the prototype frigate, though I knew the resulting wormhole would be much smaller and less stable than what a larger ship could generate. The attempt would also leave the jet's energy reservoirs depleted, so it could only be done once. It was a gamble, for sure, but ultimately it worked. When the *Baza* was chasing us, I realized the only way to stop it would be to open the wormhole directly on the pirate ship."

"But how did you manage to survive the explosion?" Matt asked. The mere memory of it made him squirm uncomfortably in his seat. "I was there, and I could have sworn you were caught in it. Everyone who saw your death dive was sure of it."

Ryce inclined his head. "Another second of delay, and it would have torn me apart along with the *Black Baza*. The jet fell into the wormhole just as it imploded, but luckily for me, it transported me to the coordinates I'd preset while working on it, hoping to return to the general vicinity of the Sonora-11 military outpost, where the *Lennox* was stationed."

"That's incredible," Walker said. "If you could translate the specs into a working module from memory alone with little to no resources— not once, but twice—then you could show the Fleet R & D how to do it on a mass scale."

For the first time since they'd encountered the Alraki frigate, Walker's grim expression was gone, replaced by a mix of hope and awe, something that transformed him back into the handsome, energetic officer he was at the start of this whole unfortunate covert operation.

"You will do it, Mr. Easom?" Admiral Cummings asked. His tone was polite enough, but it was clear to everyone present it wasn't really a request.

"Yes," Ryce said without hesitation. "Having witnessed it firsthand, I can attest this would give us an enormous strategical advantage, pending some modifications that would allow the technology to be more easily adapted to our computer and laser systems. But first, I must ask for something in return."

The admiral's eyes narrowed, and Matt held his breath.

As things currently stood, Ryce was the only human in the world who possessed the knowledge the Fleet so desperately sought, as it was doubtful the Alraki would give them another opportunity to capture one of their module-carrying vessels. That meant he was in a unique position to negotiate on any terms he damn well pleased. Money, fame, a new career—he could have it all.

"I want you to fix *Lady Lisa*," Ryce said. "Rodgers sabotaged her engine, and after everything she's been through, she needs a full overhaul."

"And?" the admiral prompted impatiently.

"I want the Fleet to grant Captain Spears a permit to operate as an independent contractor in every sector of the Federation, with his application fees paid in full."

There was a long pause.

"That's it?" Cummings said finally.

"Yes." Ryce glanced at Matt and reached out to take his hand, which Matt squeezed in return. "We've done our part. With Rodgers gone, all we want is to go on with our lives."

"Wait." Matt turned to his father, still holding Ryce's hand in his. "There's one more thing. I want you to drop all charges against Lieutenant Lee."

"The man is guilty of treason," the admiral said coldly. "He betrayed the Fleet. He betrayed *me*. That's not something to forgive and forget."

"Whatever. If Nora could do it for me, you can definitely do it for him," Matt said, raising his chin. This was something he refused to let his father have his way with, and he could be just as obstinate as him. It ran in the family after all. "Grayson came through for us when it really mattered. If it wasn't for him throwing his lot in with us and swaying the tide on *Baza*'s bridge at a critical moment, none of us would be sitting here. I realize he can't be reinstated to his post, but there's no reason he can't be positioned elsewhere, keeping his rank."

"I must say I'm surprised, Matthew—after what Grayson did, selling you out like that to a known criminal. You almost died, along with your people and mine." Cummings's gaze swept across the table to pointedly include Ryce and Walker.

"Yeah, well, I get why he did it. I think he's been punished enough, and his daughter sure doesn't deserve to grow up alone because her dad did everything he could to keep her safe."

The admiral pursed his lips, hesitating.

"Please, Father," Matt said quietly, abandoning his defiant tone. "That girl has been through enough. Don't let her lose the only thing she has left of her family."

"Matt is right," Nora chimed in unexpectedly. "Lieutenant Lee didn't commit this crime out of greed or misguided ideology. I believe his case calls for compassion, not blind justice."

The admiral drummed his fingers on the tabletop and finally sighed.

"Very well. I'll see what I can do for Grayson. And I hope he understands just how much he owes the two of you."

"Thank you," Matt said. "I think he will."

*

They spent the next hour relaying all the details of their mission aboard the Alraki frigate and subsequent capture by the pirates. The admiral heard them out with an unreadable expression, so Matt couldn't tell whether or not his father was impressed with his and Ryce's efforts to help Walker's team. The worried looks Nora kept throwing at Walker were much more telling, and Matt was suddenly very glad he'd gone along with Ryce's reckless extraction plan after all.

A brief discussion followed where Matt learned that the Fleet had already dispatched a military force to Charon in an attempt to detain the remaining pirates and dismantle their secret base. They'd also set a tentative schedule for Ryce to begin working with the R & D experts who had been urgently called in, but at that point, Matt was barely listening. He slumped in his chair and closed his eyes, letting his abused nerves calm.

He must have dozed off at some point because when he opened his eyes again, Nora, Walker, and his father were all gone. The star map rotated lazily above the table, and Ryce was fiddling with it, zooming in and out on various solar systems.

"Hey," he said softly, turning to Matt.

"Ngh," Matt said.

Ryce's gray eyes shone like the stars on the map, and all of a sudden, the simple joy of the sight was too much to contain. Matt leaned forward, burying his face in his hands, his shoulders shaking with dry sobbing.

Ryce touched his knee, and Matt looked up. As much as he'd have wanted to spare his partner having to witness this moment of weakness, he was grateful Ryce was there with him. This smart, courageous, selfless man had seen Matt at his absolute worst, and rather than be repulsed by it, he'd been Matt's rock again and again, no matter how many times Matt had let him down. Now that they had each other again, there were things that needed to be dragged out into the open, even if the idea of them made Matt cringe. They'd begun discussing it on the bridge of the *Baza* what felt like ages ago, but never had the chance to finish the conversation.

"Baby, I'm so sorry," he whispered. That awful scene in the *Baza*'s torture chamber when an appalling truth had been his last-ditch shot at survival still weighed heavily on his conscience. He desperately wanted to touch Ryce's face, to feel the softness of his skin, but guilt bound his hands tighter than iron shackles. "I should have told you all that stuff about you and Dylan Rodgers earlier. I should have told you the second I started suspecting it. But I wanted so badly to spare you the burden. Because once you knew, you wouldn't be able to ignore it."

Ryce's gaze was distant as he looked at the map, the bluish lighting reflected in his eyes. Finally, he turned back to Matt.

"Brinan told you, didn't he?" he said, but it wasn't with censure.

Matt nodded. "Yes. That time when we met him on Freeport 73, I asked him a few questions after you left. He'd hinted at it when he told me the story of the pirates' attack on their ship during that research expedition—when he was your mother's supervisor—and I connected the dots. I still can't be a hundred percent sure, of course; I don't have all the details. We may never know, but it all fits, doesn't it?"

"Yeah," Ryce said softly. "It does."

"I'm sorry," Matt repeated, feeling more and more miserable. Ryce was quiet, but the hurt in eyes was unmistakable. What pained him more—that his father had had no qualms about trying to kill them, or that his partner had kept such an important thing a secret? Matt suspected the answer, and he couldn't do or say anything that would fix it. How they went on from this rested entirely on Ryce, and Matt braced himself for the pronouncement of judgment.

Ryce shook his head. "It doesn't matter." He swallowed, and his voice became firmer. "I remember what I said to you. That I didn't care who my biological father was. And I still don't. Genetics aside, there was never any connection between us. His offer to spare me was so he could use me, and it ultimately meant nothing. He's not my father, not in any sense of the word."

"So you're not mad at me?" Matt asked, and an enormous fist clutching his heart loosened its ice-cold grip.

"No, I'm not mad. I understand why you did it. Besides," Ryce added with a wry smile. "I openly denounced you to Rodgers, even held you at gunpoint, so if feels to me like I'm the one who should be begging your forgiveness right now."

Matt snorted. "Oh, please. I knew it was all an act, and you wouldn't shoot me. Though God knows I sometimes deserve it."

"But in that moment, you thought I would." A shadow fell over Ryce's face as he tilted his head, avoiding Matt's gaze. "I saw the look on your face when I pointed that gun at you. You were...resigned. Ready to die."

Matt rubbed the bridge of his nose. Ryce was right. He had been ready to sacrifice himself, but not for the reasons Ryce thought, nor was he holding a grudge against him.

"It was what it was," he said, just as quietly. "It came down to a choice, and I'd choose you, Val, and Tony over myself any day, and you would do the same for us. You *did*."

"There was never any choice where you are concerned," Ryce said. "Losing you would be like ripping out my soul and shredding it to pieces."

A cold shiver ran down Matt's spine. "I know how *that* feels."

"I'm sorry I put you through it." Ryce took Matt's hand in his again, the familiar touch reminiscent of all the times Ryce had comforted him in the safe seclusion of his cabin. "I promised myself I would never hurt you, but I did, in the most awful way. All these other pretenses and secrets we both feel guilty about pale in comparison when I think about what you must have suffered. I did what had to be done to keep you alive, but—"

Matt shook his head and brought Ryce's hand to his lips, kissing his fingers.

"You're here. That's the only thing that matters. I love you, baby. So freaking much."

Ryce let out a shaky breath, relief flooding his eyes.

"I love you too. So freaking much," he said, his tone gently teasing, yet just as sincere.

"Let's not talk about death anymore. I'm too tired. I just want to go home." It came out raw and plaintive, as if Matt were a child lost in the woods in an ancient fairy tale. He didn't know where "home" was exactly, but as always, Ryce seemed to understand him perfectly.

"We'll go there together," he said and leaned over to close the short distance between them.

For a long moment, Matt couldn't say anything in response. He was content to let their lips, tongues, and hands do the talking, their language more honest and concise than any and all promises and reassurances he could have come up with. The kisses were tinged with the metallic aftertaste of fear and the bitterness of remorse, but it made them all the sweeter.

Chapter Twenty-One

Matt slouched in the copilot chair, holding a giant mug of steaming coffee in his hands and watching the looming bulk of the *Lennox* drift across the screen. Thankfully, Val had managed to fix the mangled coffee maker, thus restoring a modicum of normalcy to Matt's existence.

Nora had suggested *Lady Lisa* remain docked inside the destroyer, but after all the repairs had been completed and his shuttle returned, Matt had had quite enough of his baby being confined to dark holds, even for benevolent reasons. It made traveling back and forth somewhat of a hassle, but the sight of distant stars on the window screen was much more preferable than staring at a wall.

Ryce had spent most of his time on the *Lennox*, either working with the Fleet R & D engineers on reconstructing the blueprints for the jump module, or sequestered in conference with Admiral Cummings and various representatives of Fleet Central Command, whose faces all began to blur and blend together to Matt's eyes after a while. After giving an official statement (and repeating it a few times for good measure) he'd put his foot down and removed himself from all further discussion. His father and the brass would have to be content with Ryce and Commander Walker relaying all the valuable information regarding the Alraki vessel layout and preparedness. All Matt cared about was making sure Nora was getting better, and him being paid as per his contract.

He didn't know where they were going after this, now that the proverbial Sword of Damocles that had been hanging above his head for the past few years had finally been lifted. Sure, there were still people out there (perhaps too many people, come to think of it) whom he could consider his enemies, but none had ever instilled such fear in him as Dylan Rodgers.

They could always remain in Sonora. The busy sector presented its challenges, of course, but it was familiar grounds, and jobs were plentiful and easy to manage. Or, now that Matt had an unlimited work license, they could strike out for more distant parts, for new and uncharted opportunities, somewhere far away from the strife and violence of war.

Perhaps he could even take Ryce on a vacation on Earth, or Nova. Somewhere where they could dip their toes in the sea, feel the salty breeze and sunshine on their faces. Where they would swim naked under the velvet skies and lie in the tall grass caressing their skin. It was a daydream, for sure, but after staring death in the face so many times during the last few weeks, he was ready to make at least some of his dreams into reality.

Matt sighed and swirled the remnants of the rapidly cooling coffee. He'd been sorely tempted to add a splash of whiskey to it earlier, just to take the nervous edge off. He was proud that he hadn't. He knew the temptation of alcohol-induced ataraxia would be there for as long as he lived, beckoning to him, and that most likely, he wouldn't be able to always resist it with the same fortitude he'd exhibited during his short period of mourning. But the desperate need that had driven him to drink in the past was so much weaker, its teeth dulled now that he had other things to hold on to. And wasn't he the luckiest bastard in the galaxy for having found those things and being allowed to keep them?

"Permission to come on the bridge, Captain," Tony's voice said over the comm.

Matt pressed the door open, even though it wasn't locked, and Tony stepped inside, looking neat and put together with her hair in a tidy braid and her bag slung over her shoulder.

"All ready to go?" Matt asked.

Tony nodded. There were still a few days left until her daughter Sarah's graduation ceremony, but Tony had opted to make the trip earlier than planned. Matt knew she was nervous about the prospect of meeting Sarah, whom she hadn't seen or spoken to for years, but coming close to being killed so many times in the last two weeks was bound to change one's perspective on certain things—not to mention one's priorities.

"Val and I are going to take the shuttle to Freeport 16. There's a transport heading directly to Mars. Are you going to manage okay on your own here, Captain?"

"Don't worry about it." Matt placed his mug on the control panel and rose to give her a hug. "Ryce and I will be absolutely fine. Go and have a good time of it, you hear?"

She nodded. "I will, I promise. I've got to do this right, both for me and for Sarah. And you were right about this trip being good for Val. I actually think he's excited to do a bit of sightseeing."

Matt arched an eyebrow. "Val? Excited? I almost wish I was coming with you, just to see that. That's about as rare as a government tax cut."

Tony drew back and slapped his shoulder playfully. "I kinda wish you were coming, too, but I get why you can't. I'll keep you posted, all right?"

"You better. And I swear, once you both get back, we're taking that vacation on Nova I've been promising you. I mean it this time."

Tony rolled her eyes and snickered before exiting the bridge. Matt shook his head ruefully and retook his seat.

His commlink beeped just as he reached for the mug again. Recognizing the number for the *Lennox*'s infirmary, he nearly spilled his coffee in his haste to answer, but it wasn't Nora's image that popped onto the screen.

"Hey, Matthew." Grayson's smile was somewhat strained. Propped up in a hospital bed, he looked much better than the last time Matt had seen him.

"Hi," Matt said cautiously.

"I know you're probably not interested in anything I have to say," Grayson said after a moment of uncomfortable silence. "But I would still like to have a word with you. You deserve an explanation for my actions from my own mouth, even if you won't accept my apology."

"Look, Grayson—"

"Please?" Grayson pleaded. "You won't hear from me ever again after this if you don't want to; I promise."

Matt sighed. He really was getting soft, wasn't he?

"Fine," he said. "I'll arrange a transport."

*

If Matt never saw the interior of the infirmary again, it would be too soon. Nora was still hospitalized for observation, though she was thankfully out of danger.

Having cleared his arrival with the medical staff, Matt entered Grayson's room. Barely larger than a stall, at least it was private. Elisabeth wasn't there, but Matt assumed she was being looked after in the guest accommodations, seeing as Nora had taken it upon herself to make sure the girl was well taken care of, arranging everything from her hospital bed.

"Matthew," Grayson greeted him, sitting up against his pillows. "Thank you for coming."

"No problem."

Matt lowered himself into a chair by Grayson's bed. He briefly considered touching the man's hand where it rested above the covers, but Grayson didn't reach for him, and Matt thought better of it.

"The admiral told me what you did for me," Grayson said without preamble. "Getting him to drop the charges and clearing my record. I could never thank you enough."

"I mostly did it for Elisabeth," Matt said.

"I know. She told me she'd spoken to you, asking for your forgiveness on my behalf." Grayson's hands flexed and relaxed. "I know I don't deserve it. But I want you to know why I helped Rodgers trap you.

It wasn't because I harbored any ill will toward you. However things had ended between us, I never wished you harm. It wasn't an easy decision."

He stopped, drawing a deep breath, visibly struggling for composure. Grayson had always been good at controlling his emotions, and seeing him this upset distressed Matt. As petty as he could be at times, Matt didn't have it in him to be cruel to this man.

Matt raised his hand, forestalling whatever Grayson was going to say next.

"Don't," he said, and Grayson remained silent, watching him with wary apprehension. "I get it, okay? You don't have to explain, or apologize, or rationalize your actions. Rodgers kidnapped your daughter, and you did everything you could to get her back. I'm not saying that you betraying us like that wasn't awful, but if I'd been in your place, I'd probably have done the same."

Something eased in Grayson's face. "Thank you," he said quietly.

Matt shrugged, a little embarrassed by the magnitude of relief that flooded Grayson's eyes. He wasn't used to people placing so much importance on his opinion of them, and he could do without the pressure of that particular responsibility. But he saw it meant something to Grayson, so he went with it.

"We all have someone who's worth throwing everything away for."

Was there any point in having it otherwise?

"How's Elisabeth doing?" he asked, striking for more solid ground.

"She's fine, thank god. Shaken, but not hurt, and she's getting help."

"Look," Matt said. "I know things are…complicated between us. I'd still like it if we kept in touch going forward. Let's not be strangers anymore."

A faint smile touched Grayson's lips. He lifted his hand off the blanket, and this time, Matt took it, clasping it tightly.

"I'd like that very much," Grayson said.

*

After parting with Grayson, Matt popped over to Nora's room. His sister sat on the bed, her feet dangling off the edge and a collapsible walking cane propped against her knee. Commander Walker sat next to her, their shoulders brushing. They were engrossed in something playing on Walker's commlink, both of them smiling. He could practically see the hearts in their eyes when they exchanged glances.

It was cute and disconcerting at the same time.

The lovebirds didn't notice Matt come in but sprang apart at the sound of his polite cough like a couple of schoolkids caught groping after curfew.

"Yeah, sorry to disturb you guys," Matt said, shuffling on the threshold. "I'll come back later."

"No, no, please come in," Nora said, while Walker excused himself and practically ran out of the room. "I know this"—she gestured vaguely between herself and the spot where Walker had been seated—"must come as a surprise."

"Actually, I can't think of anything that would surprise me less," Matt said, grinning. "Seriously though. Walker's a great guy. You could do worse."

"Gee, thanks." Nora bumped his shoulder with her fist. "It's still new, you know? We haven't figured out yet how we want to proceed. He'd have to transfer to a different command, of course, but it can wait for a bit. He's going through a rough time right now, after what happened to his team."

"Yeah," Matt said, sobering. "I hope he doesn't blame himself for losing his teammates. It wasn't his fault, and that shit will eat you up inside if you let it."

Nora nodded. "It's a process, for sure, but he's dealing with it. The admiral is keeping him busy, which is a good thing all around."

Matt knew this mainly from the snippets Ryce had told him, and the little he could infer from the questions posed to him by the military officials during his official debriefing. Central Intelligence had gotten what they wanted as far as the new Alraki technology, but the pirates' unexpected involvement threatened to unravel the veil of secrecy surrounding the project, and the Fleet brass had scrambled to control any possible damages as efficiently as possible.

Matt chatted with Nora for a while longer and bid her goodbye when her strength began to wane. As he exited the infirmary, he bumped into their father.

Admiral Cummings appeared to be in a good mood, which was to say he wasn't scowling. This, of course, changed once his gaze landed on his son.

Damn it. Matt had done his best to avoid the admiral after their initial meetup. So far, he'd been doing a fine job of flying under his father's radar (owed, in no small part, to his own insignificance) and had been sure he'd continue to do so until their departure. He suppressed a sigh, bracing himself for another display of displeasure. At least Matt wasn't drunk this time.

He wasn't sure whether that was a good thing or not.

"Matthew," his father said by way of greeting.

"Admiral," Matt said dryly.

Cummings's gaze raked over him, no doubt noting the traces of fatigue under his eyes and the fading yellow bruises.

"I'm here to run something past Nora," the admiral said. "But seeing that you're here…perhaps we could talk."

Matt was sorely tempted to tell him off. Their mission was complete; he had no more obligations either to his father or the Fleet. It was the thought of Ryce that made him change his mind. Ryce, whose mother had abandoned him and whose father had tried to kill him.

Whatever differences Matt and his family had in the past, whatever they continued to have, at least he had the privilege of being able to talk to them—or refuse them of his own volition.

"Okay" was all he said.

The waiting area was thankfully empty, and they sat down at the end of the row of white plastic chairs in the far corner.

"I'm afraid I've been somewhat...unfair in my judgment," the admiral said grudgingly.

"About what?"

"You. You did everything in your power to ensure the team's success, well above and beyond anything that would have been reasonably expected. In fact, if you were an officer, I'd recommend you receive a medal."

Matt scoffed, weirdly pleased and affronted at the same time. "Keep your medals. Or better yet, award them to someone who truly deserves them. Walker, Martin, Ikeda, Shapiro. They'll have more use for them."

"Why did you help them, then? On the Alraki ship, when you and your partner came for them. You got them away from the pirates too. If you hate the military so much, why risk you and your boyfriend's lives to save soldiers?"

Matt was silent for a long moment. He wasn't sure if he was ready to have this conversation with his father. But wasn't this part of his newfound freedom, to lay past hurts and future fears to rest?

"I've done some things after leaving home, things I'm not proud of," he said. "I used to be exactly what you thought I was. Self-centered to a fault. I'd have done anything to save myself and my ship, and fuck everyone else. But I'm not that person anymore."

"What changed?"

"Everything. And nothing. I'm still flawed. I fuck up, and I hurt the people I love when I don't mean to. But I know what's right, and that love gives me the strength to see it through because I want to be worthy of it." He shook his head and looked away. "Sorry. I probably sound like a real douche, but it's true."

"Love. You mean Ryce Easom?"

Matt nodded. "I think he saved me," he said quietly. "In all the ways that count. Don't tell him I said that."

"I won't."

Matt turned to face him. A faint smile was playing on the admiral's lips. "What happens now?"

"If the reverse engineering process is successful, I'll be pushing to install wormhole generators on every ship in the Federal Fleet. There will be tests, of course, but if this works, it will give mankind the edge we need to survive."

"Not win?"

"Let's not get ahead of ourselves. Don't tell anyone I said that," the admiral added without any apparent trace of humor, and Matt smiled wryly.

For a while, they sat together in silence, and then the admiral rose from his seat and adjusted his uniform. His gaze caught Matt's, and his hand twitched at his side as if he wanted to reach out and touch him but repressed the urge.

"I'm proud of what you did out there, Matthew," Thomas Cummings said. "Remember that."

Without another word, he turned on his heel and strode toward the entrance to the infirmary. Matt watched the doors slide shut behind him.

Soft footsteps approached, and Ryce sat down in the chair beside him. He didn't say anything, and Matt was thankful for the unobtrusive commiseration.

"You heard?" he asked.

"Some of it," Ryce said. "I didn't mean to intrude."

"That's okay. Were you looking for me?"

"Yes. I heard you came to visit Grayson and wanted to catch a ride with you back to the *Lisa*."

"That means you're done here?"

"For now." Ryce shifted uncomfortably in his seat. "They asked me to stay for the implementation testing, but I—"

"You should do it," Matt said, turning to him.

"What?" Ryce's voice faltered, a shadow of old insecurity crossing his face.

Matt took his hand. Ryce's skin, where it was exposed above the cuffs of his sleeve, was covered in fading bruises, just like his own; a reminder of just how close Matt had come to losing him forever. He tightened his fingers around Ryce's.

"We'll hang around here while you work on this. There's no need to rush; we could all use some downtime."

Relief flickered in Ryce's gray eyes, and he smiled. "You don't mind being cooped up here with your father and putting up with all the Fleet chain-of-command nonsense?" he asked, his tone gently teasing.

"It's fine. I can handle him if it means you'll be doing something meaningful that doesn't involve being chased down ventilation shafts by angry aliens."

"Mmm. I know it's not my business, but...I think the admiral loves you very much," Ryce said quietly. "In his own way."

"You heard what he said. He's proud of what I did, not of me. I don't think he'll ever be proud of me in the way he'd want to be. But that's okay. I'm done chasing his approval—to be who I am."

Matt stood up, pulling Ryce after him. They embraced, their mouths seeking each other with instinctive urgency.

"What will you be chasing now?" Ryce said with a smile when they broke for air.

Your happiness. Always.

Matt shook his head. "I have all I could possibly want right here," he said and leaned in for another kiss.

Epilogue

"Matt," Ryce panted and arched backward, eyes shut as he rode the aftershocks of pleasure.

"Got you, baby," Matt murmured. "Got you."

Hearing Ryce utter his name in that small, quivering voice was like a burning arrow shot straight through his heart, setting his entire body aflame, even though he was already utterly spent.

With a final moan, Ryce collapsed against him, breathing hard. Matt shifted, wrapping his arms around him and closing his eyes, letting bliss overtake him.

A gentle breeze ghosted over their heated skin, cooling the sweat and other traces of their lovemaking, chilly but not yet uncomfortable. The crashing of waves drummed its eternal beat next to them, across a stretch of white sand that occasionally drifted on the wind, tickling their noses. This close to the edge of the water, the only smell at first was that of salt, but Matt distinguished subtle undercurrents beneath it—the iodine tinge of seaweed, the tangy sweetness of Ryce's skin. He could stay here, on this beach, suspended in this moment, forever.

Ryce stirred beside him. He propped himself on one elbow and brushed strands of overlong damp hair off Matt's forehead. He never did get around to cutting it.

"This is the best vacation ever," Matt mumbled, his eyes still firmly shut and a silly grin tugging at his lips.

"Is Nova a lot like Earth?" Ryce asked, his fingertips skimming over the adapters on Matt's temples.

"The weather is nicer here. But yeah, it feels a lot like it."

"Strange, isn't it," Ryce said wonderingly. Matt cracked one eye open to see him turn toward the setting sun. Its orange rays gilded his sharp profile, giving him the semblance of a statue of an ancient god, powerful and free. "I've seen so many suns in my life, but I've never felt one until now."

Matt slid a hand over Ryce's bare flank, reveling in the silky smoothness. It all seemed too much to take in, as though his heart was about to burst from being full.

"And how does it feel?" he asked. Making small talk while basking in the afterglow was preferable to embarrassing himself by turning on the waterworks, even if they were tears of joy.

"Wonderful. Almost as good as this." Ryce molded his body against Matt's again, kissing him sweetly, languidly.

Long minutes passed before they broke apart again.

"As much as I want to stay, I'm afraid it's getting cold," Matt said, watching the sky on the horizon turn a darker shade of red. "We should join the others. I hear there's going to be a proper shindig at the resort open pool tonight. Might as well enjoy the party."

"A 'proper shindig'?" Ryce laughed. He stretched and sat up, then reached for the pile of discarded clothes on the edge of the beach blanket. "I thought I was the one with the antiquated vernacular."

Matt made a face as he shook sand out of his T-shirt and underpants. "Doesn't get much more antiquated than speaking a dead language."

"I thought you liked it when I talk dirty in Latin," Ryce teased, pulling up his pants. Matt didn't bother with being circumspect about ogling his perfect backside right until it disappeared from view. "Perhaps I ought to refresh my repertoire."

"Hey, I'm up for anything as long as you don't cuss me out in Alraki while we're getting it on. Even I have my limits of strange."

Ryce chuckled and helped him up. They finished dressing, packed the rest of their scattered belongings in the picnic basket they'd brought along, and started off toward the line of greenery that bordered the beach. There, a narrow path wound down through the verdant foliage of a tropical forest, cleverly illuminated with hidden colorful lights that came on as dusk settled all around them.

Matt splayed his fingers as he ran his hand across the large, succulent leaves bordering the path, a little startled to find them real and not a bioengineered imitation. He smiled softly as he recalled Ryce examining the lush local flora with childlike wonder during the first days of their stay. For someone who had grown up on a barren rock of a colony and then spent most of his life on various spaceships, this must have seemed like a paradise, or a magical fairyland.

As enchanting as Nova was, a little haven of beauty and tranquility amid the horrors of the ongoing war, Matt yearned to give Ryce so much more, even though he could never hope for it to be on par with what Ryce truly deserved. He wanted to show him all the worlds they could explore together.

The path took them out of the forest and curved around a swath of green grass already glistening with evening dew. Beyond it, the lights of the resort's main building twinkled like jewels in the gathering twilight. Snatches of music drifted on the breeze, signaling that the party had already begun.

Instead of heading to the building, they halted at the edge of the grass, holding hands, looking back to where the sun kissed the sea, the horizon line broken by the vegetation.

"Are you ready for tomorrow?" Matt asked.

"I think so." Ryce's voice was thoughtful now, bordering on solemn. "Will you be there with me?"

"Seriously? You want me to meet your mother?"

Meeting your partner's parent for the first time was supposed to be daunting even at the best of times, let alone when said partner was meeting them for the first time since his birth. This was doubly true when the parent was a renowned scientist, a member of a collective of vastly intellectually superior beings. Then again, after the shock of discovering the truth about Ryce's biological father, the anxiety bar had been significantly lowered.

"Yes," Ryce said, still looking at the setting sun. "She said she wants to get to know me better, and you're an important part of my life." He inclined his head, glancing at Matt shyly. "In fact, you're more than just a part of it."

Matt's heart swelled, taking his breath away. They kissed again, some of the earlier heat returning in their touches.

"Let's go," Ryce said. A repressed fire smoldered once more in the depth of his eyes, but his smile was gentle. "Tony and Val are probably already wondering where we are."

Matt turned his back on the spectacular sunset, looking skyward where the first stars peeked through the purple curtain. Somewhere up there, his *Lisa* waited, safely nestled inside an orbiting space station. Soon, the vacation would be over, and their tight-knit crew would be back to the daily grind of hunting down one odd job after another, doing their damndest to stay afloat in a universe determined to pull them under.

He couldn't wait to get back to it all.

They clasped their hands together and started off toward the beckoning lights.

Acknowledgements

Huge thanks to the entire NineStar Press team and especially to my editor, Elizabetta.

About Isabelle Adler

A voracious reader from the age of five, Isabelle Adler has always dreamed of one day putting her own stories into writing. She loves traveling, art, and science, and finds inspiration in all of these. Her favorite genres include sci-fi, fantasy, and historical adventure. She also firmly believes in the unlimited powers of imagination and caffeine.

Email
info@isabelleadler.com

Twitter
@Isabelle_Adler

Website
www.isabelleadler.com

BookBub
www.bookbub.com/profile/isabelle-adler

Other NineStar books by this author

Staying Afloat Series

Adrift

Ashore

The Castaway Prince Series

The Castaway Prince

The Exile Prince

Fae-Touched Series
A Touch of Magic

Frost
Irises in the Snow
The Wolf and the Sparrow
In the Winter Woods

Coming Soon from Isabelle Adler

The Homecoming Prince

The Castaway Prince, Book Three

"I'm glad to say you look slightly less awful today," Stephan said.

His tone was teasing, but it masked a very real concern. Warren's bout of illness had been so prolonged and so grave that for a while Stephan had feared the worst.

Those days had been nothing short of horrible. He'd known plenty of wretchedness and weathered plenty of dangers, but nothing could ever come close to the long hours spent by his lover's sickbed, holding his hand, wiping the sweat off his brow, and hoping that the next rattling breath wouldn't be the last while Warren thrashed about with fever.

"Always such a sweet talker," Warren said.

A feeble smile played on his lips as he brought a cup of tea to his mouth. He sat up on the narrow bed, propped against a stack of pillows. The only room they could afford at the inn had a tiny fireplace, which gave off more smoke than heat. It was barely enough to fight the mid-autumn chill seeping through the windows and walls. But Stephan had piled all the blankets he could find on the bed, and the tea was hot and strong, at least.

Stephan took his own cup, savoring the warmth that spread through his fingers.

"You should go downstairs to the common room and warm by the big fire," Warren said, having undoubtedly noticed him shiver. The illness did nothing to lessen his usual perspicacity. "Maybe get something to eat too."

Stephan shook his head. They were running too low on funds for him to luxuriate in more than one meal a day now, and they'd already eaten lunch. Besides, he wouldn't leave Warren alone in a drafty, cramped room while he enjoyed himself downstairs. Had their roles been reversed (as they so often had been) Warren wouldn't have moved from Stephan's side even for a moment unless for some dire need.

"I don't actually mind the winter," Stephan said wistfully. "We've been traveling through hot-climate lands for so long, the nip in the air is refreshing. It reminds me of home."

Warren raised a skeptical eyebrow, but Stephan was being truthful. He'd loved Segor; the short time spent living together in the port city of Varta, free to express their love for each other, had been the happiest in his life. But when they were forced to flee, pursued by his brother Robert's assassins, things had begun to go awry. The South Isles, where they'd found a temporary refuge, had proved too much of an extreme environment for them to thrive in. When Warren had fallen sick, even the local physician advised he return to the familiar climate of the continent—which they did, despite the risk inherent in such a journey.

"I do miss Seveihar sometimes," Stephan confessed, coming to perch on the edge of the bed with his cup of tea. Warren folded his long legs, making room for him. "Even the winters at the castle, with the winds whistling through window cracks, and those endless creaking staircases. I always knew the cold and the snow would abate eventually, and then it'd be spring again, and then summer. The summers were always so beautiful there, up in the mountains."

"I remember," Warren said softly. Traces of hoarseness still clung to his voice, but already he sounded so much more vital than before. "I remember how you loved to roam the woods around the castle. Until..."

"Until it became too dangerous for me to go out on my own," Stephan said. "It still is."

The old pain of realizing his own brother hated him enough to plot his assassination flared back into life. The worries and tribulations of the last few weeks had almost made him forget the true reason for his self-imposed exile, but he knew better now than to think it was all behind him. The events that drove them from their safe little haven in Segor into the dangers of the unknown had demonstrated all too clearly that they couldn't afford to let their guard down again.

Warren reached for Stephan's hand, threading their fingers together, and they exchanged a brief, bitter smile. Some of Stephan's anger and disappointment dissipated into their shared warmth, as they always did.

"I'm sorry," Stephan said.

"For what?"

"I seem to always bring danger to our doorstep. Even when we move halfway across the world."

"And if it weren't for you, I'd never have seen anything of the world."

"Don't joke. You fell sick because of me. If I hadn't been so careless in Varta, we wouldn't have had to travel so far, putting so much strain on you. It's my fault."

"It's not," Warren said. "And if I had a choice, I would have done it again. All of it. I would do anything just to be with you."

Stephan shook his head, swallowing around the lump suddenly lodged in his throat.

"I love you," he said, ignoring the treacherous crack in his voice. "So much."

Warren's hand on his tightened, and his eyes flashed in the low lighting, illuminated by the same surge of desire that washed over Stephan. That smoldering look made Stephan's heart beat faster, filling him with the kind of hope and relief for which he'd yearned for days.

He took the half-empty cup out of Warren's hand and leaned down to brush his lips against his, tasting the strong flavor of steeped herbs.

It took some effort to pull back. He wanted nothing more than to sink further into Warren's embrace, but the faint wheezing in Warren's chest reminded him of the need for prudence.

"It's late. I'll go downstairs to fetch us some dinner," Stephan said, rising from the bed. The desire to see Warren hale again outweighed the need to be frugal.

"I'm not that hungry. At least, not for food. Can't you stay?"

"You need to eat to get your strength back," Stephan said sternly. "If you can kiss, you can chew."

Warren rolled his eyes and sighed dramatically, settling back on the pillows. "Fine. Just please hurry back."

*

The inn in which they were currently staying couldn't exactly be called disreputable, but it came too close to it for Stephan's liking. Its location near the docks and cheap prices meant the common room was always crowded and a bit too stifling, filled with loud voices and drunken laughter. But seeing as their coin was scarce, they couldn't afford being too snooty about accommodations.

Stephan made his way over to the counter, pointedly ignoring the leering looks and dirty comments his appearance never failed to garner from the sailors drinking away their shore leave. He wore nothing more provocative than a linen tunic and loose matching pants in the Segorian style he'd come to favor, but his delicate features and long hair, held up in a loose bun, tipped the scale toward femininity—which perhaps wasn't the best choice under the circumstances.

They would have to move soon, Stephan contemplated as he handed the server an empty tea pot and waited for his order of fish chowder. Preferably somewhere with fewer people jostling about.

"Here you are, love," the server said, setting his tray on the counter in front of him.

The chowder looked a bit watery, but the half loaf of bread that went with it was fresh and steaming, as was the replenished pot of tea.

Stephan thanked her and picked up the tray. As he turned, his gaze met that of a man, dressed in heavy, northern-style riding leathers. A narrow white scar ran from the hairline of his temple down his cheek, barely skirting his left eye and giving it a droopy appearance. The man, who looked to be about thirty, leaned casually against the counter, nursing a tankard of ale just like any other patron, but Stephan caught a glimpse of a scabbard hanging on his hip under his woolen cloak. When he noticed Stephan studying him, the stranger averted his eyes, focusing his attention on the general din of the room, but it was a fraction too late.

Stephan's heartbeat quickened. Unless his imagination was running away with him, the stranger's regard had been anything but frivolous.

He ducked his head and climbed the stairs to their room, struggling to balance the dishes in his hurry. He slammed the door shut with the heel of his foot and set the tray on the side table.

"Warren, listen—" he began, but a loud knock on the door interrupted him.

His eyes must have gone wide because Warren sat up, his content expression transforming into alarm.

The knock came again, even more insistent this time. Stephan stepped back and grabbed a butter knife off the tray, placing himself between the door and the bed.

"Who is it?" he called, hoping his voice sounded steadier than his nerves. Behind him, Warren shuffled on the bed, throwing off the covers.

"Lady Lasia?" a muffled voice answered. "Please, I need to speak to you."

Stephan's breath hitched, and he glanced backward at Warren. His lover's face mirrored his own confusion. Who would know to call him by the sobriquet he'd used during his sojourn in Esnia all those months ago?

"Don't open," Warren whispered. He lowered his feet to the floor, holding on to the bedpost, his shirt hanging loose on his too-thin frame in a way that made Stephan's heart momentarily clench.

"Please," the voice repeated from outside. "I mean no harm. This is about your sister."

"Nessa?" This time, Stephan didn't bother hiding his surprise. Acting on an impulse, he lowered his useless weapon and stepped to the door.

"Stephan, don't!" Warren warned, but it was too late. The door swung inward, hinges creaking, and a man stepped inside—the same man who'd been looking at Stephan so intently downstairs.

Also by Isabelle Adler

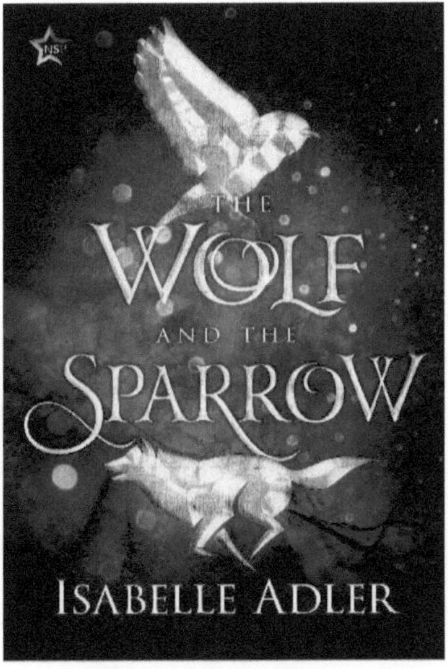

The Wolf and the Sparrow

Derek never wished to inherit his title as a result of a bloody battle. With the old count dead and the truce dependent on his marriage to the rival duke's son, Derek has no choice but to agree to the victor's terms in order to bring peace to his homeland. When he learns of the sinister rumors surrounding his intended groom, Derek begins to have doubts—but there can be no turning back from saying I do.

After the death of his wife, Callan of Mulberny never expected to be forced into another political marriage—especially not to someone like the new Count of Camria. Seemingly soft and meek, it's only fitting that Derek's family crest is a flighty sparrow, worthy of nothing but contempt.

Another war with the seafaring people of the Outer Isles looms on the horizon, and the reluctant newlyweds must team together to protect those caught in the circle of violence. Derek and Callan slowly learn to let go of their prejudices, but as they find themselves enmeshed in intrigue fueled by dark secrets and revenge, their tentative bond is all that keeps their world—and their lives—from plunging into chaos.

The Castaway Prince

Ostracized by his family for his sexual identity, Prince Stephan is forced to flee his homeland before his older brother ascends the throne.

Stephan has been drawn to feminine things for as long as he can remember, so when the dire need for secrecy arises, he seizes the chance to don the perfect disguise. With the help of his loyal servant, Stephan picks his way through hostile territory, hiding his identity by posing as a woman. His only hope for asylum lies with the man who had been his friend and lover three years ago. But when that man also happens to be the crown prince of a rival country, things are a bit more complicated.

With war looming on the horizon, the danger of discovery grows by the moment. With all odds stacked against him, will Stephan find a safe place where he can be his true self, or is he doomed to remain a castaway?

A Touch of Magic

After returning to the straight and narrow, Cary Westfield hopes to rebuild his life as a stage magician. Only thing is, the success of his new show is entirely dependent on a strange medallion inherited from his late grandfather—an amulet that holds a rare and inexplicable power to captivate the wearer's audience.

Ty prides himself on his ability to obtain any item of magical significance—for the right price. When a mysterious client hires him to steal a magical amulet from a neophyte illusionist, he's sure it will be a quick and easy job, earning him a nice chunk of cash.

As it turns out, nothing is sure when greed and powerful magic are at play. When a mob boss with far-reaching aspirations beats Ty to the snatch, Cary and Ty form an unlikely partnership to get the amulet back. The unexpected spark of attraction between them is a welcome perk, but each man has his own plan for the prize.

All bets are off, however, when it is revealed the magical amulet holds a darker secret than either of them had bargained for.

Connect with NineStar Press

www.ninestarpress.com

www.facebook.com/ninestarpress

www.facebook.com/groups/NineStarNiche

www.twitter.com/ninestarpress

www.instagram.com/ninestarpress